A WEEK FROM SUNDAY

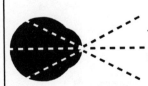

This Large Print Book carries the
Seal of Approval of N.A.V.H.

A WEEK FROM SUNDAY

DOROTHY GARLOCK

THORNDIKE PRESS

An imprint of Thomson Gale, a part of The Thomson Corporation

THOMSON

™

GALE

Detroit • New York • San Francisco • New Haven, Conn. • Waterville, Maine • London

THOMSON
GALE

Thorndike Press® Large Print Basic.
The text of this Large Print edition is unabridged.
Other aspects of the book may vary from the original edition.
Set in 16 pt. Plantin.

LIBRARY OF CONGRESS CATALOGING-IN-PUBLICATION DATA

Garlock, Dorothy.
  A week from Sunday / by Dorothy Garlock.
    p. cm.
  Set in 1930s Louisiana, a young woman makes a new life for herself after she runs away from home.
    ISBN-13: 978-0-7862-9858-7 (hardcover : alk. paper)
    ISBN-10: 0-7862-9858-8 (hardcover : alk. paper) 1. Large type books.
  I. Title.
  PS3557.A71645W44 2007b
  813'.54—dc22   2007032090

Published in 2007 in arrangement with Grand Central Publishing, a division of Hachette Book Group USA, Inc.

Printed in the United States of America on permanent paper
10 9 8 7 6 5 4 3 2 1

Lindy, this one is for you!

RUNAWAY BRIDE

Crimson and gold, purple and blue
Through the stained-glass panes
The light shines through.

I stand in the hallway of what was my
   home
'Mid the gleaming possessions
That once were my own.

Gone, all gone, like my parents so dear
And in their stead
A man I loathe and fear.

Be ready, he says, to become my wife
A week from Sunday
You begin your new life.

I've just time to run, just time to hide
From this day forward
I'll be a runaway bride.

— F.S.I.

CHAPTER 1

Shreveport, Louisiana, 1935

"I'm terribly sorry, my dear. Your father will be missed."

Adrianna Moore listened to the older woman's condolences with a slight nod of appreciation before moving on. The small parlor was filled with smartly dressed men and women, all wearing black, who had come to pay their respects to the recently deceased. Some of the faces she recognized, mostly older gentlemen who had done business with her father over the years, but nearly all of the names escaped her. She knew she should say something, at the very least thank them for coming, but she couldn't manage to get the image of her father's coffin out of her head. It all seemed a horrible dream. Her sadness kept her mute amid the soft murmur of voices and the clink of coffee cups against their saucers.

The funeral itself had been a quiet affair.

Thankfully, the Louisiana spring had cooperated; although drizzly rain had been falling for days, the morning had dawned with warm sunlight and only a light breeze rustling the treetops. High on the lone hill of the cemetery grounds, they'd laid her father to rest. Now, with that business concluded, she was required to play the role of hostess, a task that normally she'd be well equipped to handle. Today was anything but normal.

She moved from guest to guest, each stopping her for a few measured words of sympathy. She looked into forlorn faces, hands gently holding hers. Adrianna knew that they all meant well, but the things she was hearing only intensified her grief:

"Charles Moore was a lion of a man."

"Regardless of the crippling effects of his polio, he never let it get the best of him."

"I can't begin to tell you how much I learned from him about the banking business. It's a debt that I can never repay."

"He'll be watching down on you, Adrianna." A matron wiped tears from her fat cheeks.

Once, when an older gentleman with enormous jowls was telling her of a hunting trip he'd taken with her father before he had become stricken with polio, she found herself desperately fighting back tears. It wasn't the story that had upset her; she'd heard it a half dozen times before. What made her cry was the realization that her father had *become* a story, a legend in town. It had taken all the strength she could muster to get through the day, but somehow she'd managed to keep her composure through it all.

Finally, as the last rays of the spring sun disappeared over the horizon, all of the mourners had gone, leaving Adrianna alone in the large home she'd shared with her father. Built from the earnings of Moore Bank and Trust, the stately manor house had been constructed with the finest of materials. The interior was decorated richly but tastefully: a marble fireplace, an antique clock from Germany, as well as a crystal chandelier that hung over the dining room table.

This home was the only one she'd ever really known. Her mother had died when Adrianna was just fifteen years old. Her father had never remarried. Charles Moore had done everything for his only child. She'd wanted for nothing: piano lessons, private tutors, all the best that his banking fortune could buy. When his own illness had worsened, confining him to his bed or the wheelchair that he despised, she'd done her best to give him the same degree of comfort he'd always given her. But still his health slowly and steadily deteriorated.

Now he was gone and she was alone.

After the mourners left, she went through the downstairs rooms dimming the lights. Glancing up, she caught sight of her reflection in a mirror. At twenty-five years of age, Adrianna Moore had a head of dark brown curly hair that fell to her shoulders. Her soft, oval face was defined by high cheekbones and a warm complexion. Her father had always told her that her deep-set, emerald-green eyes were exactly like her mother's. He called her his "beautiful princess." At the moment, wearing a simple black dress, mourning the loss of her remaining family, she felt anything but beautiful; she was heartsick and exhausted.

"I daresay you get more stunning with each passing year."

Startled by the voice behind her, Adrianna whirled at the sound, her hand reflexively rising to her chest. With slow, measured steps, a man crossed the room toward her. In the scant light, she had to peer intently into the shadows to see her unexpected guest. Finally, there was the spark of recognition, a spark that sent a shiver down her spine.

"Oh! It's you, Mr. Pope. You startled me."

"How many times must I tell you, my dear, to call me Richard?"

He eased out of the gloom to stand before Adrianna. In his late forties, Richard Pope was a man who exuded an air of supreme confidence. Short, with a long face that was marked by full red lips, he had colorless eyes that, over a bulbous nose, looked straight into hers. His clothes were immaculate, his shoes polished to a perfect black. The sweet-smelling pomade he rubbed into his thinning salt-and-pepper hair made Adrianna's stomach churn.

"I didn't realize you were still here," she said, ignoring his comment.

"I was showing Judge Walters and his wife to the door and walked with them out onto the porch. I don't know if you recognized him . . . the wisp of a gentleman whose wife is as fat as he is thin," he explained. "He has always been very important to Moore Bank and Trust, and I wanted to give him my assurances that everything concerned with the company was in good hands. It's all about impressions, you know."

"Thank you for your help today, Mist— . . . Richard," she corrected herself. "What with the funeral arrangements, and all of the guests, I don't know if I could have managed without you." She hated to admit it, but he *had* been very helpful. With his legal guidance, her father's bank had continued to grow ever larger and more prosperous. Adrianna was certain that the only thing that mattered to Richard Pope was acquiring more and more money. As Charles Moore's health worsened, taking him away from the day-to-day operations of his bank, Richard's influence had grown. For the past several months, he had been essentially overseeing the business.

"It's the least that I could do. How are you managing through all of this?"

"All right, I suppose. I don't think it has fully sunk in yet — that he's gone, I mean. He was always positive about things. Even after my mother passed away, I could never imagine the same happening to him."

"And yet it did," Richard said matter-of-factly. "He did die." Walking over to a small bureau, he proceeded to pour himself a generous glass of brandy from a beveled decanter. As he contemplated the amber liquid, a thin smile spread across his face. To Adrianna, he looked like a wolf preparing to sink his fangs into its defenseless prey.

"I'm sorry to have to leave you," she said

hurriedly, wanting desperately to get away from the man, "but I am going to retire for the night. All of this has left me exhausted. Please let yourself out." Quickly, she turned on her heel and made for the staircase on the far side of the room. But before she could take even a couple of steps, his voice stopped her.

"Actually, my dear, there are things that you and I need to discuss. Business matters that cannot wait even for a night. I'm afraid that you'll just have to bear with me for a while longer."

Turning back, Adrianna felt a slight flare of defiance course through her body. She wanted to tell him that *he* would have to wait for *her,* but something in the way he was looking at her kept her from responding. From what her father had told her over the years, recounting his lawyer's smashing victories in court, Richard Pope was not the kind of man you wanted for an enemy.

"What sort of business matters?" she asked. "I'm afraid I don't know much about banking."

"Charles left a good man at the helm. It's not about the bank. Not really." Richard chuckled before swallowing the entire drink in one gulp. "It's actually about you, my dear. You and your future."

"What . . . what are you talking about?" Adrianna asked in confusion.

"I suppose that I shouldn't be shocked by your lack of understanding, sweet Adrianna. After all, you've been cuddled a bit too close to your father's weakened chest all of these years."

"I don't think I like your tone, Mr. Pope," she managed, hoping that her voice sounded stronger than she felt.

"There is no offense intended, I assure you," Richard said apologetically and went back to the bureau to pour himself another drink. "But let us call a spade a spade. You've always had household help. You've never worked outside this house a day in your life. You've never wanted for anything. Charles made sure that you were always provided for, and it wasn't until the very last that he saw the error of his ways."

A sickening feeling suddenly washed over Adrianna. Her knees were weak. *What in the blazes is this pompous ass talking about?* Keeping silent, she waited for him to continue.

"His greatest fear was that you would find yourself all alone, incapable of taking care of yourself," Richard explained. "As I was his closest confidant for all of these long years, it was only natural that he would turn to me to see after his most precious treasure. And that is why he decided to make me executor of his estate. I am completely in charge of you, your money, the bank, the house and everything in it. It's all under my supervision."

"What?" Like a thunderclap out of a clear sky, Richard's words struck Adrianna with dramatic force. Stumbling on shaky legs, trying desperately to stay upright, she managed to grab hold of a nearby chair and steady herself. Her eyes filled with tears, and her voice cracked as she said, "You must be joking!"

"Not in the slightest, my dear. The last legal document that your father ever signed was a change in his will . . . a change that made me executor."

"But not of me!"

"Yes, of you."

"I'm of age."

"Of course you are, but I'm in charge of your money."

As shocked as Adrianna had been by her father's passing, what Richard Pope was telling her shook her even more. *How could what he is saying be true? How could her father have done this to her?* Richard was lying. He had to be! With anger rising in her breast, she gave voice to her disbelief. "This can't be! My father wouldn't leave my future in the hands of someone else! He wouldn't!"

"And he didn't . . . not entirely."

"But you said that he left you in control."

Slowly, Richard crossed the room until he stood before her. She could smell the brandy on his breath. His smile nauseated her. Summoning what strength she had, she straightened her back and boldly returned his gaze.

"He hasn't left you without the means to provide for yourself. This was all part of his plan. All of this," he said, gesturing around the room, "the house, the bank, can still be yours. You can have everything to which you have grown accustomed."

"How?"

"By marrying me."

The words were no sooner out of Richard's mouth when Adrianna's hand shot up toward his face. She'd meant to slap him, the man's boldness on the day of her father's funeral providing the breaking point; but before she could make contact, the lawyer's hand grabbed her own in a tight, painful grip. With a strength she couldn't resist, he yanked her toward him until her body was pressed against his. Try as she might, she couldn't break free.

"Oh, sweet Adrianna," he said, licking his lips. "Haven't you noticed the way that I have looked at you all of these years? I have wanted you from the first moment I saw you. I knew that it would come to this . . . this union between you and me. Your father knew it, too."

"You're . . . you're hurting me," Adrianna pleaded.

"We will be married a week from Sunday. Because of your father's recent death, we'll have a quiet ceremony. I'll have the judge at my house when I come for you. We must keep up appearances, my dear. It wouldn't do to have people gossiping about my wife." His hands tightened on her arms.

"Let . . . let me go."

"I will never let you go!" His grasp tightened even more. "You and I *will* be married!"

"Please . . ." Adrianna sobbed, the tears now flowing freely down her cheeks.

She would never know if it were her words or the sight of her tears that finally broke through Richard Pope's euphoria, but he suddenly released her and stepped away, his hand darting to his pocket where he pulled out a handkerchief and wiped the tears from her cheeks. When he looked down at her, his eyes were flat but still menacing.

"I meant what I said to you, Adrianna," he warned, his voice deep and serious. "By making me the executor of his estate, your father gave his permission for me to provide for you for the rest of your life. To that end, we will be married. The sooner the better."

Stifling a large sob that filled her throat, Adrianna looked at the man through wet eyes. Never in her life had she been so repulsed by another human being. No matter what, she would not give him the satisfaction of seeing her fear.

Richard once again grabbed Adrianna by the wrist. While his grip was not as tight as it had been before, it was still tight enough to cause her anxiety.

"Pack what you'll need. Everything else can be dealt with later. I will come for you a week from Sunday. Dress appropriately for your wedding." Gripping Adrianna's chin, he turned her head until she was looking directly into his face. "This is for the best, my dear. In time, I am certain that you will come to love me every bit as passionately as I love you. As husband and wife, you and I will be the jewels of this town, just as your father intended."

After releasing her, Richard strode across the room and pulled open the door. "Remember . . . a week from Sunday," he said, and then he was gone.

After she heard the door close, Adrianna finally allowed herself to crumple into a chair, tears streaming down her face. Following so soon upon her father's death and funeral, this was more than she could endure.

Even if her father had worried about her well-being, he would never have given control of his estate to a man like Richard Pope! The lawyer must have manipulated him into signing the papers when he wasn't of sound mind. In those last days, Charles Moore had been robbed of all he had built over his lifetime. Now that bastard Pope was trying to steal her!

But what could she do? She could try to challenge the will, to take the matter to a judge, but how was she supposed to compete with a lawyer like Richard? No, that would not work. But what other choice did she have? Pack up her things and wait for him by the door? He was planning to come for her a week from Sunday. That left her only eight days!

CHAPTER 2

Adrianna's hands gripped the steering wheel tightly as she peered through the rain-streaked windshield to the road beyond. Ominous gray clouds blotted the afternoon sky. The darkness they created was occasionally broken by flashes of lightning. But what scared Adrianna most was the driving rain and shifting winds that threw themselves against the sides of her car. Her arms ached from keeping the vehicle on the road. It seemed as if the heavens themselves were against her.

"I should have stopped in that last town," she muttered to herself.

The car's single windshield wiper coughed and burped as it did its best to clear off the water, but it was fighting a losing battle. Still, watching the blade move back and forth was lulling, like the metronome she'd used when taking her piano lessons as a child. But with every pass, as the wiper scraped against the glass, it spoke to her, reminding her of the words that had changed her life forever.

A week from Sunday . . . a week from Sunday . . . a week from Sunday . . .

"Today is that Sunday," she reminded herself grimly.

From the moment that the door had closed behind Richard Pope, Adrianna's mind had been set. She would leave and nothing would stop her! Still, the eight days that her father's lawyer had given her had gone quickly, and there had been much for her to do, all of which had to be managed with the utmost secrecy. With each step in the preparation of her departure, the knowledge that she would never return became clearer. As she'd gone around Shreveport to visit friends and loved ones, she'd done her best to say her goodbyes without emotion, fearful that any slip would betray her intentions. Once, when she'd been ready to leave a treasured friend, she'd felt tears begin to overwhelm her. Unable to stop, they had run hotly down her cheeks. To her relief, her friend had taken her show of sadness to be grief for her father and had embraced her tenderly. She never allowed anyone to know that she was planning to leave forever.

Of all that she'd needed to do, the most

difficult task had been deciding where to go. As an only child, she had no brother or sister to run to, nor were there any cousins whom she knew well enough to impose upon. Her family was made up mostly of elderly aunts and uncles on her father's side who lived in or near Shreveport; running to them would offer her no sanctuary. In the end, she'd decided on one of her mother's relatives, Aunt Madeline who lived in Mississippi, as her only option. After the passing of her own mother, Madeline had come to stay with her and her father in Louisiana for a couple of months. Adrianna remembered her as a warm, friendly woman who was quick to offer comfort. *Surely, she'll be happy to see her niece!* Still, fearful of rejection, she'd decided not to call or write Madeline of her arrival. She'd have to hope for the best.

A week from Sunday . . . a week from Sunday . . .

Stifling a yawn, Adrianna kept her eyes focused straight ahead. She'd been on the road for hours after getting up before dawn in order to make her escape. Her father's car had received little use since its purchase; once Charles Moore's health had started to deteriorate he'd rarely gone out. Adrianna had learned to drive from necessity and had become confident in her ability. Leaving the house at first light, she'd overcome her selfish desire to look back, and pressed onward. The rain began an hour out of Shreveport, and had steadily grown worse. She was one of only a few drivers foolhardy enough to brave the bad weather, and she'd had the roads mostly to herself. The raging downpour was nerve-racking, but she had left Shreveport; she had done what she'd set out to do.

Although the thought of leaving her home had frayed her nerves, she had to admit to a twinge of excitement, too. She was moving on into the unknown. From this day forward, everything would be different. As loath as she was to admit it, Richard's claim that she had had an easy life handed to her by her father *was* partially true. Once she was settled she'd need to fend for herself: find a place to live, a job with which to support herself. In short, she'd need to start living.

From around a slight curve in the road, a town suddenly came into view. A small, weather-beaten sign announced it as Lee's Point. Adrianna had never heard of it. Through the rain, she could see a scattering of houses on the outskirts that grew denser as she neared the town's center. This was followed by a row of businesses lining the main street like towels hanging from a clothesline. No one was in sight, not surprising, given the weather. Since she'd left Shreveport and moved into the countryside, she'd passed through many towns similar to this one, although they seemed to be spread farther and farther apart as the miles went by.

For the briefest of moments, she thought about stopping and riding out the storm. Surely the town would have a restaurant where she could have a hot meal. Besides, a bit of rest would do her good. But before her weary arms could pull the car into a parking spot, the image of Richard Pope's gloating face filled her thoughts, and she knew it would be foolish to stop, even if it were only for an hour or two. She'd stopped only once since leaving Shreveport, to get a sandwich and go to the restroom, and even then she'd hurried as quickly as she could. The fear of his finding her was too great to ignore. If she were to be found . . . As quickly as she'd come upon Lee's Point, the town was behind her and lost to view.

"Damn you, Richard Pope!" she swore.

Instinctively, Adrianna shivered at the memory of Richard grabbing her by the wrists and telling her that they would be married. She still couldn't shake her revulsion at the way he'd looked at her and the words he'd spoken; they'd been burned into her thoughts ever since. He'd been so confident, so sure that she'd come along willingly. She was repulsed by the very thought of becoming his wife! He had somehow managed to get control of her father's fortune, but he would *never* get control of her.

By now, back in Shreveport, he must have come to the house and discovered she was gone. She could only imagine how surprised and angry he would be. However, it was after he'd sufficiently calmed down that he would become truly dangerous. He was a calculating man, a trait that had made him both successful and wealthy as a lawyer, and he *would* come looking for her. The farther she went, therefore, the harder it would be for him to find her.

A sudden flash of lightning illuminated the sky above her. In the brief glare, she could see the trees bowing deeply in the face of the pounding rain and punishing wind. A broken branch skittered across the pavement in front of her car before disappearing into the gloom of the thick trees that lined the road. The storm was worsening. A pang of regret gnawed at Adrianna's stomach;

maybe it would have been a good idea to have stopped at Lee's Point after all. But it was too late now to turn back.

It was also too late to pull the car over to the side of the highway. Since Shreveport, the conditions had worsened. While these county roads were paved, they were narrow and full of cracks and holes. The shoulders were a quagmire of mud. If she were to go off the hard surface the wheels would become stuck in the mud and she wouldn't be able to get out; she'd be at the mercy of a passing traveler's willingness to help, and she hadn't seen another vehicle for quite a while. No, it was better to keep going.

A quick glance in the rearview mirror showed the belongings that she'd tossed haphazardly into the backseat. She'd limited herself to the things she would need immediately, mostly clothing. She had also added a few family heirlooms that she couldn't bear to part with. Treasured most of all was a photograph of herself and her mother that had been taken shortly after her birth. For as long as she could remember, it had sat on her father's bedside table. The beautiful mother-of-pearl picture frame had greeted him every morning. The thought of Richard Pope having it made her heart heavy. She'd also scrounged up as much money as she could find. It hadn't been much, since most of her funds were tied directly to her father, but it would be enough to get her started.

Before she could break contact with the mirror, she took a long look into her own face. Her hair was a tangled mess. Exhausted, bloodshot pupils stared back from under heavy lids. Deep, dark circles ringed her eyes, giving a clear indication of her stress and fatigue. *But what could she expect?* She hadn't managed to sleep for more than an hour or two at a time since Richard Pope had upended her life with his ridiculous demands. Her very bones ached with the weariness of her heart. As each of the eight days had passed, the uneasiness had increased. She wasn't sure how much more she could have taken.

The blare of a horn split through the noise of the storm, startling Adrianna's attention away from the mirror. Her eyes snapped back to the road. Through the rain-streaked windshield, she was horrified to see another vehicle coming directly at her! *While she'd been looking at her reflection, deep in thought, she'd drifted across the center of the road and into the path of another motorist!*

"Oh my God!" she cried out.

With all the strength her tired arms could

muster, she yanked at the steering wheel, desperately trying to pull the car back to safety. Hand over hand, she turned and turned, but nothing happened. With horror, Adrianna realized that the wheels were sliding; with all the water and mud on the road, the tires were skating across the concrete surface. Even taking her foot off of the gas did nothing to stop her headlong plunge into a collision. All she could do was watch helplessly.

As the distance between the vehicles shortened, time seemed to slow to a standstill. It was as if she were in a movie, with every pass of the windshield wiper carrying the film forward another frame. Her arms were locked tightly at the elbows, her whole body tense and rigid, preparing for the impact she couldn't prevent.

Another fork of lightning pierced the sky, lighting up the dark afternoon gloom. In that brief flash, Adrianna received a clearer view of the other vehicle. It wasn't another car but a small truck, its back end covered with a soaked tarpaulin. Inside the truck's cab, two men stared back at her.

The very moment that the lightning's glare vanished, time leapt forward. With a sickening crunch, Adrianna's car slammed into the pickup truck's driver-side door. The screech of metal grinding against metal was deafening. The force of the blow shattered the car's windows, sending shards of glass raining down into the cab. As if she were a doll, Adrianna was thrown against the door, her head pounding hard into the frame. The pain was enormous, her vision clouded and spun, but she refused to lose consciousness. Even now, her hands tried to move the wheel.

Her car bounced off the truck and flew back toward the center of the road. The force of the collision had been so great that it tipped the smaller vehicle up onto two wheels. All of the belongings she'd brought from Shreveport flew into the air and whirled about as if they were in the thrall of a tornado! Adrianna's heart was in her throat as she waited for the car to come back to the ground, but the force of the crash was too much. Slowly but surely, the car continued over until the passenger's side door slammed against the concrete. The vehicle's frame shook violently.

Still moving, the car slid forward on its side. Scared out of her wits, Adrianna somehow managed to hang on to the steering wheel, her body suspended above the wreckage below. Finally, after what seemed forever, the mangled vehicle came to a stop.

Hot, searing pain filled Adrianna's arms, and she gave in to it and released her grip. With a thud, she fell among shards of glass and her belongings.

"Ohhh!" she sobbed as her head whirled with pain.

Rain fell through the broken windows, wetting her face and soaking her clothes. As she looked up through the drops, she could see out the remnants of the front windshield. By some miracle, the windshield wiper continued to run, wiping at glass that was no longer there. In her frazzled mind, Adrianna could still hear the noise it was supposed to make. And the words that had tormented her from the moment they'd been spoken were running through her mind as she finally gave in to the searing pain and fell into unconsciousness.

A week from Sunday . . . a week from Sunday . . . a week from Sunday.

CHAPTER 3

Adrianna was first aware of rain splashing against the windowpane. Cracking open her eyes she wondered why the windshield wiper had stopped. She winced at the overhead light and closed her eyes quickly. A pounding ache washed over her; she felt nauseated, and a dizziness throbbed in time with the beat of her heart. Tentatively she reached up to touch her forehead and felt the coarseness of bandages.

Where am I?

With determination, Adrianna forced her eyes open again, bracing herself for the light. She was lying in a bed: a sheet covered her body, and her head rested on a soft pillow. The room was painted white, and the wall opposite the bed was lined with cupboards and closed with glass doors. Her eyes could not focus well enough to see what lay behind them. A pile of white linens sat next to a sink. Glass jars lined a long countertop.

The smell of alcohol permeated the air.

"I see that you're awake," a voice said beside her.

Startled by the nearness of the voice, Adrianna turned her head slowly to see a woman sitting next to her. Green eyes regarded her intently through round, black-rimmed glasses. Dark hair streaked with touches of gray was pulled back from the woman's face in a tight bun. She wore a white coat, and hanging from her neck was a stethoscope. She had been writing in a small notebook, which she closed and placed on her lap.

"Where am I?" Adrianna spoke the words aloud.

"You're in Lee's Point. I'm a doctor."

"Doctor? Am I hurt? What happened?" Adrianna asked weakly. The inside of her mouth felt horrible, as if her tongue had grown to twice its normal size. Even her teeth hurt.

"You had an accident and were brought to my office. I'm Dr. Bordeaux," the woman explained. "Your car slid into the path of a truck a few miles east of town."

Even as the doctor spoke, memories came flooding back. The hopelessness she had felt as her car slid across the wet pavement, the anticipation of the collision, the jarring force of metal hitting metal, and finally the cold blackness as she sank into unconsciousness.

"Were the people in the truck hurt?" Adrianna asked, her mind in a deep, cotton-filled haze.

"Yes and no." The doctor looked over her shoulder at the closed door to the room. At that moment a masculine voice, harsh and heavy, resounded down the hallway.

"Doctor?"

"Oh, for goodness sakes." The doctor turned from the bed. "That man!" The sound of heavy footsteps came rapidly down the corridor. "He's like a bull in a china shop," the doctor said irritably and moved toward the doorway. It was suddenly filled with the body of a big man.

"Where is she? Where's the stupid woman who slammed into me?"

"Don't shout, Quinn. She's here, and she's just coming to." The doctor put her hand on his chest and backed him out of the doorway and into the hall. "Go down to the kitchen and have a cup of coffee. We'll talk later."

In the few seconds the man had stood in the doorway, Adrianna's eyes took in everything about him, and he frightened her as no other man had ever done. Not only was he big, but his hair was jet black, thick, and wild. His brows were as dark as his hair and drawn together over a large, bony nose. He had high cheekbones, and his flat cheeks were creased in deep grooves on each side of his wide mouth. It was a rough-hewn face with a jaw set in an almost brutal anger. His large, slanting eyes gleamed beneath a brush of thick lashes. They darted around the room, passed over her and away.

Thank goodness, she thought.

The man had to be a lumberjack. His jeans were pushed into the tops of calf-high boots. A flannel shirt was tucked into the waistband, the sleeves rolled up to the elbows. Dark hair covered muscular fore-arms. Adrianna could still see him in her mind's eye as the doctor's voice retreated down the hallway.

"Who was that?" she asked when the doctor returned. Adrianna spoke softly, as if she were afraid the man would hear her.

"Quinn Baxter, the driver of the truck." The doctor pulled a chair up close to the bed and sat down. "He's a real fistful of a man, isn't he?" She bent over and looked into Adrianna's face. "Is your vision clear? I'm afraid you might have a slight concussion."

"I can see just fine, but I feel slightly sick to my stomach." Adrianna's eyes were full of misery when she looked at the doctor. "When can I leave here?"

"Is someone expecting you?" When Adrianna didn't answer, she said, "I need to know your name. The sheriff will be asking about the accident."

"My name is Adrianna Moore. But do you need to tell him?"

The doctor looked at her skeptically. A question floated through her mind. *Is this lovely girl running from the law?* She could think of no other reason why the woman didn't want the sheriff to know who she was.

Adrianna could almost hear the thoughts running through the doctor's head and quickly said, "I'm not wanted by the law, but there's somebody back in Shreveport that I don't want to find me."

"Your husband?"

"No, I'm not married."

"Quinn will have to report the accident."

"Does he have to know my name?"

"I'm afraid so."

Tears came into Adrianna's eyes as she knew she had no choice but to tell this kind woman why she had left Shreveport. The doctor took her hand and held it while she told about her father's death and Richard Pope trying to take control of her life. When she finished the doctor patted her hand and sat quietly for a while.

"What did you plan to do?"

Adrianna spoke over the sob in her throat. "I wanted to get as far from Shreveport as I could. I need a job. I can't withdraw the money from my account at the bank or Richard will find out where I am." The doctor stayed silent as she continued. "All I've ever done is take care of my invalid mother and then my father until he died two weeks ago. About the only thing I can do is play the piano. I played for weddings and funerals at my church."

"Let me think about this for a while. I want you to stay here overnight. Maybe we can work something out." The doctor's mind was busy mulling over a solution that would depend on that bullheaded man down the hall. She could hear the murmur of voices as Quinn talked with Gabe Le-Blanc, his best friend. The two men were as different as a dog and a cat. Although they were of equal size, Gabe's voice was soft and musical, while Quinn's was like a buzz saw when he was irritated.

Dr. Bordeaux went down the hall to her kitchen.

Adrianna closed her eyes and wondered if she had made a mistake telling the doctor about Richard. But it was too late now.

"Calm down, *mon ami,*" Gabe was saying as the doctor entered.

"What in the hell am I going to do for a piano player?" Quinn exploded.

"Not having a piano player is the least of your worries." Gabe gave a snort of laughter.

"They're used to that honky-tonk piano. The louder the better."

"Maybe you could play a record."

"Yeah." Quinn looked at his friend as if he'd lost his mind. "Goddammit," he cursed. "Why'd this have to happen now?" He looked at the bulky bandage on Gabe's hand. "Are you sure you can't play with one hand?"

Gabe knew his friend was frustrated. He'd had a lot on his mind lately, trying to keep the supply of logs going to the mill, looking after his brother, and attempting to keep the tavern going so that Jesse could get the medical attention he needed. Dr. Bordeaux had said there was a place in Atlanta that might be able to help him.

The doctor poured herself a cup of coffee. "The woman will be all right. She may have a slight concussion, and I'm keeping her overnight." The doctor went to the door.

"Do you need some pain pills, Gabe? That was a really bad cut on your hand. You're lucky the glass didn't cut a tendon."

"Thanks for fixing me up, Doc. What do I owe you?"

The doctor smiled. "I'll take two quarts of blood and a hunk of boudin."

"You'd get that anyway, Doc. The boudin, not the blood." Gabe's dark eyes swept caressingly over the doctor's face as she smiled at him and left the room. He had loved this woman for the past three years, and she had no idea he even thought of her in that way. But he did. He'd walk through fire for her. Quinn was the only person who was aware of Gabe's feelings for the doctor.

"Every bottle in the back of that truck was broken," Quinn said irritably.

"Not every bottle, *mon ami.*"

"But damn near it," Quinn snorted. "The Whipsaw needed that liquor. Where are we going to get the money to replace it?"

Gabriel LeBlanc shrugged his wide shoulders. In his early forties, he had ink-black hair and dark eyes. The broad smile he normally wore was tempered by the pain that now raced through him. His left hand was wrapped tightly in bandages and throbbed ferociously. The cut had gone almost to the bone, and he'd wager a month's pay that he would not be using the fingers for several weeks.

"We'll come up with the money. We always do. Ain't no use in worryin'."

Quinn stopped moving and looked hard at Gabe. The man had been by his side for a long time, ever since Quinn's father had passed away. As Lee's Point's only tavern, the Whipsaw served the men who worked in the mills north of town, as well as the Cajuns. It took a hard worker with a steady hand to operate it. Quinn had found the perfect man in Gabe. More than just his helper, the Cajun was his best friend.

"I got more worries than money," Quinn continued. "I took the day off from the mill to make that run with you." For all his life he'd worked as a logger; his father's death hadn't changed that. Juggling both responsibilities, he had made the best of it . . . for Jesse. "Taking time off isn't the easiest thing for me. Times are tough. You see all these fellas coming through town looking for work. One of these days they'll find someone else to cut their logs."

"Good." Gabe chuckled. "You get fired, then I'll have some help."

"Very funny. Your ass isn't the one on the line."

"Is that right? How many jobs do you see

for a one-handed musician?" Gabe raised his left hand for emphasis. A wave of pain shot through it, and he winced.

"The loggers want music. There isn't a Cajun alive that doesn't want music when he drinks."

"What about Karl? He can play. Those two sing-along nights pay the bills."

Quinn frowned. Karl was one of the Whipsaw's fill-in bartenders, little more than a kid. Quinn had heard him plunking away at the keys one night. He would have sworn a jackass had a better ear for music.

"When we need someone to drive the customers away, we'll hire Karl to play the piano."

"He's not that bad. Who else do we have?"

Unable to answer, Quinn started to pace again.

The thunderstorm had finally begun to let up. A light rain still splashed against the windows, but it looked as if the sun was try-ing to break through. Soon it would be hot and humid. In his mind Quinn played the crash over and over again. The car had come at them so quickly, he knew there was noth-ing the woman could have done to avoid hitting them. The damage to his truck had been minor, far less than the damage to her car.

"That damn woman," he muttered.

"Stop blaming her," Gabe said. "The storm was a humdinger. She wasn't used to driving in it. When the car got away from her, we were in the way, that's all. It could have happened to anyone."

"That's just like a brainless woman," Quinn argued. "They don't have the sense to stay off the road when they've had no experience driving in a storm. I've got a notion to go in there and give her a piece of my mind."

Quinn's frustration continued to grow. Lately, one problem had piled up on top of another. *Goddamnit!* He strode to the door and yanked it open. Before he could pass through, a strong hand grabbed his shoulder.

"What are you going to do?" Gabe asked.

"What does it look like? If I lose the tavern it will be her fault," he snarled as he glared at the Cajun. "And if you don't want another busted hand, you'd better let go of me."

Gabe's eyes held Quinn's for a moment before he said quietly, "You'd fight a one-handed man?"

"Damn right I would!"

Quinn entered the room, and the woman looked up at him expectantly. He had intended to give her a tongue-lashing, to tell her what a poor driver she was and how she had damaged his business, maybe beyond repair, but something happened as he approached the bed. His eyes took in the figure, so slim it barely made an impression on the bed. She looked different from the way he remembered when he had carried her from the wrecked car to his truck and then into the doctor's office.

She was vulnerable and unbelievably beautiful.

Adrianna stared at the man who had barged into the room. She figured him to be somewhere in his middle thirties. He was tall, with long arms and legs. Thick black hair was pushed back from his face as he looked at her. His jaw moved, but no sound came out. His piercing gray eyes seemed to pin her to the bed.

As she stared back, Adrianna felt a strange sensation wash over her. This man was unlike any she had ever met before. Certainly he was different from the young accountants and lawyers she'd met during the course of her father's business dealings. They were refined and professional. This man was neither. She felt her face redden in embarrassment.

"Quinn Baxter," Dr. Bordeaux said, entering and breaking what had become an awkward silence. "This is Miss Adrianna Moore."

Looking at the strange man, Adrianna saw a flicker of annoyance cross his face, but it disappeared just as quickly. The look that replaced it mirrored the harsh weather that had caused her accident.

"What in the hell were you doing on the highway?" His voice sounded like sandpaper to Adrianna's ears. His rugged features grew sharper with each word. "I don't know where you came from, but people around here have sense enough to stay off the roads in bad weather if they don't know how to drive in it."

"I'm sorry," Adrianna managed to say.

"That's not good enough. Do you have any idea what that accident has cost me? I've got a business to run. Almost every damn bottle of liquor I was bringing back was busted. It's going to cost you plenty to replace it."

"Quinn Baxter!" Dr. Bordeaux interrupted, stepping in front of him and cutting off the hot glare he had fixed upon Adrianna. "I will not have you stomping into my office to take out your frustrations on my patient."

"You know how he can get, Doc," a softer voice said. "He ain't happy unless he's got something to complain about." Adrianna peered around the doctor and saw a man leaning casually against the door. *"Bonjour,"* he said. He was probably a bit older than the rude creature with the wild hair, but he had the same rough features. Unlike the other man, he had a warm smile.

Adrianna noticed the bandage on his hand. "Oh no," she blurted out. "Is that from the accident?"

"I'm afraid so." Gabe's smile grew wider. "I think that's one reason Quinn here's got his back up."

"That's his problem, Gabe." Dr. Bordeaux crossed her arms over her chest and glanced at the wild man. "It's not a good enough reason for you to come in here yelling like an ignoramus."

"Since you've got all the answers, Sarah," Quinn said, "why don't you tell me how in the hell I'm supposed to produce a piano player when Gabe's hand is busted?"

"It isn't broken." The doctor wrinkled her nose at Quinn. "It's cut and will take a few weeks to heal, that's all."

Without a moment's thought, Adrianna said, "I play the piano."

The conversation stopped as the three

turned to stare at her. As her eyes moved from face to face she saw a mixture of different emotions: interest, surprise, and the last was the disbelief on Quinn's features.

"What did you say?" Quinn asked, moving past the doctor and placing one rough hand on the bed's headboard. He stared down at her, his eyes narrowed.

Her heart pumped painfully. "I can play the piano," she repeated. "I've been taking lessons since I was a little girl. My father insisted upon it. He said one who had a good grasp of music was an intelligent person."

"I guess that lets me out," Quinn said. "What kind of music do you play?"

"All kinds. But mostly classical. Mozart is my favorite." A smile crossed her face. She was happy that she could be of help, but her smile quickly faded as she saw a frown form on Quinn's face. Hurriedly she added, "I can play anything if you have the sheet music."

At that the man's frown deepened. His eyes locked on hers. Adrianna could see the thoughts were whizzing around in his head. Turning to Gabe, he said, "Have you got sheet music at the Whipsaw?"

"Of course, but . . ."

"Then it's settled."

"What's settled?" Adrianna asked.

Quinn moved down to the end of the bed so he could look at her. He made her nervous, but she did like to look at him.

"The way I see things" — he grinned down at her — "you owe me for the damages you caused."

"I said I was sorry," she said quickly.

"Seeing that I'm such a nice guy," Quinn continued, ignoring her apology, "I'll be willing to overlook the busted bottles and damages to my truck. Congratulations, Miss Moore. You're my new piano player."

CHAPTER 4

"It's completely out of the question," Dr. Bordeaux argued. "The Whipsaw is no place for a woman like Miss Moore."

"The hell it's not," Quinn snorted defensively. "There are plenty of women who come to the tavern. It's not like I'm running a whorehouse. Besides," he added with a nod toward Adrianna, "she owes me for the damage to my truck and what was in it."

"He's got a point, Doc," Gabe added.

"Damn right I do!"

As much as she hated to admit it, Adrianna saw a degree of truth in what the big galoot was saying. She did not like to owe anyone for anything. She would play the piano in his damn bar.

"You play for church singin', don't you?" Gabe said.

"Of course."

"That's what you'll be doing at the tavern.

49

We have sing-alongs two evenings a week." He winked at the doctor. "Of course, they're not church songs. The sing-along nights are our best nights, and without the big crowds on those two nights, the business would probably go down the drain."

The thought of playing the piano in a smoke-filled room with a bunch of strangers made Adrianna's stomach roil. It seemed that this big, rough, unfeeling man wasn't going to let her get away without paying her debt to him. She had just run away from one problem and found herself another.

Have I jumped out of the skillet into the fire?

The conversation continued as if she weren't even there.

"Are you going to get her a room in a hotel?" Dr. Bordeaux asked. "Don't tell me you'd let her stay in the Lamplighter."

"Hell, no," Quinn barked. "I'll not put her there, but she probably couldn't afford to stay at the Bellevue Hotel."

The words that he spoke startled Adrianna. The truth was, she wasn't without money. She could probably afford to stay at the hotel, but she didn't want him to know it. She had scrounged every nickel she could find in the house and what she had saved for shopping. It was stashed in her purse in the bottom of one of her suitcases.

"Isn't there a rooming house in town where I can stay?" she asked irritably.

"She could get a room at Ma Parker's place," Gabe suggested.

"Absolutely not," the doctor disagreed. "The girls who live there have some pretty wild parties."

"It'd be like putting a kitten in with a bunch of tomcats," Gabe said as he glanced down at the girl on the bed.

"I have a suggestion." The doctor looked at Quinn and then back at Adrianna. "Quinn, you have plenty of room in your house, and I think Jesse would benefit from being with someone like Adrianna. That girl you have working there isn't very stimulating company for a teenage boy. Besides that, I think Adrianna would be good for him."

"How do you figure?"

"She's had nursing experience taking care of her father. Between the two of us, I think we can work out a routine of exercises for Jesse so that he will be able to do more to help himself. You don't want him staying in that bed for the rest of his life, do you?"

"Now just a minute," Adrianna interrupted. "I'm not going to stay with *him*." She looked at Quinn as if he had just crawled out from under a rock. "And who is Jesse?"

"Why not?" Quinn snapped, irritated by her haughty attitude. "You don't think my house is good enough for you?"

"I didn't say that. It wouldn't be proper for me to stay there. Besides, you don't like me, and I don't like you. It would not be very pleasant."

The doctor looked from one to the other. "You're both adults. You can put your dislikes aside for Jesse's sake, can't you?" The doctor then explained to Adrianna that sixteen-year-old Jesse had been in a school bus accident and at the present time was unable to use his legs.

"My place isn't the fanciest house in Lee's Point, but there's plenty of room. I can certainly afford to feed one more mouth. Besides, she's so skinny, it's evident she doesn't eat much." He smiled, suddenly warming up to the idea. "I guess if Jesse can put up with her, I can too."

"Well, thank you very much. And how much do you want for your room?"

Quinn grinned, the smile softening his rough features. "Oh, you'll work for your room and board. Lola is always complaining that she has too much to do."

"Who's Lola?"

"She's our housekeeper, and she takes care of Jesse when I'm not there." He cocked a brow at the doctor and Gabe. "You'll like Lola. You two should hit it off."

"Quinn . . ." Gabe started to say something, but one look from his friend cut him off. "But Quinn . . ." Gabe persisted. He looked at the doctor for help, but she turned toward the door.

"She should spend the night here, Quinn."

"Fine with me."

Adrianna looked at the three people standing at the foot of her bed. Between them they had decided what she would do and where she would stay. If her car was in running order, she would tell all three of them what they could do with their plans for her, then go on down the road.

Gabe and Quinn walked out the door. Quinn said over his shoulder, "See you tomorrow, Annie."

"My name is Adrianna," she called, and the sound of her voice echoed down the hall. She couldn't remember when she had spoken so loudly.

Quinn smiled.

Gabe looked at his friend and frowned. "You know that Lola will be mad as a hornet when you bring her home." The two men stepped out of the doctor's office and into a light, drizzling rain. Gabe slipped his bandaged hand inside his coat pocket.

"What about Jesse? What's he going to think about you bringing another woman into the house?"

"I'm sure he gets tired of Lola's company. I do."

Gabe chuckled. "So she hasn't got you in bed yet?"

"Hell, no. I know her game. She'd claim I got her pregnant so I'd have to marry her. That's not gonna happen."

"The *mademoiselle* won't stay long, if Jesse takes a dislike to her. He can be a little shit when he wants to be."

"I'd be a shit too if I was in his shape."

"Does he let Lola help him into the chair?"

"No, he's afraid she'll let him fall."

"You can't always be there, *mon ami.*"

"My God, I don't understand why this should happen to a good kid like Jesse. He had such high hopes of going to college and playing football."

"He can still go to college."

"You know damn good and well he can't. Someone would have to be with him every minute of the day, and I can't do that. Besides, he hasn't finished high school yet."

"Miss Moore seems to be a well-educated woman. Maybe she can teach him at home."

"I don't think we can count on her. She

won't hang around this place long," Quinn said.

"She doesn't seem the type of woman to be roaming around the countryside alone."

"Maybe she's an ax murderess. She may have killed a husband or robbed a bank." Quinn gave his friend a lopsided grin. "You can't go by looks these days, you know. They say Bonnie Parker looked just like an average girl, and you know what she did."

"I don't think you can compare the young *mademoiselle* to Bonnie Parker."

Adrianna put in a restless night. When she got up, she felt weak and her head ached. Her relief at getting away from Richard had faded, and she was now worried about another man managing her life. She had to admit, the two were as different as sunshine and rain. She had seen the softening in Quinn when he spoke of his younger brother. The only thing she had seen in Richard was his determination to force her to marry him.

After she dressed, she went in search of the doctor. She had never known a woman doctor, but she liked this one. She had to find out what happened to the belongings she had in her car as well as when it could be repaired.

The doctor's office was quiet, but she could hear a voice coming from another room. She peered into the room at the front of the house and saw a woman sitting at a desk. The woman looked up, returned the phone receiver to its hook, and smiled.

"Hello, you must be Miss Moore." At Adrianna's nod, she continued: "The doctor is out right now but should be back soon. She'll want to see you." The woman had light brown hair that was pulled back in a bun. Wire-rimmed glasses perched on her nose. She wore a neat blouse tucked smoothly into a dark skirt and a pleasant smile. "How are you feeling?"

"I'm weak, and I have aches in bones I didn't know I had."

"I'm not surprised. I saw your car."

"You did? Where is it?"

"Quinn had it pulled into the garage."

"All of my things are in it."

"No." The woman shook her head. "Quinn took everything out and put it all in the doctor's garage."

"Why didn't he just leave it in the car?"

"You'll have to ask him. He told Dr. Bordeaux that he'd be back about noon. I understand you're going to his house. I'm glad. Jesse needs someone besides that woman Quinn has staying there. You haven't had breakfast."

"I didn't expect to eat here. I can get something from the café."

"Dr. Bordeaux wouldn't hear of it. Would a roll and coffee be all right? By the way, my name is Mildred Bacon."

Adrianna held out her hand. "Hello, nice to meet you. I can get my own coffee if you tell me where to go."

"The kitchen is just down the hall. I'll go with you. I'm not busy now. Gabe put a bell on the door to let us know when someone comes in. Now I'm not so tied to the desk."

Adrianna followed the woman to the pleasant kitchen. The rain had stopped during the night and the sun was shining through the east windows. Peering out the window, Adrianna could see that the doctor's office was close to the business district of town. She turned to Mildred, who was pouring her coffee and putting a cinnamon roll on a plate.

"Is this a very big town?"

"It depends on what you consider big. I think the population is somewhere near two thousand. Compared to Baton Rouge or New Orleans we are really small." Mildred pulled out a chair from the table and motioned for Adrianna to sit down. "Most of the people here work in the timber business. About half of the population is Cajun."

Adrianna sat down and picked up her napkin. She hadn't realized that she was hungry until she smelled the warm roll.

"The doctor was called out this morning. One of the timber men cut his foot with an ax. His boy was waiting on the steps when she got up this morning."

"I've never before met a woman doctor."

Mildred poured herself a glass of iced tea. "Dr. Bordeaux came here about eight years ago with her husband, who was also a doctor. Folks around here resisted being cared for by a woman. But she gradually became accepted, and when her husband died, she stayed and took over the practice. Now folks don't know what they would do without her."

At the jingle of the bell on the door, Mildred set her cup down and hurried from the room. Adrianna heard the voice of a man demanding to see the doctor.

"Where's the doc?"

"Dr. Bordeaux?" Mildred plainly didn't like hearing the doctor called "doc."

"Is there another doctor here?" the man asked irritably.

Mildred ignored his sarcasm. "Dr. Bordeaux isn't here right now, Mr. Thatcher.

She should be back shortly."

"Exactly how long is 'shortly'?" The man looked as if he hadn't shaved in a week. His eyes were bloodshot. The hands holding his worn felt hat moved nervously around the brim.

"Is there an emergency?"

"Hell yes, it's an emergency! My wife is bleeding. It's not yet time for the baby."

"The doctor went north of town to the Kilburn farm. Mr. Kilburn cut his foot with an ax."

"Kilburn's place? I have to go right by there going home. I'll stop and tell the doc."

"That's a good idea. If you miss her, I'll tell her as soon as she gets back."

The man slammed his battered hat onto his head and hurried out the door. Mildred turned to look at Adrianna standing in the doorway.

"Poor man. He looks worried," noted Adrianna.

"He should be. His wife is only sixteen. He's old enough to be her father." Mildred shrugged. "The men around here seem to marry younger and younger girls."

"Why is that?"

"Who knows?" Mildred answered the ringing telephone. "Dr. Bordeaux's office."

"Mildred, this is Quinn."

"I know who it is. What's on your mind, Quinn?"

"Tell that prissy woman that ran into me that I'll be by when I get through with work to take her to the house."

"You're not nice, Quinn."

"Who said I was?"

"Don't give me any back talk, Quinn Baxter. I'll box your ears the next time I see you."

"If you do, I'll kiss you right on Main Street."

"You're all talk, Quinn Baxter. You wouldn't dare!" Mildred hung up the telephone and turned to Adrianna. "He'll be by for you later."

"I'd like to talk to the doctor before I leave."

"Why don't you go back to your room and rest for a while? She may not be back for several hours if she has to see about Mrs. Thatcher."

"I don't know this Quinn Baxter. I'm not sure I want to go to his house. All of this was decided so fast."

"You'll be perfectly safe with Quinn. I'd trust him with my seventeen-year-old daughter, and that's saying a lot. He sounds gruff, but he's really a pussycat when you get right down to it. The doctor said you

60

might be able to help Jesse with exercises. If you do that you'll be Quinn's friend for life."

"I'm not sure I can help him."

"Neither Quinn nor Dr. Bordeaux expect miracles." When Mildred saw the apprehension on Adrianna's face, she continued: "Don't worry. If it doesn't work out for you to stay there, Dr. Bordeaux will help you find another place."

"But I've got to get a real job."

"Gabe said something about you playing the piano at the Whipsaw."

"That's for the two nights a week they have a sing-along. I'm doing that to pay for the damage I caused when I slid into his truck. After that's paid for, I'm sure it wouldn't pay enough for me to live on."

"The Whipsaw is a rowdy place, but with Gabe and Quinn there, you'll be all right."

"Is Quinn at the tavern every night?"

"I don't know about that, but Gabe runs the place — and by the way, he can make that old piano talk. He plays a ragtime style that sets the feet to tapping and the hands to clapping."

"They needn't expect me to do that. I've only played for church services, weddings, and funerals."

"Don't worry," Mildred said for the second time.

Adrianna wished people would quit telling her not to worry. None of them knew her circumstances. None of them had a man like Richard Pope trying to run their lives. Even now, her stomach turned at the thought of marrying him. Being his wife meant she would have to sleep with him. *Oh my Lord, I'd almost rather die than do that!* A shudder went through her and she closed her eyes for a moment. Mildred looked at her curiously.

"Are you feeling ill?"

Adrianna opened her eyes. "Oh, no! I was just thinking about something very unpleasant." She looked down at her wrinkled skirt. Fastidious person that she was, it bothered her to be untidy. "I think I'll go lie down for a while."

It was late afternoon, and Adrianna was dozing on her bed when Mildred came to the door of her room. "Quinn's here. He's early."

Adrianna groaned inwardly and got up from the bed. She dreaded facing that big uncouth man again. He made her nervous. She didn't feel threatened by him as she had by Richard Pope, but he scared her in a way no other man had ever done. She cringed when she heard the heavy footsteps coming down the hallway. The door flew open and Quinn stood before her.

His hair looked as if he had been in a tornado. He had a scowl on his dark face, and his teeth were clenched. She could see the muscles dance in his cheek. He wasn't liking this.

"Mr. Baxter," she said, "I don't like this arrangement any better than you do. As soon as my car is fixed I'll be on my way and mail you a check for the damages to . . . your supplies."

"How do I know your check would be any good? Come on, I don't have all day. Let's go."

CHAPTER 5

Adrianna tried to keep up with Quinn's long strides as he led the way down the street. She was fuming because he didn't trust her to mail a check for what she owed him. The businesses that lined Main Street began to give way to residential houses; most of them were identical to those near the doctor's office. A couple of blocks from the church, Quinn turned to the north onto a side street.

"You doing all right? It's not much farther."

Ahead, a tall row of hedges lined the street. Their branches and small green leaves still glistened from the rain. Tiny flowers had begun to pop from their tight buds and filled the air with a sweet, fresh fragrance. A scattering of petals had been loosened by the rain and lay on the pavement.

They turned up a walk and approached a

two-story white home, fronted by a wide porch. Adrianna noticed a pair of bentwood chairs on the porch and a swing at the end. With the sun beginning to set, bright light was reflected off the long, slender windows that lined both stories. A door led out onto a small roof porch. An abundance of shrubs flourished around the porch; a small magnolia tree stood at the end. A patch of yard at the side of the house had been set aside for a vegetable garden, although it was obvious from the tangle of weeds overrunning it that it hadn't been tended to lately.

As Adrianna walked up the steps and onto the porch she was aware that the house at one time had been splendid, but time and neglect had made it rather shabby. Quinn pushed open the door and walked ahead of her into the house, set her suitcase down, then held open the screen door for her to enter.

"Come in, Annie." As he looked down at her, his eyes softened for an instant as if he were apprehensive about her being in his home.

Adrianna's heart thumped. She wasn't sure if it was this big man who caused it or her fear of the future in this house. She looked around. A tall stairway rose from the entry to the upper floor. To the right of the foyer was a living room; a couch, a library table covered with a tasseled scarf, an upright Victrola and an RCA radio were the only furnishings. Adrianna was dismayed by the clutter and disarray; nearly every surface was buried in papers, magazines, and books. She was trying to come up with a compliment about his home when something caught her eye. Above the couch hung a pair of oval picture frames: a sweet-faced woman with her hair piled on her head and a rather stern-looking man who appeared uncomfortable in a stiff collar, suit, and tie.

The sound of footsteps came from another part of the house, and a woman with a mass of dark hair emerged from a doorway, wiping her hands on an apron. Her face appeared to be freshly made-up: spots of rouge on her cheeks, eyebrows darkened with pencil, and thick mascara on her lashes. Her mouth was a streak of deep red. She smiled brightly at Quinn, the corners of her mouth turning up, but when she saw Adrianna her smile faded.

"Annie," Quinn said, "this is Lola Oxnard. Lola, this is —"

Lola interrupted: "Is she the one?" Her eyes traveled from the top of Adrianna's head to the tips of her toes. Her look was one of disapproval, and Adrianna knew immediately that the woman resented her being there.

Adrianna held out her hand. "I'm glad to meet you."

Lola touched her hand briefly to Adrianna's. "Ya are?"

"Of course I am," Adrianna said firmly, determined not to let the woman intimidate her. She was aware of Quinn looking from one to the other. When he spoke, it was to Lola.

"Did you get the room ready?"

"Of course I did," she said in the same firm voice Adrianna had used, and Adrianna knew she was mocking her.

Quinn picked up the suitcase and headed for the stairway as Adrianna followed.

Lola watched them ascend the stairs. "Bitch," she muttered under her breath. "I'm not going to let you come in here and spoil things for me. I'll make you wish you'd never come to Lee's Point."

Quinn flung open a door at the top of the stairs and nodded for Adrianna to enter. She was surprised when she entered the large, airy room. The furnishings were old but well cared for. A large, four-poster bed stood against one wall covered with a faded quilt. A rocking chair sat next to the window. A beautifully embroidered scarf hung over the back. The room was clean and not as cluttered as the rest of the house.

"This was my mother's room," Quinn explained.

"Are you sure you want me to use it?"

"I'm sure or I wouldn't have brought you here. My mother spent a lot of time in here during her last days. She was proud of her needlework, and I'm trying to preserve it for Jesse. He isn't interested in it now, but he might be someday." Quinn walked over to the dresser and ran his fingers over the embroidered scarf that lay on it. "She liked to make pretty things." He hushed abruptly, wondering why he was telling her this.

"It's truly a beautiful piece of work," Adrianna said, and she meant each word.

"Since she left us," Quinn said, "I've tried to keep the room the way she would. You'll see the rest of the house is not very well kept. Lola isn't much of a housekeeper, but she watches over Jesse. I've not the time to do much with the rest of the house, but this room is different. I keep the door closed, and Lola knows not to mess it up."

"How long has your mother been gone?" Adrianna asked hesitantly.

"Five years." His eyes avoided hers. "Some days it seems like it's been forever, while on others it seem like it just happened."

"I understand how you feel. I lost my mother ten years ago and my father a few weeks ago."

"No brothers or sisters?"

"No. I was the only one." Adrianna's heart beat loudly in her chest. She stood silently and stared into his gray eyes.

Quinn looked away. "Lola should have supper on the table in a few minutes. Come on down when you're ready."

After he left, Adrianna went to the window and looked down at the street. *What in the world am I doing here in the home of this strange man?* There was something about him that made her uneasy. She was sure that Lola, the housekeeper, didn't like her. She would have to be careful not to step on her toes. Quinn would have to tell her exactly what he wanted her to do to earn her room and board.

She heard voices coming from downstairs and wondered if Quinn Baxter ever talked in a quiet tone. Although his voice was loud, it was not unkind, and she figured he was talking to his younger brother. Well . . . she wouldn't be here long. She could call the bank and get the money to pay him, but she was sure Richard would find out and come for her. She'd do that as a last resort.

Adrianna ran her comb through her hair

and, on sudden impulse, touched her lips with her Tangee lipstick. With a handkerchief, she blotted some of it off thinking about the bright red Lola was wearing. Her estimation of Quinn had slid down a notch after she met the housekeeper; surely he could have hired someone a little bit more refined to keep his house.

Dr. Bordeaux had told her about Jesse's accident. She tried to imagine how difficult it would be at that age to be unable to go to school with other kids. The doctor said that after the accident, Quinn had taken his brother to doctors in Jackson, Mississippi. They had told them there was nothing they could do for him, but they had given him a schedule of exercises that would help. Dr. Bordeaux said Quinn was busy and the housekeeper had been negligent about seeing that the boy did them.

Adrianna took one last look in the mirror and went down the stairs. As she stood hesitantly, not knowing if she should go to the kitchen or not, Quinn came out into the hall.

"Annie," he called. "Come meet Jesse."

"My name's not Annie," she retorted as she passed him to enter the room. Her eyes focused on the young man on the bed. He was propped up against the headboard. In her peripheral vision, she saw a chair with large wheels that sat in the corner of the room. Books and magazines were scattered on the floor, along with a dirty plate and glass.

"Jesse," Quinn said in a quiet voice that Adrianna had never heard him use before. "This is Miss Moore. Her name is Adrianna, but I think we can call her Annie." He grinned when he saw the frown come over Adrianna's face. "She's the one who slid into me on that damn curve at Baker's Corner. I swear that corner is jinxed."

Adrianna stepped closer to the bed and held out her hand. "Hello, Jesse. I see you like to read."

"Yeah. What else can a cripple do?" He ignored her hand.

"Now, Jesse," Quinn said, but the boy didn't look at him. He continued to flip the pages of a magazine.

At that moment, Adrianna saw a great sadness hanging over Quinn, as well as a touch of helplessness. *There is far more to this man than what is seen at first glance.*

Lifting a small pile of books off a chair, Quinn moved the chair close to the bed for Adrianna to sit on. He stood at the end of the bed, his eyes on his brother.

"I hear you had a bad day. Lola said you

71

were impossible and rude to her."

Jesse didn't answer. After a couple of seconds, Quinn reached out and gently but firmly tugged the magazine from his brother's hands. Jesse didn't protest, but he didn't speak either, choosing instead to fold his arms over his chest.

"Do you have anything to say for yourself?"

"No." Slowly, Jesse raised his head to look directly at Quinn.

In the sparse light, Adrianna got her first good look at Jesse. He was in his mid-teens. His close-cropped black hair was identical in color to his brother's. Wire-rimmed glasses perched on his nose. The shirt he wore hung loosely on his small frame. Even though she had only glanced at the boy's mother's picture, she could see that Jesse was the spitting image of her.

"Do you have a library in town?" Adrianna asked Jesse, ignoring Quinn.

"Yeah," the boy said grudgingly.

"I'll have to visit and get some books."

"When are you going to have time to read?" Quinn murmured. "Don't forget you're going to play the piano at the Whipsaw two nights a week."

Adrianna was surprised to see a grin flirt with the corners of Jesse's mouth. When he spoke, it was just above a whisper.

"I'd like to see that."

"Did you say you'd like to come hear me play?" Adrianna asked.

"Quinn won't let me go in there."

"Why not?"

"Because he's not old enough," Quinn said as he dropped the magazine on the bed.

Jesse snorted. "You went in taverns when you were sixteen."

"It wasn't a tavern. It was a pool hall."

"Same thing."

Lola came to the door and announced, "Supper's on the table."

"I'm eating in here tonight," Jesse said, looking defiantly at his brother.

"No, you're not. You're coming to the table."

Adrianna said as she got up from the chair, "I don't think it would be much fun to eat in here by yourself."

"What do you know about it?" Jesse said belligerently.

"Jesse, don't be ornery," Quinn cautioned.

"I just asked a question," the boy said defensively.

"That's all right," Adrianna said. "I'll answer. No, I don't know. But I know how it was for my mother who had to eat in her room when she wanted so badly to come down and eat with me and my father." Adrianna went to the door. "I'll see you later, Jesse."

"You'll see him now because he's coming to the table." Quinn grabbed the wheelchair and pulled it up beside the bed. "Come on, kid. You're getting out of there."

"I should at least be able to say where I'm going to eat," Jesse grumbled.

"When I'm here, Jesse, you eat at the table. You know that."

Quinn picked up a pair of pants and threw the covers off Jesse's legs. He lifted the boy's thin, bare legs, swung them off the bed, and knelt down to shove first one foot and then the other into the legs of the pants.

"Where are your shoes?"

"Ask that bitchy cow that stands guard over me all day."

"Watch your mouth."

Adrianna turned and went into the hallway. She could hear Jesse complaining and Quinn's voice, quiet for once, talking to him. Moments later, he was pushing Jesse out the doorway and down the hall toward the bathroom. She headed for the kitchen where she heard the rattle of pans.

"Can I help?"

"No," Lola answered sharply. She ignored Adrianna, continuing to dish up the food.

Moments later she brushed past Adrianna and carried two bowls to the dining room table.

"Are you sure I can't help you with something?"

Lola's head spun around. The annoyed look on her face made Adrianna wish she hadn't offered. She heard Jesse and Quinn coming down the hall as Lola brushed past her to go back into the kitchen.

Quinn pushed Jesse to the table. Adrianna noticed that Jesse's hair was damp and smoothed back from his forehead and his shirt was buttoned; Quinn had made an attempt to make his brother presentable.

"Sit down, Annie." Quinn pulled out a chair.

"I should help . . ."

Lola, who was coming into the dining room, said sweetly, "I don't need her help." She placed a loaf of bread still in its store wrapper within Quinn's reach. "I've been doing things around here for a long time by myself."

Adrianna looked at the soiled oilcloth on the table and wondered if the dishes were clean.

Lola smiled graciously at Jesse and Quinn before seating herself at the opposite end of the table facing Quinn; it was as if she were the lady of the house.

Sitting across the table from Jesse, Adrianna watched the boy and wished that he would smile.

Lifting a spoonful of potatoes, Lola put them on Jesse's plate.

"I'm not a baby. I can help myself."

"I know you can." She smiled sweetly. "I'm just trying to be helpful."

"There's nothing wrong with my arms and my hands. Next you'll be trying to feed me . . . when Quinn's around."

Lola's face turned a dull red and she clamped her lips shut.

Quinn helped himself to the turnip greens before passing them to Adrianna. She took a small helping, then set the bowl on the table.

"Bread?" Quinn asked Jesse.

"I can reach it."

"Quinn?" Lola said when their plates were full. "Will you help me turn over Jesse's mattress after dinner?"

"Didn't we do that last week?"

"Oh yeah, I guess we did. I'm sorry, I forgot," she said and smiled at Quinn.

Adrianna heard a small disgusted sound come from Jesse. She glanced at him and found him looking straight into her eyes, then to her surprise his eyelid dropped and he winked. She didn't understand what he meant, unless he was letting her know that Lola had her eyes on Quinn.

Lola kept up a lively conversation with Quinn, talking about people they both knew, giving Adrianna no chance to join the conversation, not that she wanted to; she was too busy gathering her impressions of this strange family she had been thrust into.

When the meal was over, Adrianna began taking the dishes from the table to the kitchen. Lola didn't speak to her until Quinn and Jesse went out onto the front porch.

In the kitchen, Lola pointed to the dishpan. "You can wash."

Not for anything would she tell Lola that she hadn't washed dishes since she was ten years old. Back then Nettie, the family cook who had been with them since she was born, let her stand on a box and help. At the time, she thought it was great fun. No one scolded her because her dress was wet from neck to hem or because she had broken a cup.

After the dining room table had been cleared and Adrianna was elbow-deep in the dishwater, Lola suddenly left the kitchen. Adrianna heard her voice on the porch with Quinn and Jesse, but not clearly enough to understand what was being said.

Well if she thinks I can't clean this kitchen, I'll show her. I've watched our cook at home and she would be horrified at the mess here.

An hour later, Adrianna stood back. Her eyes swept over the kitchen. The dishes were washed, scalded, and dried. The stove was clean, as were the pots and pans. She took a soapy cloth to the oilcloth on the dining room table, then dried it with a towel. She found a broom on the back porch and swept the dining room and the kitchen. When she finished, she stood at the door leading to the porch. Lola was laughing at something Quinn said. Their voices reached her as she turned and went slowly up the stairs to her room. But when she heard her name, she turned back and listened. . . .

"Where is Adrianna?" Quinn asked.

"She said she was tired and went upstairs."

"Did she help with the dishes?"

"Are you kidding?" Lola said with the toss of her head. "She thinks she's above doing dishes."

"We'll see about that." Quinn got up to push his brother's chair. "Ready to go in now?"

"Why?" Jesse said irritably. "Are you wanting to get me back in the bed so you can leave?"

"I've got to go to the tavern. You know that."

"Why did you put Cowboy in the shed?" he asked Lola.

"I always put the dog in the shed when the doctor is coming."

"Well, the doctor didn't come, so let him out." Jesse demanded. "Miss Prissy Tail will just have to get used to him if she's going to stay here."

Adrianna slipped quietly up the stairs to her room.

CHAPTER 6

Richard Pope ran his fingers absentmindedly over the baubles scattered across
Adrianna's bureau. He touched a perfume
decanter, then a jeweled compact case, and
finally a hand mirror, all of them left behind
in their owner's hurried flight. They, just
like him, had been abandoned. While in this
they shared a similarity, in one way they
were spectacularly different — each of the
accoutrements was cold to the touch, in
great contrast to the rage that boiled in his
chest.

"She was certainly in a hurry!"

All around him was near darkness. He
hadn't bothered to turn on the lights to her
bedroom, preferring to let his eyes wander
in the gloom. In what little light remained
of the day, he could see open drawers,
clothes in haphazard piles, and a discarded
suitcase that lay half-hidden under the bed.

Jerking a pair of her silk panties out of a

drawer, he held them to his face for a long moment, breathing in the scent, then opened the fly of his trousers and stuffed them inside. They felt so good against his maleness. It wasn't the first time he had taken a pair of Adrianna's panties. He sometimes carried a pair in his coat pocket; fondling them made him feel closer to her. He rubbed himself with her silken garment until his erection was stiff and throbbing. If she were here, he would be tempted to slap her for causing him to have to obtain satisfaction in this way.

At some point during the last seven days, Adrianna had decided to reject his offer of marriage. She had moved about this very room, deciding what to take and what to leave behind. What Richard now stood amongst was the unworthy and unwanted. It was the trash . . . and he had been left behind with it. With a hiss of air through clenched teeth, he turned and hurled the perfume decanter against the wall; the sound of it shattering was balm to his frustration.

It wasn't supposed to have been this way!

He'd spent the week since Charles Moore's funeral busily getting ready for their wedding. On top of the day-to-day operations of his law firm, he'd worked tirelessly preparing his home for his bride. He'd ordered the house to be cleaned from floor to ceiling. He wanted everything to be perfect when he brought her to her new home. Today was to have been a celebration. Today was to have been their wedding day!

Even now, as he stood in her bedroom, a priest was waiting for him and his bride-to-be. He'd invited only a select few guests, all men and women of substance. The food was ready. Champagne was chilling in the tubs of ice. *How will I explain it when I come back without her?* Some lie or other would have to suffice. The embarrassment would undoubtedly pass, but at that moment, its sting was like a knife in his gut.

As the sweet smell of perfume began to fill the bedroom, he paused and rubbed his crotch again with her silk panties, then left the room and descended the stairs.

When he'd let himself in, he had known immediately that something was wrong. He'd called out Adrianna's name only to be met with silence. With each step up the stairs, the knot in the pit of his stomach had grown tighter. Even before he'd opened the door to her bedroom, before his hand had even touched the knob, he'd known that she wouldn't be there.

In the end, the error had been his. He had assumed that Adrianna would be intelligent enough to see that his intentions were in her best interest; that assumption had been a great overestimation. She had been too naive to accept the simple truth that lay before her, but it was not all her fault. The coddling she had received from her father had spoiled her. She wasn't capable of knowing what was best for her, namely to have Richard Pope for a husband.

But where had she gone? This was the question that truly needed answering.

Moving more deeply into the house, Richard found himself in the room in which he had declared his intentions to Adrianna. Turning on a pair of lights affixed to the wall, he could see her standing there in his mind's eye, her luxurious hair piled high atop her porcelain face, the grief of her father's recent passing mixing with the excitement that must have pulsed through her veins as he had spoken.

Why had he not taken her right then and there?

Even as he thought the question, he knew the answer: because he was a gentleman and such coarse behavior was not becoming to a man of his standing. He had not taken her; but if he had forced her, she would have been so shamed that she would have gladly married him, thinking that she had been ruined for any other man.

Opening a decanter, he poured himself a glass of brandy, which he drank in one large gulp. The amber liquid burned as it moved down to his stomach to mix with the bile and anger he was brewing on his own. He drank another glass quickly, before he had a chance to think better of it.

On the mantel above the fireplace was a photograph in a silver frame. He snatched it from its resting place and looked deeply into the image. In the picture, Adrianna stood slightly behind her sitting father, one hand placed upon the older man's shoulder. As he stared at the image, he ran one finger across the young beauty's face. She looked so very delicate, like a tender flower that needed constant care. Richard remembered the day the picture had been taken. He'd stood in the background, waiting behind the photographer.

"That's always been my lot!"

From the moment he'd come into Charles Moore's employ, all of the success that the bank had achieved had been because of him and him alone. As Charles's illness had become increasingly debilitating, he'd removed himself from more and more responsibilities. Each and every one of those had then fallen to Richard. But was he allowed to claim the credit he had earned? Was he allowed to bask in the glow of his own success? *No!* He had to stand in the background, just as he had when this picture was taken. Well, no more! Never aga—

A sudden noise from the rear of the house stopped him in his tracks. Cocking one ear, he waited for another sound. Moments later, he heard it again. *Someone was here!* Setting the picture back down on the mantel, he hurried over and snapped off the lights, returning the room to darkness.

As he moved down a hallway toward the sound, his heart pounded in his ears with such force that he would have sworn that it could be heard by others. Another sound, the clinking of dishes, reached him. He pressed forward, creeping carefully, cautiously, but with purpose. *Could it be that Adrianna has returned? Has she come to her senses after all?* Light spilled from a crack in the door that led to the kitchen. Taking a deep breath, he flung the door open.

"Ahhh!" a woman's shrill voice shrieked.

It was not Adrianna. His prospective bride was dainty and beautiful, but the woman he found in the kitchen was plump and especially homely. Her eyes bulged widely underneath her mop of straggly hair. One heavy hand flew to cover her heaving bosom. She was one of the Moores' housekeepers, and his mind raced for her name. *Was it Stella? Blanche? Pansy?* Somehow, all of this served only to make him angrier.

"Where is she?" he thundered as he grabbed the woman's arm.

"I-I-I don't know what . . ." she stammered through ragged breaths.

"Don't play stupid with me, you bitch!" As he spoke, he shook her viciously. Her large breasts jiggled as she was rocked one way and then the other. "I know damn well that you've got your eyes and ears glued to the goings-on in this house! Where the hell did she go?"

"I saw . . . saw Miss Moore pack up her . . . things but I don't know . . ." Before she could manage any more, Richard raised one hand and slapped her hard across the face. The force of the blow knocked her head into the wall and she immediately burst into tears. She sobbed and tried to cover her face with her hands. But he grabbed her wrists and forced her hands down.

"Shut up your damn bawlin' and look at me!" he shouted. In that moment, Richard was so angry he feared he would kill her if that was the only way to discover Adrianna's whereabouts. Even as the thought settled over him, he was not surprised. He was tired of the battle to get what was justifiably his. He'd not allow it, especially not from *this* ignorant clod!

"Mr. Pope . . . Mr. Pope," she pleaded, her face red and blotchy. She tried to choke down the sobs but could not. "Miss Moore asked me to come back and clean the house today and to take what I wanted from the garden. She didn't tell me where she was going or why, I swear it!"

"You're lying."

"I'm not! Honest, Mr. Pope! I only talked to her for a few minutes. She gave me a bag of her old clothes and paid me for today. I have worked for Miss Adrianna and Mr. Moore for a year. She gave me a key and trusted me to come and clean after she was gone."

"When did she leave?"

"I don't know, sir. But the day I was here, she put some things in the car."

"What things?"

"Boxes and stuff like that."

"I will ask you one more time," he said, raising his hand as if to strike her again. "Where did she go?"

"I swear to you, sir," she said quickly, fearful of another blow. Her eyes moved frantically across the lawyer's face, as if she were searching for some crumb of compassion, anything that would make him believe she was telling the truth. "I don't know where she ran off to! She didn't make no mention!"

"Why do you say she ran off? Maybe she just went to visit someone. Damn you! Don't you spread the rumor around that she ran off."

"I won't, sir . . . I swear I won't."

Looking into the woman's frightened eyes, Richard knew she wasn't lying, that Adrianna wouldn't entrust a secret to this stupid woman. He had to try a different tactic. "Then where do you *think* she went?"

"I . . . I . . . don't know."

"Come on, you fat fool!" he shouted, grabbing her by the shoulders and shaking her viciously. "If she didn't tell you her destination, you must be able to guess where she went. You've been here long enough to know her habits!"

"I don't know!" she pleaded. "She ain't got no family around here no more. All of Mr. Moore's brothers died years ago! You got to believe me! You just got to!"

"Has she ever mentioned anything about the relatives on her mother's side?" Richard continued to press. "Did she have any family that she would know of? You'd better come up with something or you'll spend the next year in jail. I'll swear you were stealing from this house."

"No! No! I never did! I swear I have never taken anything that Miss Adrianna didn't give me."

"It makes no difference if you did or not, I'll say you did, and you know my word carries a lot of weight in this town."

"But sir!"

"Goddamnit! What about her mother's brothers or sisters? I'm asking you for the last time."

A flicker of recognition flashed across the woman's face and her mouth quickly opened but was abruptly shut. Whatever she knew, she was reluctant to part with. An eruption of fury raged in Richard's chest, and he raised his hand to strike her another blow, this one sure to be harder than the first. But before he could let it loose, the dam of her silence broke and she blurted out, "Her mother's sister lives in Mississippi, I think."

"Where in Mississippi?" he demanded, the hand still raised as a threat.

"I don't know what town."

"Do you know her aunt's name? Well,

never mind. I can find out."

Suddenly, everything became clear to him — what she had done, how she had done it, and most important, where she had gone. It was as if a lightning bolt had blazed through his head, illuminating all that had been hidden. Shoving the housekeeper aside, he went out the rear entrance of the house and across the short lawn to the garage that sat at the rear of the property. Yanking open the twin doors, he found just what he had expected.

Charles Moore's automobile was gone, taken by his wayward daughter. *How dare she take the car.* It was "his" car. It had been left to him in Charles's will. He had already put the title in his name.

She has stolen my *car.*

As he stood in the cool night, the light wind pushing the wisps of his thinning hair in a bizarre dance, Richard Pope's mind raced. As a lawyer he had been making decisions affecting life and death for years, and he knew what he had to do. If she had gone to Mississippi — and he had no reason to think anything else at this point — it would be easy to locate her with his resources. *Won't she be surprised when she arrives and finds me waiting there for her.* He immediately began to feel better.

"Oh, my sweet Adrianna," he said as he rubbed himself with her panties again. The anger that had filled his chest upon entering the house was slowly dissipating. As he calmed, he began to even look forward to the chase — wherever it might lead — and the challenges that lay ahead. "I'll play your silly game for a while, you little hussy." He chuckled. This time when he found her he would no longer be the gentleman she had known. He would show her, in no uncertain terms, that he was the master and she belonged to him.

CHAPTER 7

Quinn hurried down the steps, through the squeaky wrought-iron gate, and out into the gloomy night. As he walked toward the Whipsaw, his hands thrust deeply into his pockets, a light breeze stirred the leaves of the treetops, bringing with it the fresh smell of impending rain. Even though this day's storm had passed, another would surely be close behind. Springtime in Lee's Point was nothing if not wet! On the far horizon, the sun had nearly set. Deep crimson and purple streaks colored the tops of the billowy clouds.

Quinn's father had named the tavern the Whipsaw, thinking it appropriate for the logging community. A whipsaw was a narrow, seven-foot, two-person, crosscut saw with hooked teeth, used to cut logs into planks.

Operating the Whipsaw was not a labor of love for Quinn; that honor had belonged to his father. As he had built the home in which Quinn now lived, John Henry Baxter had constructed the tavern with his own two hands, tending and caring for it as if he were a farmer trying to raise fields of crops. At first, the new business struggled to make ends meet but, through years of hard work and dedication, it had managed to find its legs and thrive. People had come from miles around to find a place to forget their worries for a while. It was assumed that the Whipsaw would always be a fixture in Lee's Point.

That assumption had held true until the day John Henry Baxter died.

While Quinn had respected his father, he had never admired John Henry, and he'd certainly never wanted to follow in his footsteps. John Henry had been a pious man who rarely imbibed in the stock that he traded; he truly believed that you could achieve anything you wanted . . . providing you were willing to sacrifice for it. To that end, he had worked day and night, tirelessly trying to improve his lot, even if it meant neglecting his family. Such dedication had won him a heart attack and an early grave.

Quinn had marched to a different drummer. He'd chafed at going to school, but gone anyway and given it his best effort. He had attended church for his mother's sake but was not interested in the piano lessons she had pushed upon him . . . although they might have come in handy, given the current circumstances! His father had wanted him to follow in the family business, but instead, Quinn had left home to go to the mill, promising himself that he would never be a tavern operator. He'd held that promise for nearly eight years. His father's death had forced him to go back on his word.

Running the tavern had proven to be far more of a challenge than he had thought it would be. The responsibilities weighed heavily on his shoulders. He was determined to make the Whipsaw a success for Jesse's sake. Jesse would need a way to make a living after he finished school. Luckily, he'd made one very good decision: hiring Gabe LeBlanc to tend the bar. Together, the two men had somehow managed to keep things running smoothly.

As he rounded a corner and moved onto Main Street, Quinn could see people milling about. After many long, hard hours of work, followed by the quiet of a family meal, quite a few of Lee's Point's residents longed to get out and relax. For many, relaxation meant nothing more than visiting friends for a game of cards. Others found church socials more to their taste. But for a large number, a night of singing and dancing, fueled by a touch of liquor, did the trick. To that end, there was the Whipsaw.

He waved a few greetings, shouted a "hello," turned another couple of corners and minutes later was standing in front of the tavern. The Whipsaw was a squat one-story building that was only half as wide as it was long. A pair of rectangular windows looked out onto the street, spilling scant light from inside. Above the front door, a weather-beaten sign in desperate need of a new coat of paint spelled out the bar's name.

Suddenly, Quinn thought of Adrianna. He'd been hard on her today, certainly harder than he'd needed to be, but he couldn't deny that the accident had made him irritable . . . for a number of different reasons. The way she'd entered his life had been abrupt, much like the accident itself, but she now was a part of it . . . for a while anyway. Still, she was different from any woman he'd ever met. She was educated, well-mannered, and even a tad delicate, a far cry from the women he'd known. When she spoke, people listened; what she said, as well as the simple sound of her voice, seemed to grab hold of him, refusing to let go. *What am I thinking, bringing her to this place?*

Shaking his head, he pushed open the door and entered the bar.

The first thing that struck him was the sound: pieces of conversation mixed with bursts of laughter and the clinking of glasses. Occasionally, the scrape of a chair leg against the hardwood floor carried across the din. Men and women sat in groups at the mismatched tables and chairs that were set haphazardly about the long, rectangular room. Some of the tables had cloth covers draped over their scarred tops, but most were bare. The light was much gloomier than the tavern's mood; a dull glow came from the fixtures that were stuck to the walls and the naked bulbs that hung from the ceiling. Smoke from cigars and cigarettes floated above the tables. The Whipsaw wasn't the fanciest place, but it was clean. Although it was still early in the evening, the tavern had begun to fill up. Even on a weeknight, there was a good chance that the Whipsaw would have a decent crowd.

"Well, if it ain't Quinn Baxter, I done do swear!"

Quinn turned at the sound of the voice to see a disheveled mess of a man ambling toward him, a drink in one gnarled hand. Roy Long had been a fixture in the town for as long as anyone could remember. Topped with straggly white hair, his wrinkled face wore a perpetual stubble. Soiled clothes hung loosely from his rail-thin frame. Somewhere in his late fifties or early sixties (no one was really sure how old he was), Roy swore that he was a distant relative of Huey Long, the man who had been Louisiana's governor up until a couple of years earlier. Since Roy, often quite drunk, was prone to exaggerate, no one gave this tall tale much credit.

"Evening, Roy," Quinn greeted the older man.

"Damn shame what happened to all that there booze, I done do swear!" Amongst other things, Roy Long was known for the way in which he often ended his sentences. The phrase was like a caboose that always managed to hang on to the runaway loco-motive that was his everyday speech.

"I don't think we're in any danger of run-ning out," Quinn fibbed slightly. As he spoke, he caught a whiff of the man's odor, his unwashed smell harsh even by the standards of the working people of rural Louisiana. If you wanted to talk with Roy, upwind was the best place from which to do it. "I wasn't too happy about the accident. Losing my booze was bad enough, but I'm mad as hell about my truck being messed up. Delmar thinks it's fixable." Quinn edged around Roy and slid an empty chair under a table.

"If it's fixable, ol' Delmar ain't gonna have too much of a hard time with it, I reckon." Roy cackled as he ran leathery fingers over his rough chin. "Ain't a contraption made that he ain't worked on one time or other. That boy could take a mule's tail and make it into a hind leg if he set his mind to it, I done do swear!"

"You're probably right. Maybe he should take a look at Gabe's hand," Quinn joked, glancing at his friend.

"That ain't but nothin' a little time'll fix. He's a young fella. He'll heal right up, good as new," Roy explained sagely. "If it happened to an old bird like me with one foot already in the grave, ya might be havin' yourself a wake tonight."

"Good thing you weren't driving then," Quinn said with a chuckle.

Suddenly, a look of seriousness overtook the old man. "If Gabe's got hisself a busted wing, who's gonna play the pian'r for the sing-along? Ya ain't gonna put it off, is ya?"

Once again, Quinn's thoughts were drawn

to Adrianna. Looking up, his eyes found the Whipsaw's piano, tucked into the far corner to one side of the bar. He'd purchased it from the church a couple of years earlier when they'd decided to buy a new one. It had its share of nicks and scrapes and was in dire need of a tuning, but it more than met their needs. When they needed it for entertainment, it was pushed out toward the center of the room; but for now it sat silent, its black and white keys covered. In a couple of days' time, Adrianna would be perched on the tiny stool, plunking out a tune. She would look as out of place as a sunflower in a rose garden.

"I got it covered," he answered.

"For heaven's sake, I hope so," Roy said with relief. "But if ya ain't, I done played the pian'r at one of my cousin Huey's fancy parties, I done do swear! Just let me know!" With a slap of his knee that sent his beer sloshing onto the floor, Roy roared with laughter and headed off in search of new drinking companions.

All along one wall of the tavern stood the long, dark mahogany wood bar that John Henry had purchased shortly after he'd opened the Whipsaw. While the tables and chairs looked worn, the bar itself stood out for its class and beauty. Nearly twenty-five feet long, with tall beveled columns that were matched by the work area behind it, the bar had been a source of great pride for John Henry. He'd spent so much time polishing the wood that it still glowed softly. A trio of mirrors backed the bar. The glass was clean and unblemished. Gabe stood behind the counter trying to clean a beer mug with one hand and was failing miserably as Quinn approached.

"You'll have to practice," Quinn joked.

"It's a hell of a lot harder than it looks," the Cajun growled.

"How does the hand feel?"

"Throbs a little bit, but it's nothing a drink or two won't take care of." With a wink, he added, "But that doesn't mean I won't go and visit our beautiful doctor again."

"What you need to do is go over there and tell the woman how you feel about her. She can fix your busted mitt, but she can't read your mind." The two men had had a long-standing discussion about Gabe's romantic interest in Sarah Bordeaux. From the moment she'd come to town, he'd been smitten, even though she was happily married. He knew it was a hopeless love. His interest in her had never been brought out into the open for fear that she would reject him.

He'd never let his feelings be known to anyone other than Quinn. Hardly a week went by without Quinn trying to prod him into action. So far, Gabe had resisted.

"The time will come," Gabe said matter-of-factly.

"Don't wait until you're as old as Roy over there," Quinn said with a thumb toward the old drunk. "Somehow I don't think she'll be very interested by then, especially if you smell as bad as he does."

For the next hour, the two men worked together behind the bar, drawing mugs of beer and pouring drinks. The cash register bell rang loudly with every sale. Between customers, Gabe filled Quinn in on the Whipsaw's inventory, particularly an accounting of the tavern's liquor supply. It showed that they would have enough to last for at least five days, or until another purchasing run could be made.

"What about *la petite belle fille?*" Gabe asked, the French of his Cajun upbringing resurfacing. "How did it go introducing Adrianna into the household? Was Jesse up for it?"

"That went about as well as could be expected," Quinn admitted.

"Well, *mon ami . . .*"

"Well what? Why don't you come right out

and ask?"

"I don't have to. You know what I mean. Did Lola pitch a fit?"

"No, she was quite decent."

"When you were around," Gabe snorted.

"I think Annie will be able to hold her own with Lola."

"Annie? I bet she likes that."

"She wasn't too happy about it, but I can't get my tongue twisted around 'Adrianna' all the time. Besides, I think 'Annie' suits her."

"Why don't you give Lola a week off?" Gabe grinned mischievously.

"Why would I want to do that? She might quit. Then what would I do when Miss Moore leaves?"

"Don't worry about Lola quitting," Gabe hurried to say. "She'll stay there hoping to get her hooks into you. She likes your nice house. It's a palace compared to the one she grew up in."

Quinn put his hand on Gabe's shoulder. "Give this ol' boy some credit for knowing the ways of women."

"I don't think you know them as well as you think you do. Lola is not going to give over to Adrianna easily. She'll do her best to turn Jesse against her by making herself look good. She'll find fault with Adrianna every chance she gets. Keep your eye on her. Adrianna may not have come up against such a cat as Lola."

"Dr. Bordeaux wants Jesse to get outside more. He spends most of his time reading. I'm going to build a ramp out the back door so if Annie can persuade him to go out, she can take him out by herself. That is, if she can get him into the chair."

"Readin' isn't all bad. He might get to be as smart as me."

"Hell, that wouldn't take much."

"Watch your mouth, *mon ami.* Some dark night you might find yourself a meal for the gators."

"It seems the last few years those damn gators are getting braver and braver. I saw one walking along Taylor Road the other day."

"He wasn't far from the bayou." He chuckled.

Quinn had discussed Jesse's depressed attitude about his injuries with Gabe. His friend always put the best face on everything and frequently stopped by to visit the boy, often bringing him books and magazines.

"Dr. Bordeaux says there's a place up in Memphis that could possibly help Jesse adjust to being in the chair. I haven't mentioned it to him because I want him to walk if at all possible, even if it's on crutches.

He's got this idea in his head that he doesn't want any of his school friends to see him in the chair."

"With time . . . he'll walk," Gabe reassured him. With a sly look crossing his face, he added, "But enough about Jesse. I want to know all about the lovely young lady, and I want to know now."

"Annie?" Quinn said defensively. "What about her?"

"Come now, my friend!" Gabe frowned as he put his hands on his hips. "Do you take me for a fool . . . and a stupid one at that? I saw the way you were lookin' at her! A blind man could have seen that somethin' was working in your mind!"

"You're imagining things," Quinn said as he hoped that his face wasn't giving him away. The truth was that he had felt *something.* He just didn't know what. Carrying on the lie, he said, "She's going to come in here, play the piano, repay her debt to me, and be on her way. That'll be that."

"I hope that you're only lyin' to me, *mon ami,* and not to yourself." The Cajun laughed. "And if you are on the up-and-up, maybe I'll have to forget all about Dr. Bordeaux and try for somethin' else."

"She's not your type."

Gabe laughed again, his dark eyes sparkling. "I suppose she's yours?"

"She's not my type either. She'll shake the dust from this town as soon as her car is ready to go."

"Then it's up to you to see that she stays awhile. If you can't do it . . ." Gabe knew his friend was bothered by the turn of conversation, and he couldn't resist goading him more.

"What the hell can I do? Break your other hand? At times I think it would be a pleasure."

"Then you'd have to wash and dry *all* the glasses." Gabe grinned and tucked the rag he was using under the counter.

Before Quinn could even open his mouth for further banter, a sight at the front door stopped him in his tracks. A young man wearing a very prim-looking shirt and tie had stepped inside, glanced around with an expression that could only be described as disdain, and, when locking eyes with Quinn, made a beeline for the bar.

"Aw, shit," Quinn muttered.

Gabe, hearing Quinn's curse, looked up and let loose with one of his own. "*Mon Dieu!* It was such a nice night!"

Walking toward them was Dewey Fuller, a man who had been Quinn's enemy most of his life.

CHAPTER 8

Dewey Fuller stood on the other side of the long bar and stared at Quinn through narrowed eyes. He'd approached without a word, his hands gripping the rail. His boyish face was punctuated by a thin mouth turned down in a sneer. Quinn returned the silence. Even when a lumberjack at a far table let loose a belly-jiggling laugh that seemed to shake the room, neither man so much as blinked.

"Evenin', Dewey," Gabe said, attempting to break through the tension. When no response was forthcoming, he reached under the bar and grabbed a glass and a bottle half-full of whiskey. "I reckon you stopped by to have yourself a drink or two. Well then, one whiskey comin' up." The Cajun poured an inch of the dark liquor into the glass and slid it easily across the countertop to the other man.

"Obliged," Dewey muttered before quickly

downing the drink.

All the while, Quinn watched him closely. Dewey Fuller was a prim man whose dress and manners were a far cry from the norm in Lee's Point. Always attired in a suit of the latest style, he had sandy-blond hair slicked back with a sweet-smelling pomade that made Quinn's nose turn up in disgust. His skin was unblemished and smooth, the result of a life in which he'd never had to use his hands to provide for himself. The only mark of note was a thin scar that ran like a razor along the left side of his jaw. When he'd tipped his head back to drink the whiskey, it was as clear to see as the sun in the sky. No matter how hard he tried to avoid it, Quinn's eyes were always drawn to the scar. What choice did he have but to look? After all, he'd been the one who had given it to him.

"We need to talk," Dewey declared matter-of-factly as he slammed the empty glass down on the bar. Quinn was filled with a sudden anger at the realization that the man would never so much as offer to pay for the drink. He wasn't surprised by the emotion; no Fuller had ever paid for what he could just take.

"I don't have anything to say to you," Quinn replied.

"I'm not here to listen to you, but you're damn well going to listen to me." Looking around the Whipsaw, his nose wrinkling at the sight, Dewey asked, "Do you have somewhere we can go to talk? This isn't the kind of thing I want everyone to hear."

"If you've got something to say, spit it out here," Quinn declared defiantly as he crossed his arms over his broad chest and stood his ground. "Gabe's the only one who'll hear, and I don't keep any secrets from him."

"My father said it was for you and you alone."

"I don't give a shit what your father said!" Quinn barked as he pointed a finger sharply at the smaller man. His face reddened and his lips parted to form a snarl.

"Goddamnit, Quinn!" Dewey spat.

"Gentlemen! Try to keep your voices down," Gabe interjected, moving to position himself between the two men. He'd seen enough of their arguing over the years to know that things would soon escalate out of control. If it was going to happen, it shouldn't happen in the tavern.

"You don't have to leave, Gabe," Quinn started to say before Gabe waved him off.

"There ain't no point in my bein' a part of this business. What's to be said is between the two of you, *c'est la vérité,*" the barman explained. With a deep chuckle, he added, "And with the two of you out of my hair I'll be able to get some work done, at least as much as a one-armed barman can do!"

Quinn shrugged. "We'll go to my office then."

"Fine," Dewey agreed.

Quinn walked out from behind the bar and headed for the door that led to his office. He nodded a greeting to a couple of regulars, hoping that he'd done enough to mask his anger. Never once did he look back to see if Dewey had followed him, knowing full well that he was there; the man was like a tick that wouldn't let go.

"Damn," he muttered under his breath.

With every step, the bile in Quinn's stomach rose ever higher. He dropped into the rickety chair behind his desk and watched the man who had followed him into the office. The space was small, little more than a glorified broom closet, and the tight quarters allowed no room for decoration. Besides the chair in which he sat, it held only a crate full of empty bottles near the door and a desk fashioned from a couple of boards and two stacks of leftover bricks.

Without a chair of his own in which to sit, Dewey paced back and forth.

"Let's get this over with," Quinn spat.

"What I have to say to you won't take long," Dewey began in a voice that was at once both restrained and confrontational. "My father sent me to speak to you about the money you still owe him."

"I know all about what I owe your father. It was a sneaky trick for him to buy up my loan papers from the bank."

"Sneaky or not, he's becoming concerned about the loan," the dapper man said sarcastically as he brushed dust from his sleeve. "I'm not sure if you're aware of this, but the general idea of borrowing money from someone is that you will eventually pay him back. My father has been waiting for nearly a year, and I'm afraid that his patience is wearing a bit thin."

Quinn winced inwardly. From the moment Dewey had come through the Whipsaw's door, he'd known that he'd come to talk about the money that Quinn had borrowed from the bank. A year earlier, when business had slumped because of a depression in the lumber industry, Quinn had been at his wits end trying to keep the tavern afloat. With no other avenues open to him, he'd taken a loan from the bank, not knowing the bank had the option of selling the loan to an individual. Preston Fuller had stepped in, and Quinn had suddenly realized he owed his father's old enemy money. He'd struck a deal with the devil.

"I'm working on it. I'll have it soon —"

"In a couple of weeks," Dewey cut in, finishing his sentence. "Isn't that the same tired story you've told me the last three times that we've had this talk? You can't possibly expect me to go back to my father and give him the same old line. He'd take me for a fool!"

"If the shoe fits," Quinn challenged.

Dewey stopped his pacing and moved toward the makeshift desk. His mouth opened and his hand rose as if it were about to be used to punctuate a point, but it only hung in midair. Composing himself, he said, "This isn't about you and me. This is about the money you owe and nothing more."

"It's about more than money."

"No, it isn't."

"Bullshit! It's always been about the history between your father and mine. That was the reason he snuck in and bought my loan from the bank. He figured I wouldn't be able to pay and that he'd get the Whipsaw."

To that, Dewey had no answer except silence. Quinn knew he had heard the stories of how Preston Fuller had claimed that John Henry Baxter cheated him out of a business deal, and a friendship that had been thirty years in the making had blown away like so much smoke. This simmering dislike had in turn festered into something worse: out-and-out hatred. Even with John Henry's death, forgiveness was not forthcoming.

"I need to give him something," Dewey finally said.

"I don't have anything to give."

"Then do what you should have done from the very beginning and sell this dump to my father. He'll get it by some means so you might as well recover something out of the bargain."

"I'll never sell the Whipsaw!"

"Who's being the fool now?" Dewey argued as he came toward the desk. Gripping the front planks, he leaned down until he caught Quinn's gaze and held it steady. A whiff of his pomade carried across the desk, but Quinn had become too angry to notice. "You and I both know that you aren't cut out to do this work. You're a lumberjack! You're not the kind of man to stand behind a bar running a two-bit dive and you know it!"

"I've managed so far," Quinn argued, even though the sharp blades of truth in Dewey's words cut him to the quick. He'd had the same argument with himself since the day his father had died.

"Managed?" Dewey repeated incredulously. "All you have managed to do is drive yourself further into debt. Do you have so much pride that you can't admit you've made a mistake? Do you want to have all this taken away from you?"

"Shut up!" Quinn bellowed, his voice echoing around the small room.

"You're not just failing yourself, you know," Dewey pressed on, ignoring Quinn's order. "If you think you're doing Jesse some kind of favor by holding on to this rat hole, you're mistaken."

"Keep him out of this, you son of a bitch!" He struggled to contain his temper, but with every word out of Dewey's mouth, he began to lose the fight.

"Why should I? You borrowed the money. You can't blame my father because he bought up the note. Why are you trying to save this for Jesse? He's going to be a cripple for the rest of his life!"

"He's going to walk!" Quinn shouted.

"Goddamnit, Quinn! Face the facts! Jesse is never —"

Before Dewey could utter another word, Quinn was out of the chair and across the

113

desk. His calloused hand found the softness of the smaller man's throat and, with the strength of a wild animal, he hurled him across the room and into the door with a resounding crash. As he struggled to gain his balance, Dewey's foot collided with the crate of bottles, setting the glass clinking.

"Let go of me," Dewey struggled, one hand clawing at the vise that held him in place. The rage that had taken Quinn was beginning to ease off. When he finally spoke, it was more of a growl than a spoken word.

"Don't you ever call Jesse a cripple again!"

"Quinn . . . I . . . I . . . didn't mean any disrespect."

Thoughts raced through Quinn's head. A part of him wanted to break the man's neck and be done with it, consequences be damned. But common sense prevailed.

Quinn had taken on the responsibility of running the Whipsaw for one reason and one reason only: so that his brother would have something to live on. He could manage the place even if he was still in the wheelchair. All the work that he had put into the tavern, all the hours that he and Gabe had spent trying to keep the place going, would have been for nothing if he lost it to the Fullers. He let go of Dewey, and the man crashed to the floor in a heap.

"Oh . . . oh . . . Jesus!" Dewey rasped.

Striding back toward the desk, Quinn kept his back turned to the younger Fuller. The only sound in the room was the ragged breaths Dewey sucked down his strained throat. Quinn expected the man to slink out the door and go running back to his father, but he surprised him by talking in a voice no louder than a whisper.

"The . . . the last thing . . . I wanted was to come here and talk to you about this, but my father insisted. He thinks that because we were once friends, I could talk some sense into you."

Quinn turned and faced the fallen man. As they stared at one another, his mind raced back to a time when they weren't enemies, no matter how badly their fathers spoke of each other. There were summers spent down by the river and in the woods. There were the laughs, tears, and occasional fistfights of fast young friends. But all that, as with their fathers before them, had changed. It was gone forever.

"Our friendship is dead," Quinn said matter-of-factly.

Composing himself, Dewey rose to his feet and nodded. "Then it's business."

"I guess so."

"Then we're right back where we started."

Dewey sighed as he rubbed his hand against his damaged throat; the skin above his shirt collar was raw and red. "I need something to take back to my father."

"I told you —"

"And I told you that my father is serious," Dewey cut him off. "If you don't give me something, he's going to have the front door padlocked shut. He's been talking with Sheriff Beauchamp the last couple of days, so I know this time it's no empty threat."

A heavy weight settled squarely on Quinn's chest. He'd been pushed into the corner several times before, but never as soundly as now. There was no doubt that what Dewey was saying was true; Preston Fuller wasn't the type of man to play games, especially not where money was concerned. If he tried to stall, he could lose everything. Deflated, Quinn walked back behind the desk and knelt to the floor. There, wedged between a pair of bricks that supported his meager table, was a small roll of bills. It wasn't much, only a hundred dollars, but it was his last bit of emergency money. He'd hoped to use it to replace the liquor they'd lost in the crash with Adrianna, but this was more pressing.

"Here," he said, tossing the bills to Dewey. "Tell your father that it's all I've got. It'll have to do for now."

Thumbing through the bills, Dewey said, "I think this will hold him off, but only for a while." He paused for a moment before adding, "I know you don't see it the same as I do, Quinn, but you should really reconsider selling."

"Damn it, Dewey! Just give me a receipt for this money and get out."

Without another word, Dewey Fuller wrote out a receipt, set it on the desk, shrugged his shoulders, passed a hand through his slicked hair, and left the office. As the door clicked shut behind him, Quinn was left to himself and the thought that raced through his head.

What the hell am I going to do now?

Chapter 9

As Adrianna awoke from a night of fitful sleep, her eyes wandered around the room. In the early morning light that came through the window, she could make out the faded wallpaper, the walnut chest, and an ancient-looking washstand, absent the pitcher and bowl that had once sat upon it. For a long moment she wondered what she was doing in this strange place, then rolled over in the soft bed and closed her eyes.

A feeling of dread pressed hard against her chest at the thought of going downstairs to face that formidable man and his spiteful housekeeper. She'd always been the sort to get along well with others, but this was different. *I've never met anyone as belligerent as the woman who works in this house!*

Her body was tense and achy. The night before, she had come up to the room after washing the dishes and cleaning the kitchen, a chore she had not done since she was a child. The work had been harder than she'd remembered, and she'd been dead tired as she climbed the steps. No sooner had she washed herself, put on her nightdress, and stretched out on the bed, than she was asleep.

"Nothing has gone as I'd hoped," she whispered into the sheets.

When she'd left Shreveport, she'd had such high hopes of quickly getting to her aunt's house in Mississippi. Never in her wildest dreams could she have imagined she'd be sleeping in the house of a strange man and planning to play the piano in his tavern.

Oh, my Lord! Wouldn't Richard Pope have a fit if he knew?

The sudden sound of footsteps on the stairs reached her. Throwing back the sheet that covered her, she swung her feet to the floor where they rested on a faded rag rug that lay beside the bed. Knowing that she would have to dress before she could go downstairs and use the bathroom, she hurriedly pulled on her stockings, slipped her feet into her shoes, and reached for the dress she had thrown over her open suitcase. Taking out her hand mirror, she glanced at herself and began to pull a brush through the tangles in her shoulder-length dark brown hair. The face that looked back at her was fresh. She had slept soundly and was well rested, ready to take up her duties and pay for the damage she had caused. Once her debt had been repaid . . . *I'll be out of here like a shot!*

Opening her door, she stepped out into the hall and listened. The murmur of voices rose from the kitchen below. That *man* was talking to his housekeeper. A flicker of a thought ran through her head, and she wondered if he was sleeping with the woman. With a shrug, she realized that even if he were, it wasn't any of her business.

On her way to the stairs, she passed an open door and glanced inside. She knew at once that it had to be *his* room. Clothes were hung over the chair. The covers were thrown back from the bed as if he had just climbed out of it. There was such a mess that she wondered if yesterday's storm hadn't stopped by on its way out of town!

Adrianna passed on down the hall. Somehow, the fact that his room was so close to hers bothered her. It wasn't that she feared he might force his attentions on her. The doctor wouldn't have suggested she stay here if there had been a danger of that. Still . . .

She continued on down the steps. The

door to the bathroom was ajar. She opened it and went inside, making sure to lock it behind her. The room was steamy and smelled of soap and shaving cream. A straight-edged razor and a shaving mug with a brush sat on a shelf above the lavatory. After relieving herself, Adrianna pulled the chain to flush the toilet, fastened her clothes, and looked around. Everything was filthy! She was sure the room hadn't been cleaned in quite a while. The linoleum floor was in need of a good scrubbing, as was the lavatory. The towel that hung on the rod was dingy and damp when she blotted her face with it.

Adrianna glanced at her reflection in the mirror above the shelf, looked down to make sure the bodice of her dress was buttoned correctly, then opened the door and went out into the hall. Making her way to the kitchen, she paused hesitantly in the doorway. Quinn sat at one end of the kitchen table, Lola at the other. When he looked up to see her, Quinn stood.

"Come in and have a seat," he said warmly.

I guess he does have some manners after all, Adrianna thought.

Before seating herself, Adrianna hesitated. Glancing up from her end of the table,

Lola looked anything but happy to see her. Adrianna raised her head and looked directly at the woman. "Am I intruding?"

"Certainly not," Quinn answered before Lola could open her mouth. "I wanted to talk to you about Jesse before I left for work."

"You work days *and* nights?" Adrianna asked with surprise.

"I leave the tavern around midnight," he answered with a wave of a half-eaten piece of toast. "Gabe does most of the work anyhow. After I leave, he shuts everything down."

"That doesn't give you much time to sleep, does it?"

"A fella can't get much done if he spends his time sleeping." He chuckled. "Besides, my job at the mill pays the bills. If they cut back hours, I'll have more time to spend at the tavern."

"But Quinn," Lola said through lips puckered into a pout, "I was hoping that if they cut back at the mill you'd have more time to spend here at home with your family."

Quinn looked at Lola strangely, the corners of his mouth turned down in a slight frown, before glancing in Adrianna's direction. She looked from him to Lola with questioning eyes.

"Did you see if Jesse was awake?" Quinn asked, breaking the silence.

"He was still asleep." Lola frowned. "I wish you would do something about that dog he keeps in his room. Every time I go in there, he growls at me."

"Cowboy wouldn't growl at you if you tried to be friends with him. Jesse told me you kicked him," Quinn chastised the housekeeper. "Thing is, dogs have memories like your old grandmother . . . they don't forget anything."

Stifling a laugh, Adrianna nonetheless beamed broadly. "The dog's name is 'Cowboy'? That's sort of unusual, isn't it? Most dogs are named 'Rover,' 'Blackie,' or 'Spot.' "

"Cowboy fits the pup," Quinn explained, his gray eyes fastened to her face. "He's the sort that likes to roughhouse and run about on his own. What about you? Do you have a dog at home?"

"I like dogs, but I'm afraid we couldn't have one. They made my father sneeze."

Lola, resenting the sudden attention Quinn was giving to Adrianna, got up from the table in a huff and went to pour more coffee for herself and Quinn, completely ignoring the other woman. "That dog is far more trouble than it's worth. He eats everything in sight. Right now he's sick and threw up all over this morning. He should stay outside," she said.

"Cowboy is sick?" Quinn asked.

"It's what I said. He threw up this morning."

Like a cloud passing over a clear sky, Quinn's face suddenly turned from mirth to seriousness when he added, "That dog means the world to Jesse. What's the matter with him? Did he eat something spoiled? As soon as he quits throwing up, he stays where Jesse wants him to stay."

"I don't know what's the matter with him," Lola said defensively. "He probably got out and ate someone's garbage."

"Well, keep an eye on him. Jesse would be heartbroken if something happened to that dog." Turning from Lola, he asked, "Would you like some coffee, Annie?"

"Are you talking to me?" she responded, turning to face him.

"It's your name, isn't it?"

"No, it's not. My name is Adrianna."

"I like Annie better." He shrugged. "Now, how about coffee?"

"I can get it myself," she answered, rising from the table and going to fetch her own cup. "I don't want to cause more work for Lola."

Quinn caught the barb of sarcasm in her words. It was as obvious as the stars in a clear night sky that Adrianna knew Lola resented her being there. He'd given Lola strict orders to be civil to the new boarder. Apparently, he hadn't made himself clear enough.

Draining the last of his cup, Quinn stood up. "Now if you'll both excuse me, I'm going to check on Jesse."

Lola's eyes followed him as he left the room. After she'd heard the sound of the door to Jesse's room closing, she sat her cup down on the table with a bang. As she stared at Adrianna, her eyes were full of malice. It wasn't until that very moment that Adrianna fully realized the extent of the woman's hatred. *Is she afraid that I'm going to try to steal Quinn away from her?* She certainly didn't need to worry about that. They came from two different worlds.

"I don't want you here," Lola hissed.

"It's obvious," Adrianna answered, and she set her cup down gently.

"A decent woman would be embarrassed to live with a couple about to be married."

The shock of the woman's words hit Adrianna square in the chest. *What on earth is she talking about?* Quinn had never mentioned anything of the sort. "I didn't know you were engaged to him."

"We're keeping it a secret for the time being because of Jesse. Quinn is afraid that the boy will become agitated thinking I was taking his brother away from him. He could even end up in a home for cripples." With a sneer, she added, "Besides, I have no idea what you could possibly do for Jesse that I haven't."

"I might be able to give him more time," Adrianna answered defiantly, screwing up her courage and straightening her back. "The household chores certainly seem to take up much of yours."

"Yes, they do. There's a lot of work to be done around here," Lola replied, completely failing to recognize the true meaning of Adrianna's words.

"I can see that."

With a wayward eye, Adrianna looked at the dust that caked the furniture and the curtains that hung at dirty windows. She'd hate to even hazard a guess as to the last time they'd been washed.

What in the world does this woman do all day?

Seeing the door slightly ajar, Quinn pushed

it open and went into the room. Cowboy lay on the bed beside Jesse, who in turn sat with his back propped against the headboard. He was looking at an issue of the *Saturday Evening Post,* one of the magazines Gabe had brought him.

Quinn greeted his brother warmly. "I didn't know you were awake." He tried to keep his eyes from roving over the boy's thin frame. "Why didn't you call out?"

Jesse looked up and grunted. "I knew you'd come sooner or later."

Quinn reached over and scratched behind Cowboy's ears before gently tugging at the dog's neck in order to coax him from the bed. The dog stood and stretched, then wagged his long tail happily, glad to see Quinn.

Quinn had found Cowboy when the dog was just a pup. He had been wandering along the side of the road that led from town to the mill. The dog's long black and white hair had been full of cockleburs, his paws were cracked and sore, and he had been tired and hungry. But from the moment Quinn had brought him home, Cowboy and Jesse had been inseparable. Most anytime Jesse had ridden his bicycle into town, Cowboy could be seen trailing along behind. After a while he became protective of Jesse and had once jumped on the back of a boy who'd accidentally knocked Jesse to the ground when they'd been playing ball. Even after Jesse had found himself in the wheelchair, Cowboy had remained a loyal and steadfast companion.

"Are you ready to use the bathroom?" Quinn asked.

"I guess so." Jesse frowned. He seemed agitated, as if something was preying on his mind. Finally he spat it out: "How am I gonna pee in the can with that strange woman in the house?"

"Tell Lola to close the door and reach under the bed for it, like you always do."

"Aw, shit," the boy swore. Quinn couldn't imagine what the difference would be with Adrianna in the house, but it had been a long time since he'd been fifteen. "How long is she gonna be here, anyway?"

"I'm not sure. Dr. Bordeaux thinks she might be able to help you."

"Help me? How the heck is she gonna do that? She isn't no doctor."

"Maybe she can help you in ways that don't have anything to do with your legs," Quinn explained as he sat down at the foot of the bed. Cowboy took it to mean that he didn't have to move either and lay back down. "For one thing, she could help you with your schoolwork. The teachers will send books to the house. There's no reason why you can't graduate next year if you put your mind to it."

"How's all that going to help a cripple?"

"You keep calling yourself that and you're going to start believing it," Quinn chided his brother. "What happened to you didn't do anything to your brains, did it?"

"Sometimes I'm not so sure."

"Do me a favor and at least give it a try."

"That's the same thing you told me when Lola showed up," Jesse explained. "You said it'd only be for a while, and she's been here for months. Now you're gonna have two women lazing around the house doing nothing but listening to *Ma Perkins* and *My Gal Sunday* on the radio."

"Is that why you don't like Lola?"

"That's only one of the reasons I don't like her," Jesse said with exasperation, dropping the magazine in a heap on his lap. "If she kicks my dog again, I'm gonna throw that slop she brings me to eat right back in her face! She's only here for one thing, and that's to get her hooks into you. She doesn't care if I lie here all day with nothing to do."

"You can mark one of those worries off your list," Quinn said reassuringly, laying one hand on his brother's leg. "I'll never marry anyone you don't like. That's a promise."

"I'll hold you to it."

Quinn stood up from the bed and moved the wheelchair close to the side. He threw back the covers, lifted his brother in his arms, and set him in the chair. "Let's get you to the bathroom, and then I'll come back and empty your pee can. After that, I'll tell Lola to clean up this room."

Once Quinn had maneuvered Jesse's chair into the hallway, he lifted the boy and took him into the bathroom, setting him on the toilet. While his brother took care of his business, he filled the lavatory with warm water and handed Jesse a wet cloth to wash his face and hands.

"You're going to need a haircut soon, kiddo," Quinn joked.

"Oh, boy," Jesse groused.

"At the very least, you should have a bath. I can't tell who smells worse, you or Cowboy."

Even with soap on his face, Jesse shot his brother a hard look. "Very funny!" the boy said sarcastically. "With a mouth like yours, maybe you should have a comedy show on the radio!"

Dressed in shirt and pants, his hair mostly

tangle free, Jesse was wheeled into the kitchen by his brother. Adrianna and Lola had been sitting quietly since shortly after Quinn had left the room, but now the cleaning woman's demeanor changed drastically.

"Well looky who we have here!" she exclaimed excitedly, rising from her chair and rushing to the boy's side. She tried to fuss over him, pushing his hair back from his forehead with her fingers, but he moved his head to avoid her touch. "Let's get you some breakfast! I've got toast and the strawberry jam you like."

Through it all, Jesse ignored her, his eyes locked on Adrianna. He hadn't really looked at her the night before and now, upon closer inspection, he had to admit she was quite pretty. Compared to her, Lola looked like a floozy. Something about her reminded him of one of his teachers at school, although he noted that she looked like she hadn't done a hard day's work in her life. She might even be kind of snooty. He couldn't stop a smile from curling his lips at the thought of her playing the piano at the Whipsaw.

Before Lola could continue her fussing, Quinn interjected. "I've got to get going. Somebody make sure Cowboy gets out a time or two during the day. Poor fella is probably chomping at the bit to get out-doors."

"He doesn't mind me at all," Lola said.

"If you kicked me," Jesse spat, "I wouldn't mind you either."

"I didn't kick him, honey," Lola explained weakly, trying to lay the sweetness on thickly. "I was just pushing him away with my foot. All I wanted was to move him out of the way."

"Bullshit!" Jesse blurted out, stifling Lola. As soon as he swore, Jesse glanced at Adrianna. She showed no reaction to the crude language and continued eating her toast.

Quinn stepped in and moved Jesse's wheelchair up close to the table. He then leaned down to say softly, "You better watch your language, Bucko. We've got a lady in the house." Turning to Adrianna, he added, "I'll be off now. You and Jesse can figure something out, I suppose. Maybe you could help him with his schoolwork."

"I'd like that," Adrianna said, flashing a wide smile. "What grade are you in, Jesse?"

"I just finished the tenth grade," he mut-tered.

"Do you have any books? Have the teach-ers given you any assignments?"

"Yeah, I have a couple that my teacher

brought me," he said a little louder. He straightened up a bit in his wheelchair and looked directly at Adrianna. "But she's only been here a couple of times. Like everyone else, she thinks I'm a lost cause."

"Well, I sure don't think that way. As long as you have your wits about you, and it certainly seems to me that you do, you can do anything you set your mind to."

"Yeah . . . I guess so."

Quinn stood at the door listening to the conversation. Maybe Miss High-Toned Moore had more gumption than he'd given her credit for. Smiling, he slammed his hat down on his head and went out the door.

CHAPTER 10

Adrianna straightened her shoulders and, taking a deep breath, rapped lightly on Jesse's door before opening it and going inside. Propped up in his bed, he looked over the top of his magazine before going back to his tales of organized crime and pirates. Cowboy lay on the bed, enjoying the way his master's hand absently scratched behind his ears. As Adrianna came farther into the room, the dog gave a low growl from deep in his throat. Giving him a quick glance, she walked across the room and threw open the shades.

"Do you mind a little light?" she asked over her shoulder.

"Would you care if I did?" the boy retorted.

"Of course I would." She smiled warmly. "I'm here to help, not to tell you what to do."

"You can't do anything to help, 'cause I've

got these useless legs."

"Maybe they're not as useless as you think."

"Oh, I get it," the boy said with a crinkle of his nose. He finally closed the magazine and tossed it onto the heap on the bed. "So you're one of those, huh?"

Confused, Adrianna asked, "One of what?"

"You're one of those women who goes around spreading sunshine and light." He folded his arms across his chest and said, "You don't know everything. You don't know nothin' 'bout me."

A part of Adrianna found Jesse's attitude a bit amusing, but she knew she couldn't dare laugh at the boy. Matter-of-factly, she said, "I admit I don't know everything. But if there's one thing I do know it's that if you don't help yourself, you'll sit in that chair for the rest of your life. *You* are the only person that can change that."

"How in the hell can I do that?"

"That's what we need to find out. It's different for each person. But even those who don't regain the use of their legs still manage to lead very productive lives."

"Yeah, yeah," Jesse said dismissively, looking out the window.

"You still have the use of your arms."

"But hell! I can't walk on them," he answered angrily.

Adrianna moved over and sat down on the edge of the bed. "I knew a man in Shreveport who had both of his legs amputated. He used his arms to swing himself out of bed and into his chair. He had no trouble going wherever that chair could take him. If you're willing, you could build up your arm and shoulder muscles until you could do the very same thing."

"You've got great plans for me, don't you," he sneered.

"All the plans in the world won't do you any good unless you want to make them work. It's up to you. You can lie in this bed and feel sorry for yourself, or you can use what you have and take control of your life." When he didn't answer her, she pressed on. "Your brother could hang a bar above your bed so you could grasp it and pull yourself up. You might be able to strengthen your legs. Dr. Bordeaux would know for sure."

"What if I don't want to do that?" Jesse spat.

Coolly, Adrianna fixed him with a hard stare. "If it's something you don't want to do, we'll not work on it."

"You said that before."

"I thought it was worth repeating. Either

way, the first thing we need to do is give you a proper washing."

"Are you saying I stink?" Jesse's tone was incredulous. The bridge of his nose was crinkled in a harsh sneer. "Quinn already hauled me to the bathroom today."

"What you need is more than just wiping yourself with a towel," she explained as gently as she could. She didn't want to hurt the boy's feelings by being too harsh. "The more you can take care of yourself and keep clean, the better you'll feel."

Jesse looked like he wanted to say more, to argue, but finally barked, "Bring the damn wash water and then get the hell out! That is, unless you want to look at my bare ass."

"You won't get rid of me with crude talk like that."

"What's crude about 'ass'?" Jesse frowned. "Everybody has one."

"You're right about that." She turned and left the room before he could see the smile spreading across her face. As she closed the door, she said, "I'll be right back."

Downstairs in the kitchen, Adrianna looked under the sink and was starting on the cupboards, looking for a pan, when Lola's sharp voice, coming from the doorway, startled her.

"What do you think you're doing?"

"I'm looking for a wash pan so that Jesse can wash himself," she said evenly, staring at the belligerent woman.

"Wash Jesse? Quinn gives him a bath every week."

"He needs to wash every day," Adrianna persisted. "Now, where's a pan?"

"Oh, you're just bound to have your way, aren't you?" Lola complained as she brought a large graniteware pan from the pantry. She shoved it at Adrianna before stalking out of the kitchen, up the steps, and into Jesse's room.

"What the . . . ?" Jesse blurted out, pulling his shirt over his bare chest as Lola barreled into the room.

"I'm sorry that you have to put up with her, Jesse," Lola began in an annoyingly fake tone of voice. "Good God Almighty! She walked in here like she owns the place! I can't wait for Quinn to set Miss Prissy straight!"

Jesse looked up at Lola with one eyebrow cocked. Even a blind man could see that the only thing she was interested in was Quinn. *She'd just as soon spit on me as look at me,* he thought. He was suddenly glad that his brother had brought Miss Moore to stay with them for a while. If nothing else, life with these two women in the house would break up the monotony.

Before he could give her a piece of his mind, a tap sounded on the door and it was opened again. Adrianna entered with a pan of warm water, a wash cloth, and a towel hung over her shoulder. Lola, a sly look on her tight face, didn't move an inch out of the other woman's way. As Adrianna pulled up a chair with her foot, Cowboy reluctantly got up from a light sleep and moved.

"Now might be a good time for you to go outside," Adrianna said to the dog. "At least until Jesse is finished washing himself." Then, to Lola: "I know that you have chores to do. You may want to get started on them."

Nearly beside herself with anger, her face a red mess of lines and raised veins, Lola left the room in a huff without a single word of response. Cowboy trudged along behind her.

"Miss Moore," Jesse said anxiously, "if he goes out, Lola won't let him back inside."

"Don't worry, I'll let him in. And by the way, call me 'Adrianna.' After all, you don't hear me calling you 'Mr. Baxter,' do you?"

Jesse almost grinned at that. "Quinn calls you 'Annie.'"

"He also calls me 'stupid woman driver,' 'idiot city woman,' as well as a few other choice things. Now that I think about it, maybe 'Annie' isn't so bad after all." Both of them chuckled at her joke, and Adrianna knew that there was more to this boy than met the eye. "Is there anything else I can get you? If not, I'll go out while you wash."

"I'll need a clean shirt. Lola would be able to find one, but she's probably sore as hell."

"That'd be my fault. She isn't happy that I'm here."

"She's afraid you'll spoil her chances with Quinn."

"She needn't worry about that. Your brother and I don't like each other very much."

"Why not?"

"Let's not talk about that now," Adrianna said, moving toward the door. With a hand on the frame, she said, "I'll find you a clean shirt while you're washing. When I come back, we'll talk about your schoolwork. I need to do something to earn my keep."

"I thought you were playing the piano at the Whipsaw?"

"Between you and me" — she winked conspiratorially — "I think he'll fire me from that job when he finds out I don't know how to play rowdy tunes. I doubt Mozart or Chopin would be too popular in a saloon."

"Gabe could show you how to play the rowdy ones," Jesse explained.

"Enough about that. You'd better wash before the water gets cold."

Leaving the room, Adrianna was pleased with the progress she had made with Jesse. She had inveigled him to talk to her. With work, she was certain he'd be able to improve his condition. She wondered if Quinn would be willing to make some changes to Jesse's room, a few bars here and there, so that he could strengthen himself. Regardless, even with the tools available to help him, he'd have to *want* to get better.

When Adrianna reached the kitchen, she found it empty. Noticing a laundry basket propped in one corner, she began digging through its contents in search of a shirt for Jesse. Most of the clothes were clean, all of them wrinkled. *What in the world is that woman doing in this house?* She imagined that there were cleaner pigsties! Selecting the best of the lot, she went off in search of the cleaning woman in order to ask about an iron and ironing board.

"Lola!" she called, but there was no answer.

Searching from room to room, she found no one. Before she could head back upstairs to search some more, Cowboy's bark called out from the yard. Crossing the first floor, Adrianna pushed open the screen door and stepped out onto the porch. The dog stood in the yard, his tail wagging.

"Come here, Cowboy," she called. "Come here."

The dog hesitated for a moment, as if he had second thoughts, before trotting back toward the house. Adrianna let him pass her and was about to follow him into the house when she caught a sight that stopped her heart in her tracks. Lola stood silently in the corner of the porch, her arms crossed over her chest, a cigarette smoldering between her lips. The look on her face was one of seething anger, her eyes boring holes through Adrianna's flesh.

"I hate you," Lola muttered, the cigarette's tip dancing before her.

Without a reply, Adrianna turned her back and went into the house.

"What grade are you in, Jesse?"

The subject of schooling had been one that Adrianna felt some reluctance to broach; she didn't want to do anything to damage the progress she felt she'd made. Still, her father had always stressed the importance of an education, and she wanted to do as much as she could for the boy while she was here. She pulled up a chair and sat down beside the bed.

"I've finished the tenth grade," he explained. His eyes were downcast as he said, "I had just started the eleventh when it happened."

"The accident? Do you mind talking about it?" she asked tentatively.

"Yeah, I kind of do," he said, but added, "although sometimes I think about it in the night. I dream about the accident once in a while. I can hear the crash and feel the bus roll over onto its side and hear the kids yelling, but that's usually when I wake up."

"The school bus?" she pressed.

Jesse nodded. "There were twenty-two kids on it. Three of them were killed, as well as the driver, and some others were hurt pretty bad. Most everybody says that because I lived, I'm lucky. To that, I say bullshit. I'd bet if they were in my place, lucky is the last thing they'd feel."

"I'm sorry," Adrianna offered.

"It just ain't fair."

"Not everything in life is fair, Jesse. For some reason, known only to God, your life was spared while others were taken away. Remember, He only puts upon us as much as He thinks we can bear."

"To that, I'd say the same thing . . . bull—"

"Shit," Adrianna finished for him. They looked at each other and laughed.

"Quinn said I shouldn't talk nasty in front of you. He said you were kind of refined."

"I'm not so refined that I've never heard someone say nasty words before." She smiled. "Even though I've been a bit sheltered, my ears have heard plenty of swearing. That word you're so fond of was also the favorite of our cook back home. Nettie was always careful not to say it when my mother was around. I felt special that she'd say it in front of me."

"This was back home in Shreveport?"

"Yes."

"Did you live in a mansion?" Jesse asked bluntly. "Are you rich?"

"I wouldn't say that we were rich," she said, shrugging her shoulders, "but we were comfortable. My father worked hard for many years to ensure we were provided for. He owned a bank."

"Then you were rich."

"All of the money in the world won't make a person happy," Adrianna explained. "I would have given it all to have had a brother or sister. You don't know how lucky you are to have someone like Quinn to care for you."

"I guess I never thought of it that way."

A thought had been nagging at the back

of Adrianna's mind, and she hesitated only for a moment before asking about it. "I understand that Lola and Quinn are engaged," she began. "I'm sure that it won't make any difference in his taking care of you."

Jesse's eyes grew as large as saucers as a deep chortle burst from his mouth. His whole body shook on the bed as the belly laugh rolled through him. "Where in the hell did you hear that?"

"Lola mentioned it."

"That's Lola's wishful thinking! She's the biggest fool in town if she believes she can get him into her bed. It'll be a cold day in hell before Quinn marries her."

Suddenly embarrassed about having mentioned the subject, Adrianna got up from her seat and picked up a magazine that lay on Jesse's dresser. It was a pulp magazine called *Detective Action Stories.* This particular issue featured a story called "Five Doors to Death." "Do you like to read, Jesse?" she asked.

"Sure. A fella in my condition has got lots of time for it."

"That's good." She smiled warmly. "Because I'm sure there will be plenty of reading to do for your schoolwork. If we're going to have you graduate with your class, we'll need to get started as soon as possible. Maybe I should talk to one of your teachers so that I'll know what to instruct you in."

"You're going to teach me?"

"I'm qualified. I graduated from Centenary College."

"What good is it going to do for me to graduate?" Jesse groused. "Even if I were to get my degree, it won't matter. It's not like anyone will hire me. Who would want a cripple?"

"If you keep thinking about yourself in those terms, that's all you'll ever be."

Jesse turned his head away from her and looked out the window. If Lola had her way, she'd be leaving soon. He didn't want to get too fond of her.

"Do any of your friends visit?" Adrianna asked.

"Not all that often. They're all busy with baseball practice after school. It's not like I blame them or anything. Who'd want to spend time with a cripple when you could play ball?"

"Jesse Baxter!" she exclaimed as she strode back over to the bed. Even as her tone was harsh, he could see that her eyes were soft. "I've had just about enough of that nasty word. If you say that word one more time, I'm going to wash your mouth out with soap."

"At least I won't stink," he said, his eyes twinkling with mischief.

Adrianna couldn't help but laugh at the joke. "Then I'll have to come up with something that will be a true punishment. How about if every time you say that word, I'll give you extra schoolwork and make you go without supper? Is that harsh enough?"

"Going without supper wouldn't be a punishment. Even Cowboy won't eat some of the slop Lola fixes." Hearing his name, the dog got up off of the floor and came to lay his head on the side of the bed. Jesse's hand reached for the animal's head and scratched lightly behind his ears. "It's pretty bad sometimes, isn't it, Cowboy?"

"How did you come to give him that name?" Adrianna asked.

"I guess it's because I've always wanted to be one," Jesse explained. "Besides, the name suits him. He likes to roam far and wide when he gets the chance, and he doesn't mind eating whatever's handy. One of us should be able to see something outside this house."

"Did you hear him growl at me when I first came in this morning?"

"That's because he wasn't sure of you."

"I'm not sure of myself," Adrianna admitted. "I don't know what my duties here are . . . not exactly, anyway. I know that I'm to spend time helping you and play the piano at the tavern, but as for the housework, I'm clueless."

"If you listen to Lola, you'll be expected to do it all."

"Lola wasn't the one that hired me. I don't owe her anything. My debt is to your brother, and I intend to pay him back for the inventory that I destroyed." She moved over to the windows and gazed out into a sunny sky. "It's a beautiful day. This afternoon, we could go out onto the porch, and you can tell me more about this town."

From a crack in the door, Lola looked into the room, her eyes hatefully locked on to the woman who was ruining her life. *That bitch!* She'd been listening for several minutes, and it was obvious that the slut was doing her damnedest to turn Jesse against her. The stupid boy was falling right into her trap! That little shit had better watch what he said! If everything went as she planned, the rich bitch would soon be gone. If he were to ruin her chances with Quinn . . .

I'll make his life miserable! After all, I've done it before!

CHAPTER 11

Adrianna sat in a wicker chair on the porch, the mid-afternoon sun warming her face. Looking through the leaves on the elm trees, she could see a strand of wispy clouds spread out across an otherwise flawless sky. At this time of the year, the weather felt comfortable; it would be a few more weeks until the humidity of the wet land became clinging and unbearable.

Jesse sat on the porch beside her. She'd had to cajole him to come outside, but she'd finally managed to break his reluctance, and they'd wheeled his chair out into the fresh air. He was thumbing through another of his magazines, but she could tell that he was enjoying the day. Even Cowboy had gotten into the act; he lay on his back in the grass, the sun warming his belly.

"This is much better than that stuffy old house," she muttered aloud.

"Mmmm." Jesse grunted absently, licked

his finger, and turned another page.

The other thing that was pleasant about this beautiful day was that she was out from under Lola's watchful eyes. After they had taken their retreat outside, Lola had remained in the house. Once, Adrianna had caught a glimpse of the housekeeper as she'd peeked out of a window, but so far she had left them alone. Hopefully, it would stay that way.

Adrianna had stood to go back into the house to fetch the two of them some iced tea when the front gate swung open, and a familiar figure strode up the walk wearing a jaunty, small-brimmed hat.

"*Salut, mes amis!*" Gabe called. "What a beautiful day, *n'est-ce pas?*" The Cajun's smile was as bright as the weather. He bounded up the short steps and then leaned against one of the porch columns, his thick arms crossed over his broad chest.

"It's nice to see you again, Mr. LeBlanc," Adrianna greeted him.

"Oh, no, no, no, *mademoiselle,*" Gabe chided with a shake of his head and a cluck of his tongue. "The only Mr. LeBlanc I have ever known is my father, and I'm afraid that he hasn't been seen in these parts for many a year. You must call me Gabe, *chérie,* or I will think *mon père* has returned from the dead."

With a laugh, Adrianna agreed. "Gabe it is, then."

"Much better."

"How is your hand today?" Adrianna asked.

"It would be a lie for me to tell you it does not hurt." He shrugged. "But I am sure that it will not be long before I am as good as new. Besides, I believe a trip or two to the doctor's office will make up for any discomfort."

"Good excuse for you to visit the doc, huh, Gabe?" Jesse snickered.

"There's nothing worse than a smart-mouthed kid," the Cajun said and winked at Adrianna. Then, back to the grinning boy: "I see that you are deep into the latest *Argosy*. I'm sure you'll agree with me that *Monsieur* Hammett is one fine writer, no?"

"Do you read pulps too, Gabe?" Adrianna asked.

"But of course! Jesse and I share them."

For the next fifteen minutes, the three of them sat on the porch and talked, first about the mystery stories, then about the town of Lee's Point. She learned that Gabe lived with his mother and a sister a few miles out of town on the bayou in a house his family had lived in for generations. It was easy for Adrianna to talk to him. She found him extremely likeable; his personality was warm and inviting. However, the thing that endeared him to her was the way in which he brought Jesse into the conversation. To him, Jesse was just another person, not a boy in a wheelchair who needed his pity.

"I thought it might be a good idea for us to go to the Whipsaw," Gabe said to Adrianna. "You should play a song or two and get used to the piano."

"I really should see what I'm getting into," she said, grinning up at Gabe.

"You'll be sorry," Jesse chided.

"There are a couple of songs that are popular right now," Gabe explained, ignoring Jesse's pointed comment. "They're the ones that are used for the sing-along. I dug around *pour trois heures* until I found the sheet music for most of them. But not to worry, if you can read any music at all, with a little practice, you'll play them better than me."

"She's a lot prettier than you, that's for sure," Jesse joked.

"You'd best watch yourself or I'll roll you down these steps."

As the man and boy joked with each other, Adrianna felt her heart beat faster.

What was she getting herself into? She hadn't lied when she'd told Quinn that she could play the piano, but she doubted that the patrons of the Whipsaw would enjoy listening to Mozart or Chopin.

But still . . .

"Why don't you come along with us, Jesse?" Adrianna asked.

"Aw, no," the boy said with a shake of his head. "I'll just stay here and read. It's not like I can do anything to help and besides, I'll only slow you down if you have to push me."

"Nonsense!" Adrianna insisted. It seemed to her that too often, Jesse used his handicap as an excuse to stay in the house, locked away from the world that he could still be a part of. Not this time. "There's no reason that you can't come along with us. I'm not going unless you go. Besides, you're part owner, aren't you? Don't you want to see how big a fool I make of myself?"

"Yeah, but —"

"I do believe she is right, *mon ami,*" Gabe interjected with a wicked grin. "You should come."

Jesse looked back at both of them with a face full of indecision. He seem to want to argue more, but instead turned his head to look back through the windows into the

153

house. Adrianna couldn't be sure, but she thought he might be weighing the idea of going to the Whipsaw against staying behind with Lola.

"All right," he finally nodded, "but I want a Coke from the mercantile, and Cowboy comes, too."

"D'accord!" Gabe laughed heartily. "My treat!"

As Gabe pushed Jesse's wheelchair down the sidewalk, Adrianna and Cowboy walked alongside. She gazed out from under the shade of various businesses' awnings at Lee's Point. The town was nearly empty. A handful of automobiles and a couple of pickup trucks were parked here and there. An older woman carrying a nearly overflowing bag of apples puttered along on the other side of the street.

"This is a quiet little town," Gabe remarked as he followed her gaze.

"Have you lived here long?"

"My whole life. My great-grandfather was one of the first Frenchmen to come to these parts. He was a trapper and moved up and down the small rivers and creeks in search of game. He and his brother made a fortune selling their pelts."

"What happened to all the money?" Jesse

blurted out.

"*Je ne sais pas.*" Gabe shrugged. "I don't know. My father used to say that they had been swindled out of it by some Americans who came to the area, but I'd bet they spent it all on drink and wild women."

"I'm sorry," Adrianna said. The talk about family fortunes struck a nerve that was still raw. Her father had worked all his life to amass his wealth, and she was certain that Richard Pope had swindled him out of it. Regardless of how it had happened, she was much like Gabe's great-grandfather; what once had been hers was now in someone else's hands.

They stopped at the mercantile and bought Jesse a bottle of Coca-Cola that he greedily drank, wiping his mouth on the back of his hand. Even though Adrianna was certain that he would never admit it, she could tell the boy was enjoying being away from the house. She noticed that one of the clerks at the store had stared rather rudely at the wheelchair for a moment, but Jesse either had not seen the look or chosen to ignore it. Either way, she knew that this was a positive step in reintroducing him to the world.

As they left the mercantile, Adrianna glanced at the cars parked in front of the bank. One of them was a black Packard, like the one Richard often drove. She stopped as if her feet were glued to the sidewalk. A wave of fear washed over her. Was he here? Had he found her? She lingered behind Jesse and Gabe, scarcely breathing. Then she saw a woman come out of the bank and get into the car. She took a deep breath of relief and scolded herself for her fear. She had no doubt that Richard was looking for her, but why would he come to a town like Lee's Point?

After the mercantile, Gabe led them to the garage where Adrianna's car was being repaired. Delmar was covered in grease and as silent as he was filthy. As he grunted and nodded to Gabe's questions, Adrianna wheeled Jesse over to where they could get a look into the garage.

"Wow!" Jesse exclaimed. "Your car's a wreck!"

Still shaken after seeing the Packard, all Adrianna could do was stare at her vehicle as the accident played itself out before her eyes. The memory of the sickening crash and the shattered glass raining down from above made her cringe. Still, she could see that some improvements had been made; a couple of dents had been hammered out and a tire had been replaced.

"Delmar says he had to order a few parts," Gabe said as he joined them.

"Does he have any idea how long the repairs will take?"

"He can't say for certain, but things can be a mite slow in these parts. This isn't like Shreveport. It can take weeks for a letter or a package to find us here. Who can say when it comes to car parts?"

"You might be stuck here longer than you think," Jesse added. She couldn't tell by his tone if he meant it as a taunt or as a note of condolence. She'd resigned herself to staying in Lee's Point for as long as was needed. At this pace, would she *ever* leave?

"The Whipsaw is just down the street." Gabe smiled, showing even white teeth.

The four blocks to the tavern passed quickly. Adrianna walked most of the way with her head down; the weight of seeing her father's damaged car and looking ahead to her forced stay in the town pressed upon her. She didn't look up until she realized Gabe and Jesse had come to a halt.

"This is it," Gabe said.

"Not half bad, huh?" Jesse added.

The tavern sat in the middle of a block, its one-story frame wedged between two buildings; one a small café, the other a shoe repair shop. The front of the tavern looked shoddy; one of the two small windows that looked out onto the street was cracked, and the whole thing was in desperate need of a fresh coat of paint. As she stared at the dilapidated sign above the front door, she tried to fix a smile to her face.

"It's really something," she muttered.

"Wait until you see the inside," Jesse boasted. "Come on, Cowboy."

Adrianna held open the door while Gabe pushed Jesse's chair. The inside of the tavern smelled strongly of beer and cigarette smoke. It was all that Adrianna could do not to bring her hand to her nose. With only a couple of lights on, it was as gloomy as a cave, and she had to squint to see much of the interior. Jesse moved off on his own, rolling easily between the tables and chairs on the wood floor. Cowboy stayed close to him. A young woman was lazily sweeping the floor beneath the bar stools. She looked up at them as they entered.

"*Bonjour,* Sally," Gabe hailed her. The woman nodded a greeting before resuming her task.

Gabe led Adrianna toward the rear of the bar. In the far corner sat a lonely piano, a stool with a worn leather seat beside it. Once she was close enough to see it more clearly, Adrianna winced inwardly; there were nicks and scrapes along the side of the instrument, and the ivory on some of the keys was missing. Obviously, the piano had seen better days.

"It might not be much to look at, but it can still play a pretty good tune."

The Cajun walked over and flipped a switch on the wall. Faint light came from bulbs affixed to the walls, but at least it was enough to see by. Fetching a sheaf of papers from atop the bar, Gabe pulled up a chair and beckoned her to join him with a pat on the stool.

Adrianna sat with a squeak of the stool's rusty swivel. Gabe arranged the sheet music in front of her and she stared at the notes. The song's title was "Old Dan Tucker." She'd never heard of it, but the sheet music didn't seem complicated.

"This is one of our more popular songs. It's so well liked at the sing-along that you'll probably end up playing it a couple of times. I've plunked it out so often that I could probably do it in my sleep, *c'est la vérité!*"

With a deep breath for courage, Adrianna put her fingers on the keys and began to play. The sound that came from the piano was clunky and out of tune; she could only imagine how long it had been since it had

had a proper tuning. She tried to concentrate solely on the notes on the paper instead of the sounds, but she stumbled with her timing and had to stop.

"That piano sounds like a lumber wagon," Jesse offered from across the room.

"Didn't know you had an ear for music, gator-bait," Gabe called back over his shoulder. Looking back down at Adrianna, he encouragingly added, "It will take some time to get used to this piano, so please do not become discouraged, *mademoiselle.*"

With a weak smile, she nodded and began again. She made it further into the song but soon stumbled, the notes sounding an awful lot like the crash of her automobile.

In her heart, Adrianna had a sense of what was the matter, and it wasn't the music. It was hard enough with Gabe, Jesse, and the silent cleaning woman. How could she expect to manage with a room full of rowdy men?

"Maybe you should give her some whiskey," Jesse shouted.

"Pay him no mind," Gabe said leaning down to speak softly. "No one expects you to play perfectly, but there's no one else in the whole town who can do it, other than Mrs. Monroe, of course."

"Mrs. Monroe?" For a split second, Adrianna had hope that there was another option, someone else who could keep her from having to play. Gabe quickly snuffed that hope.

"Mrs. Monroe is the woman who plays the organ up at the church." He grinned. "She is something of a teetotaler, so I doubt that we'd be able to persuade her to enter a house of spirits, *n'est-ce pas.* I do believe that she thinks of us about as kindly as she does the devils and sinners that the good reverend preaches against every Sunday. I could never introduce Mrs. Monroe to the tavern patrons . . . they'd die laughing."

"Oh, Gabe, I'd rather you'd not use my last name when you introduce me," Adrianna said and looked up at him pleadingly. "It isn't that I'm ashamed of playing here. I just don't want someone to find me."

"*Chérie,* someone wants to hurt you?"

"No, it's nothing like that."

"Quinn would be quite upset if anyone bothered you. I daresay he might be a touch smitten." He winked.

"Oh, you . . . stop teasing me."

"We still have several hours before you'll have to play, *chérie.*" Gabe didn't comment on her rosy cheeks. "That gives us plenty of time to go over all of the songs. Let us practice as much as we can."

As she bent her head back to the piano, Adrianna attempted to focus on the music, but try as she might, she failed. Her heart beat like a rabbit's, and she was certain that her face was flushed crimson. Gabe's words repeated over and over in her thoughts.

I dare say he might be a touch smitten.

Adrianna wasn't prepared when Quinn came into the tavern. She was playing chords on the piano, while Gabe played the melody with his right hand. They were laughing and Jesse was clapping his hands.

As Quinn approached the piano, Adrianna slid her hands into her lap.

"Who in the hell brought Jesse down here?" he demanded.

"I did," Gabe and Adrianna answered in unison.

Adrianna looked up into his angry face. "Is there something wrong with him being here?

"I wanted to come, Quinn." Jesse had rolled himself over beside Adrianna.

"This is no place for a boy your age."

Adrianna felt a flash of anger. "Yes, what's wrong with him being here?"

"Why didn't you take him to the park if you wanted to take him out?"

"There's no piano in the park, *mon ami.*"

Gabe's eyes sparkled as he looked from Quinn to the pretty woman sitting on the piano stool.

Quinn turned and walked back behind the bar. *Damn, she and Gabe are getting pretty friendly. She'll find out soon that Gabe's heart belongs to Dr. Bordeaux. He's never looked at another woman since he met her.*

Gabe began to play, and Adrianna automatically joined in, making her fingers ripple over the keys as Gabe had shown her.

"We'll make a honky-tonk piano player out of you yet." Gabe smiled and she laughed, surprised at how much she enjoyed his company. It was surprisingly easy to follow his instruction and put in the extra notes.

"He'll get over his mad, Annie," Jesse said, watching her fingers on the keys.

"I don't know why he's mad . . . and I really don't care."

CHAPTER 12

Jesse was unusually talkative during supper. He bragged about Adrianna learning so quickly to play the honky-tonk piano. Lola scowled and didn't comment. Quinn smiled frequently, apparently recovered from his concerns about Jesse being at the tavern. He seemed pleased that Jesse was enthusiastic about something. Adrianna looked from one brother to the other, trying to find some resemblance. Where Jesse's features were finely chiseled, Quinn's were craggy. She reasoned it was because he worked outdoors in all kinds of weather, while Jesse had been in the house for the better part of a year.

"Gabe had a good time playing with Annie." He looked at Adrianna and grinned when he shortened her name.

Lola jumped up from the table and went to the cabinet where she brought a large spoon and poked it into the bowl of green beans. She plopped back down into her seat and spoke to Quinn.

"Have you heard how Mr. Thatcher's wife is doing?" she asked with a sly glance at Adrianna, clearly intending to shut her out of the conversation.

"Haven't heard," Quinn said shortly and continued eating.

Adrianna got up from the table. "Excuse me. I'll go get dressed."

Lola looked up quickly. "Quinn doesn't leave here until nine o'clock. You've got time to help me with the dishes, don't you? Or will it take you all that time to get prettied up?"

Adrianna paused.

"Annie won't be helping you tonight, Lola," Quinn said tersely.

Lola jumped up from the table. "Well, I declare! You said she would help me."

"Do you think you're overworked here?" Quinn asked. "You've never complained before."

"That was when there was only the three of us."

Adrianna stood uncertainly in the doorway, then went up the stairs to her room. She'd never had to justify her actions to the household help before, and she was not sure how to react. Let them thrash it out. She didn't care one way or the other. As soon as she had paid her debt, she'd be gone.

Before she and Quinn left the house, Adrianna went in to say good night to Jesse.

"Wish me luck, Jesse."

"You'll do just great," the boy said. "Gabe says you have a magic touch on that piano. I wish I could be there to hear you."

"I'll tell you about it in the morning. You'll probably be asleep when we get home."

Quinn and Adrianna walked the handful of blocks to the Whipsaw. The click, click of Adrianna's high heels striking the paved sidewalk mixed with the night sounds of the birds settling in the trees. There were very few people on the streets. A full moon had risen just above the treetops, pale in the cloudless sky. A slight breeze brought the clean smells of flowers and freshly cut grass.

"It's a lovely evening," Adrianna offered.

"My granddaddy used to call these nights 'pearls,' " Quinn said.

"Why was that?"

"Partly because of the way the full moon hung up there in the sky, round as can be," he said. "But I think part of what he was trying to say was to hold an evening like this as if it were a treasure. There aren't all that many that are this nice. When the heat soars, most summer nights are hell."

As much as she wanted to agree that Quinn's grandfather was right, that the night was a treasure, she couldn't help but feel her nerves jump at the very thought of playing the piano at the tavern. Ever since she and Gabe had gone over the songs, she'd known she *could* play them . . . but that still didn't answer the question of whether she *would.*

"Sometime I want to talk to you about getting some bars in Jesse's room so he can pull himself up and get into his chair on his own. I plan to talk to Dr. Bordeaux about exercises for him."

"Anything you can do to help him would be appreciated."

"I know a man in Shreveport who doesn't have the use of his legs, and he has developed his arms and shoulders to lift his weight. Jesse is young and has his whole life before him. I'd like to see him more independent." Enthused, she continued: "You know, he is a very smart boy. I hope to speak to his teacher and help him finish his senior year. I can at least get him motivated and, after I leave, you or Gabe can take over."

Quinn felt a prick of disappointment at the thought of her leaving. All he could think of to say was, "I'm glad you took Jesse to the Whipsaw."

"You didn't act like it this afternoon. You acted as if you could bite my head off."

"I just had to get used to the idea, that's all. I was surprised to see Jesse there."

"He enjoyed getting out of the house."

"Gabe's been taking him out some."

"He's got the right idea," Adrianna said. "It's not healthy for anyone, let alone a young man like Jesse, to spend that much time by himself, away from other people. It's no way for anyone to go through life."

"I know what you mean," Quinn agreed. "Besides, when he gets out of that wheelchair and starts walking again, he'll be able to come and work at the Whipsaw. He could help with the accounts now. He doesn't have to walk to do that. After all, someday it'll all be his."

Adrianna looked over at Quinn's profile in the moonlight. He walked with his head high; the love he held for his brother was as apparent as the full moon in the sky. Still, she was worried that he held too much faith in Jesse's being able to walk again. It was possible, even likely, that Jesse would never regain the use of his legs and forever be stuck in his chair. What Adrianna was trying to help him learn was to be more capable and confident in his current predicament. She wanted to warn Quinn, to tell him to lower his expectations, but she found she didn't have the heart.

The other subject she was reluctant to broach was that of Lola. When she and Jesse had returned from the tavern, the cleaning woman had held her tongue, but her eyes had spoken of hatred. Even when Quinn had arrived home, Lola had remained quiet, dropping dinner plates onto the table with thuds and then glaring at Adrianna all throughout the meal. Quinn hadn't seemed to notice; Adrianna wondered if he even cared.

"I like what you're wearing," Quinn said abruptly.

"Thank you," she stammered, certain that her cheeks were flushing. She'd put a lot of thought into what to wear. Not wanting to appear too formal or "city," she'd fetched a sunflower yellow dress out of her suitcase. Her father had given her the dress to wear in the summer; he'd liked the way she'd looked in it as she'd busied herself in the drawing room. She'd even let her hair down a bit and put on a touch of makeup.

"Of course, you'd stand out like a three-legged dog no matter what you wore," he said with a chuckle.

"Was that supposed to be a compliment?"

"It must not have been a very good one if

you have to ask." He shrugged. "I just meant that you're the type of woman that's just plain meant to be seen. Most of the women around here are a bit hardened by life."

"Hardened? What do you mean?"

"They've been worn down from the day-in and day-out of their lives," he explained. "About the best that they can ever hope for is to find a fella to settle down with and have a bunch of kids. They don't have any chance to go to society balls or fancy dinners."

"I'll have you know that my life in Shreveport wasn't the bed of roses you make it out to be," she scolded him. "I had my hands full taking care of my father, and his health didn't allow him to attend many parties."

"I didn't mean it like that."

"Yes, you did."

"Well, maybe I did." He turned his head in the moonlight and winked at her. "But that doesn't change the fact that you're different from the women in Lee's Point. Very different."

"Even different from Lola?" she asked tentatively.

"Oh, hell yes!" he exclaimed. "Do you even need to ask?"

Adrianna wanted to open her mouth and tell him all of the things that Lola had said about the two of them, but she couldn't find her voice. Just because she and Lola were different didn't mean that he wasn't interested in her. Besides, she didn't know him well enough to inquire. Finally she managed, "I suppose not."

The rest of the walk to the tavern was filled with small talk. Quinn pointed out the various businesses and spoke of people he knew, but Adrianna had trouble paying attention. With every step toward the Whipsaw, her nerves became more frayed. Finally, they rounded the now-familiar corner and found themselves in front of the tavern. A couple of rough-looking men were going in the front door and gave the two of them a cursory look before entering.

"Don't be nervous," Quinn murmured.

"That's a lot easier said than done."

"What's the worst thing that could happen? It wouldn't matter a bit if you hit a dozen wrong keys. They won't know the difference."

Giving him a wry smile, she said, "I don't suppose they would."

"You'll do just fine," he winked.

As they stood for a moment inside the door,

Adrianna could hear her heart pounding in her ears. Unlike the empty room in which she had practiced just a few hours earlier, the space was now nearly full. Men stood elbow to elbow at the long bar. The smoke from their cigars and cigarettes formed a haze above their heads. Other patrons sat at the tables and gathered in groups, the sounds of their voices echoing off of the walls:

"You should have seen his face!"

"He got a job on the WPA."

"Huh, they'll not get much work out of him."

"If you ain't gonna drink that, slide it on over to me."

"That tight-ass banker is a skin flint."

"I told you it ain't gonna work."

"Ahhh, shit-fire."

Adrianna had to squelch the desire to turn and run back out the front door. The conversations that floated around her made her head swim. This was far more than she had ever bargained for. She'd never performed in front of a crowd like this before! How on earth could Quinn possibly expect her to play? With her knees quaking and her insides going around and around like a Ferris wheel, she took a deep breath, tried to remember the debt she owed, and followed along behind Quinn as he headed toward the bar.

Gabe had just slid a tall glass of a dark beer across the counter to a bear of a man. As he was retrieving his payment, he looked up to see them approaching and gave a warm greeting. "It is nice to see you again, *mademoiselle.*"

She could only nod her head in reply, her voice stuck in her throat.

"It will be a good night for singing, *n'est-ce pas?*"

"Did you get that damn tap working?" Quinn cut in.

"I am afraid she is a bit of a fickle mistress, *mon ami.*" The barman grinned as he slapped his boss on the shoulder. "It worked fine to start the night, but now it's not." He gestured down the length of the bar to where a man was working on his hands and knees. "Charlie is working on it now."

"Not again," Quinn groaned. "Let me look at it."

Without another word, the two men left Adrianna standing beside the bar and went to examine the tap. Indecisive as to whether to follow, she settled on staying put; if he'd wanted her to come, he would have asked.

As she looked out over the sea of people, she felt a wave of self-consciousness wash over her. Every eye in the place was looking her over as faces peered up over their beers and people elbowed their neighbors. She regretted her choice of attire, wishing she had chosen something less colorful. She was wondering if she should join Quinn and Gabe over by the tap, when there was a tug at her sleeve.

"Well, ain't ya a pretty thing, I done do swear!"

Adrianna turned at the sound of the voice and nearly recoiled from the sight that greeted her. An incredibly old-looking man had sidled up beside her, one arm leaning against the bar. Dirty white hair fell down his wrinkled face. As he smiled at her, she could see that his mouth was like a cemetery, a tooth jutted up here and there, as if they were tombstones haphazardly planted. But the worse thing about the man was his smell, a mixture of alcohol and an overpowering body odor.

"Excuse me?" she asked tentatively.

"Ain't ya the one that's gonna play that pian'r now that Gabe's got hisself a busted wing?" the man continued, rubbing one hand against his stubbly chin. "Ya might not play like ol' Gabe, but ya'll be a hell of a lot prettier on the eyes, I done do swear!"

"Th-thank you."

"The name's Long. Roy Long," he said, extending a hand. Looking down at his gnarled fingers, Adrianna could see a thick layer of grime under most of his nails. Still, it would be rude not to return his greeting. Taking Roy's hand, she marveled at how it felt like leather. "Ya can probably tell by the last name that I done do be related to our governor."

"You mean our former governor, Huey Long?"

"Yes sir-ee-bobtail. His granddaddy and my granddaddy was kinfolk. I'll tell ya, that man was a crackerjack."

Tuning out her speaking companion, Adrianna looked over her shoulder, her eyes searching for Quinn. When she found him, he was staring back at her, a grin on his face. He chuckled to himself and winked at her before returning to the task of fixing the tap. Instantly, she felt better; if the ancient Mr. Long had any ill intentions, surely Quinn would come to her rescue.

". . . just the type, I done do swear!" Roy cackled.

"Tell me, Mr. Long," Adrianna inquired. "Does everyone participate in the sing-alongs or just a few?"

"Aw, heck! Ya're likely to have every dang person in this place up on his feet just a ramblin' along! Even an old fart like me who ain't got the voice that can compete with a jackass's bray will sometimes find hisself singin' like he was in a church choir."

"So it's an important event," she said, her heart sinking.

"You ain't just a whistlin' Dixie!" the old man nearly shouted. "But most of that's on account of the way Gabe plays that piano, I done do swear! More of these folks done show up to hear him plink away on Saturday night than show up to hear the church organ on Sunday!"

Her nerves sinking faster than a wrecked boat at sea, Adrianna was barely aware of asking, "So what . . . what would happen if the piano playing wasn't quite what everyone expected?"

"Well, now," Roy said as he took a glass of liquor from the bar and downed its contents in one gulp. He smiled his rotten-toothed smile as he said. "I reckon things might get a bit ugly."

Adrianna sat down at the piano stool as Gabe spread out the music she would be playing. As casually as she could, she blotted her nervous, damp hands on the front of her dress. Sweat beaded on her upper lip. When Gabe placed a reassuring hand on her shoulder, she tried to look at him with as much confidence as she could muster.

"Are you ready?" he asked.

Looking at the sheet music, the song's title burned itself into her mind — "Old Dan Tucker." She and Gabe had practiced it over and over earlier in the afternoon, and she felt relatively sure that she could play it without any errors . . . *relatively* sure. Taking a deep breath, she said, "I'm ready."

"Nothing to it, *mademoiselle.*"

Pulling a chair from one of the nearby tables, Gabe climbed onto the seat and whistled loudly through his fingers. The conversations that had filled the room slowly came to a stop as each head turned to look at him. Adrianna could feel the anticipation in the room.

"*Messieurs et mesdames,* if I can have your attention, please. It is now time for us to begin this week's sing-along," the Cajun began to a loud round of applause. Raising his heavily bandaged hand above his head, he continued: "As I am sure all amongst you but the blind can tell, I will be unable to perform at the piano, but do not fret, for we have a most able replacement." Holding his hand out to Adrianna, he explained, "All the way from the fine city of Shreveport, I present to you *cette petite femme,* Annie."

With exuberant applause mixed with a few whistles, the Whipsaw's patrons responded warmly. Adrianna leaned up from her stool and gave a slight wave. Quinn stood near the bar, a towel draped over one shoulder, and nodded to her. She was certain her face was flushed with embarrassment.

Sitting back down on her stool, Adrianna poised her fingers over the keys.

You can do it, you can do it, you can do it, she repeated in her mind.

Right before she played the first note, a saying that her father had told her came to mind: *The only failure is the fool who doesn't try.* Charles Moore had taken the same attitude in dealing with his handicap and refused to let it dictate the terms of his life. She was asking Jesse to do the very same thing. How could she expect less of herself?

Gabe, still standing on the chair, shouted, "Let us begin!" Then he begin to sing in a loud, clear, and surprisingly good voice:

"Old Dan Tucker's a fine old man,
Washed his face in a fryin' pan,
Combed his hair with a wagon wheel
And died with a toothache in his heel."

Taking a deep breath, she began to play. The sound of the piano, while not providing the crisp, clear notes of a well-tuned instrument, nonetheless rang out in the enclosed space. After the first tentative bars, she began to gain confidence and her fingers slid effortlessly over the keys. Once she had finished the opening refrain, she was startled when the audience joined in; deep baritones mixed with the sweet tenors and altos in a strong harmony. She was surprised by the purity of the sound and found herself joining in.

"Get out the way, old Dan Tucker,
Get out the way, old Dan Tucker,
Get out the way old Dan Tucker,
It's too late to come to supper."

The song neared its finish. The sound filled the room and bounced against the walls. Adrianna felt a great joy inside. Considering how nervous she had been when she'd entered the Whipsaw, her feelings of happiness were somewhat surprising. All the thoughts that had bothered her over the last several days drifted away: her father's passing, Richard Pope, Lola, and even her dealings with Quinn. As her fingers played the final note, the tavern crowd roared its approval.

As she turned to see Quinn's reaction, a

man stepped into her line of sight. Looking up, she had to squint through the lights above to make out his features. When she did recognize him, she was startled to see that it was the same bear of a man who had been sitting at the bar earlier. Longish black hair and matching whiskers partially covered his deep jowls. His shoulders were so wide that they blocked most of her view. She smiled uneasily, but the man's face was turned down in a frown.

"Ya really think yore somethin', don't ya girlie?" he snarled.

"Wh-what?" she stammered.

"Go back to where ya come from."

CHAPTER 13

"Goddamnit, Reuben."

Behind the counter, Quinn had watched as the man got off the stool and headed for the piano. *What the hell is he going to do?* When he and Adrianna had first entered the Whipsaw, he'd seen the large man and should have known there would be trouble; there was *always* trouble whenever Reuben Griffin was around.

Ignorant and piss-mean from the moment he could walk, Reuben had spent most of his life drifting in and out of the sheriff's jail cell. Nearly as wide as he was tall, he was the type of man who was far more likely to let his fists do the talking, whether or not any talking was needed. With a thick beard and a puffy, whiskered face, he looked almost comical; but with a few drinks in him he was anything but funny. Most of the townspeople of Lee's Point had learned to give him a wide berth. Several years earlier, he had gotten into a fight with a salesman passing through town and broken both of the man's arms and a couple of ribs. Reuben had done his time for the crime, but prison hadn't changed him.

Something *bad* was going to happen.

Gabe too saw Reuben move toward the piano and sidled down the length of the bar toward Quinn. He absentmindedly wiped the counter, but his eyes, much like Quinn's, were locked on the mountain of a man approaching Adrianna.

"I done bet ya is a touch nervous, Gabe," Roy cackled from his vantage point at the bar. "Ol' Reuben is like a caged bear, I done do swear!"

"You might be right, *mon ami,*" Gabe answered jovially, his tone a far cry from the seriousness in his eyes. Then to Quinn, "Seems like he's taking an interest in our pretty new musician, *n'est-ce pas?*"

"Ya got that right! He ain't took his eyes off'a her," the drunk put in, swiveling in his chair.

"What the hell is he doing here anyway?" Quinn asked his manager.

"I have a guess."

"You think Lola sent him here?" he ventured.

"None other."

For years, there had been a rumor floating around Lee's Point that Reuben Griffin held a candle for Lola but that she refused to return his feelings. Was it possible that she had put Reuben up to coming to the tavern and causing trouble, hoping to scare Adrianna off?

Quinn was still trying to come to grips with his own thoughts, when the sounds of glasses shattering, swearing, and fisticuffs began to fill the Whipsaw.

"You can't play that piano for shit, you high-toned bitch."

Adrianna's eyes grew as wide as saucers, her heart pounding wildly in her chest, as the gigantic man leaned closer to where she sat. His breath was even more putrid than Roy's, which she would have found difficult to believe if she hadn't been so frightened that she couldn't think clearly.

"Get away from me," she shouted, wanting to be heard over the noise in the room.

"All you high-falutin' types are the same," the man snarled. "You think you can just walk in here and start givin' orders like you're a queen or somethin'?"

With surprising quickness, the man slammed his empty beer mug down on top of the piano with a crash. The fury of his actions combined with the sudden noise made Adrianna nearly jump off her stool. Fear began to creep into the corners of her mind. *Is this man really going to hurt me in front of all of these people?*

"Get away from me," she said again, wondering if Quinn had seen the man approach her.

"I do as I damn well please, girlie." He grinned. With that unruly brush of hair, he looked more like a wild animal than a man. "Uppity bitches like you don't understand nothin' unless it's from the back of a man's . . ."

"Get the hell away from her, Reuben!" a man's voice interrupted the brute's threats. Adrianna's heart leapt! But when the man-mountain moved, she was doubly surprised to see that her rescuer was *not* Gabe or Quinn, but a complete stranger! A middle-aged man, obviously three sheets to the wind, who stood on wobbly legs next to the piano. His bulbous nose was crisscrossed with broken red veins, and he jabbed the air with a shaky finger.

"You ain't bossin' me," Reuben snarled.

Before her defender could say another word, the man he'd called Reuben swung a meaty fist that crashed squarely into his bright red nose. An audible crack filled the room like a rifle shot, the cartilage shattering and blood spilling down onto the hardwood floor. The man fell like a sack of flour, his arms and legs splayed around him.

A pregnant pause filled the tavern as everyone took in the spectacle before them. Then suddenly, like a tornado bursting forth from a clear blue sky, the room exploded into chaos. Shouts and curses flew like raindrops, a bottle whizzed toward the bar and struck a man in the temple; another man jumped onto Reuben's back and began to beat him about the ears before being tossed like a rag doll. A half-full mug of beer shattered on the wall beside Adrianna, dousing her in alcohol.

"Ahh!" she shrieked.

With an eye for self-preservation, she slid from her stool and headed for relative safety behind the piano. On shaky legs, she peered tentatively out into the melee as she tried to wipe the beer from her face with the sleeve of her blouse.

Another man grabbed a fistful of Reuben's shirt but was beaten down more savagely than the first who'd tried to interrupt him. The sound of his fist striking the man's face was like meat being slapped against the countertop in preparation for dinner. Adrianna felt her heart in her throat; as soon as he finished with his opponent, what would stop him from turning his attention back to his original target . . . *her?*

"Reuben! You stupid son of a bitch!"

Adrianna gasped as Quinn sprang into view. He stood facing the bearded man with a locked jaw and taut arm muscles ending in clenched fists. She was both horrified and excited by what she saw; he looked so fearsome and determined to inflict harm, but she could not deny that he also looked dashing. Never in her life had she seen a man like Quinn.

"Should have finished you long ago," Reuben spat.

"Here's your chance."

The big man lumbered toward Quinn and threw a punch. Adrianna cringed, certain that the bar owner would meet the same fate as the others. Instead, he effortlessly ducked under the punch and released one of his own that crashed into Reuben's rib cage. The force of the blow drove the air from his lungs with a whoosh.

"Unnhhh," he grunted.

Reuben took a hesitant step back in the hopes of regaining his balance, but Quinn was on him, determined to give him no respite. A hard left hand pounded into the bigger man's jaw, whipping his head to the side. His knees buckled and, for a brief moment, it looked as if he would go down, but somehow he managed to stay upright.

With his foe nearly beaten, Quinn's attention briefly wavered as he glanced around the rest of the tavern. Watching from behind the piano, Adrianna could clearly see Reuben as he gained a moment of clarity and balled up his fist for another swing. The man's hand was so large that the only thing Adrianna could compare it with was a Christmas ham. If he should strike Quinn while his attention was diverted . . .

"Look out!" she shrieked in warning.

Reuben threw the haymaker punch but his intended target was nowhere to be found, and the blow sailed wildly past Quinn, who had ducked safely beneath the hulking man's arm, and landed a solid body blow of his own. A grimace of pain shot across Reuben's face, and he doubled over, his hands covering his aching gut. Then, with his opponent's head lowered, Quinn wound up and smashed Reuben in the jaw with an uppercut of such force, it lifted the big man off his feet. This time there would be no stopping his fall. Like a downed oak, Reuben crashed to the floor, crushing a wayward chair beneath him as he went, its legs splayed out beneath him.

"Yeah!" Adrianna shouted with joy.

"It's over, goddamnit," Quinn shouted. "The rest of you guys settle down, or you'll be out the door on your ear."

Now with the bigger man defeated, she expected Quinn to rush over to her and see if she was all right, but instead he disappeared into the melee of bodies that surrounded him. In that instant, she suddenly became aware of the rest of the Whipsaw. While her attention had been focused solely on Quinn and Reuben, utter bedlam had erupted around them. She had no idea what everyone was fighting about. The only person responsible for starting the ruckus was Reuben, but several other brawls had broken out.

"What in heaven?" she wondered aloud.

Over at the bar, all of the stools had emptied save one. Roy Long sat with his back to the bar, looking out over the chaos with a smile that went from ear to ear. To Adrianna, it was as if he were the cat that had caught the canary. Roars of laughter came from his mouth as he slapped a palm against his knee. *He's having the time of his life!*

Adrianna was wondering if it was safe to come out from behind the piano when the tavern door flew open with a bang, and a thunderous voice somehow managed to carry over the din.

"What in the hell is goin' on in here?"

As if a thunderclap had gone off indoors, all heads stopped and turned to the voice. Through the narrowest break in the crowd, Adrianna could see the man who had asked the question. Wearing dark slacks and a sweat-stained white, button-down shirt, the man had a protruding stomach that threatened to spill over his waistline. Beady eyes stared from above a porcine nose. Still, none of these features was particularly memorable. What did stand out was the shiny revolver he held in one pudgy hand and the shiny tin badge that adorned his chest.

"What in tarnation y'all think is goin' on here?" he barked again. It wasn't so much a question as a demand that he didn't seem inclined to wait for.

"Just a quarrel that got out of control is all," Quinn offered, stepping out from behind the bar to join the lawman.

"Do you take me for a fool, Baxter?"

"No."

"Maybe I ought to close this place down." As he spoke, he waved the revolver around loosely, as if to demonstrate his authority.

Adrianna slipped out from behind the piano and sat down.

"Look, Sheriff, it was just a little argument . . ." Quinn began, but the lawman waved him off. With one hand gripping his weapon and the other hitched into his belt buckle, he began to walk through the bar, gazing from one set of eyes to another. Finally, as he neared the piano, he stopped, his eyes on Adrianna.

"And who are you, darlin'?"

When Adrianna didn't answer, he let go with a long whistle and wiped one greasy arm across his sweaty brow. "Well, it ain't hard to see what set ol' Reuben off," he said. "He was at the center of this ruckus, or I'll eat my hat. I suppose I'd be safe in saying that you had a role in this here fight?"

"Sure as shit, I done do swear!" Roy offered, his voice loud in the now quiet room.

"That's right," Gabe echoed, a touch more delicately, from the bar. "Reuben was drinking most of the night, *c'est la vérité.* As soon as the first sing-along ended, he became a wild man."

With a shake of his round head, Sheriff Beauchamp took an abandoned glass full of drink and emptied its contents onto the unconscious man's face. Sputtering and coughing, Reuben shot awake. Momentarily startled, the bearish man looked for a second as if he still had some fight in him but the wind went out of his sails as soon as he caught sight of the sheriff.

"On your feet, boy," Sheriff Beauchamp commanded, "and head for the door."

With a hangdog look on his face, Reuben did as he was told. He kept his head down for most of the way but, as soon as he reached Quinn he lifted it and shot him a glare full of hatred. The barman stared coolly back.

At the door, the sheriff turned and scolded, "Now I sure as shit didn't fall off no turnip truck today, so don't think for one second I believe this was all Reuben's fault. Things best change around here or I'm a gonna be back . . . and ain't a one of you wants that."

A few grumbles came from the crowd but nothing more.

Before he left, he leaned in close to Quinn, the smell of liver and onions on his breath. "This here's another strike against you, Baxter. You keep this up, there ain't a gonna be nothin' remainin' of your daddy in Lee's Point. Best keep that in mind."

Quinn ignored him.

As soon as the sheriff left, things returned to a bizarre normalcy. Adrianna watched as men who had been fighting one another only minutes before now slapped each other on the back and headed to the bar for another drink. She could scarcely believe what she was seeing. It was as if nothing had happened! She was overwhelmed with emotion, and tears began to well up. Before the first one could fall, she looked up to see Quinn standing before her, his hand extended.

With a mischievous grin and a wink, he said, "Welcome to the Whipsaw."

With quivering fingers, she took his offered hand and was pulled to her feet. Her eyes searched his face. "Does this happen often?"

A few coal-black clouds drifted over Lee's Point, their wispy shapes outlined boldly by the bright moon above. To Adrianna, they looked like a couple of ducks that had been separated from their flock, in much the same way as she'd been separated from the life she had known. She made a silent wish that they too would find their way home.

With Quinn's hand firmly attached to her elbow, she was retracing the route from the Whipsaw to home. It was late, a little past midnight, when they'd herded the last of the paying customers out of the bar and shooed them home. She and Quinn had offered to stay behind and help with the cleanup, but Gabe had insisted that he had things under control and bade them good night.

With every step, Adrianna became more conscious of the tall man walking beside her. Ever since Reuben had towered over her, she'd been in a state of anxiety that she wouldn't have been able to explain if her life had depended on it. Even when things had returned to normal, she'd found herself breathless and her muscles taut. Quinn had refused to let her play any longer but she'd scarcely found the calm to sit still behind the bar. Even now, an hour later, she still reverberated with the exhilaration she'd felt when she first saw Quinn leap into the fray. The cool breeze that rustled through the bushes and high tree branches did little to cool the flame that had been lit by the fight.

"Sorry about your first night," Quinn apologized.

"Is it always like that?"

"No, thank goodness." He laughed easily. In the bright moonlight she could see the broad grin that lit up his face. "The folks of this town can be a bit lively from time to time, but it usually isn't that bad. If it was, I wouldn't be in business."

"When that man started talking to me, it nearly scared me to death!" Adrianna exclaimed, her hand flying to her chest.

"That's Reuben for you. If he were only half as smart as he is strong, he wouldn't be the type of fella to start a fight. He's been that way his whole life, so I suppose it isn't fair to think he'd change now."

In her mind's eye, Adrianna could see Quinn as he stood before the piano. When Reuben had turned to him, the rage that had swept over his face was so great that it resembled storm clouds ready to burst. Tentatively, she said, "He seemed awfully mad at you . . ."

"It's been that way between us since we were kids." He sighed. "I thought it might be different as we got older, but it isn't . . . it's only gotten worse. Most of the reason is because of Lola."

"Lola?"

"Reuben has had a crush on her since they were kids. They went out together a few times," he explained. "She denies it, but in this small town people talk."

"I don't see why he wanted to insult me . . ."

"Lola probably put him up to it."

"But, why?"

"Who knows." He shrugged. "She may think you're going to take her job."

The excitement that had been churning

around in Adrianna's chest suddenly turned to anger at the thought that the housekeeper was somehow behind what had happened at the Whipsaw. How on earth could she possibly hate her enough to have someone do her harm? Her growing rage must have been as evident to Quinn as if she had spoken her thoughts aloud, because the man quickly spoke up.

"It wouldn't do you any good to confront her about it."

"Why not?"

"She'd just deny it."

Then why on earth do you have her in your house? Adrianna wanted to ask but held her tongue. She had heard Quinn criticize Lola several times, so there must have been a reason he hadn't fired her.

"I'm glad the sheriff showed up when he did," Adrianna said, changing the subject. "Who knows what could have happened . . ."

"The fighting had stopped when he got there."

Once again, Adrianna bit down before she could say more. From the grimace that had crossed Quinn's face, she knew the sheriff was something of a sore subject. Even though he had stopped the fighting, the tone he had taken with the tavern owner was not a friendly one. Quinn walked on silently, his hands jammed deeply into his pockets.

Minutes later, they turned down the street that led to Quinn's home. The tall trees with their long limbs blocked out the moon's glow, leaving their path a dark one. Up ahead, she could see no light coming from the house; everyone must have gone to bed. Quinn's mood seemed as black as the night, and she made up her mind to try to change it.

"It'll be better the next time I play," she said as confidently as she could.

At the wrought-iron gate, he stopped suddenly and turned to her. Without the light from above, she couldn't see his face, but the sound of his voice did nothing to raise her spirits. "You don't have to come back to the Whipsaw again," he told her.

"What are you talking about?" she exclaimed.

"Your debt is paid."

With the whirlwind of emotions that had coursed through her that evening, she was momentarily surprised to find her anger directed at Quinn. Even though she could not see him clearly, her hand shot out and grabbed his shirt.

"Quinn Baxter! I'll have you know that I'm not a quitter when the going gets rough," she barked at him. "I caused the accident that injured Gabe and broke your liquor bottles. We made a deal for me to pay you back, and I intend to fulfill that agreement!"

Silence greeted her.

Suddenly conscious of the way she had spoken to him, she was about to open her mouth and apologize, to soften the blow, when she felt him move toward her. He surprised her by coming closer. Her first instinct was to take a step backward, but she somehow managed to hold her ground.

"Quinn, I . . ." she began but he hushed her with a finger against her lips. *How can he see me so clearly when I can't see his finger in front of my face?* In the darkness, she swore that she could feel the heat coming off his body.

Gently and delicately, she felt his lips touch hers in a warm kiss. Once again, instead of moving away, she felt herself becoming one with it, her breath locked in her chest. Limply, her hand fell away from him and swung at her side. She closed her eyes and reveled in the moment, hoping that it would go on and on. When he broke away, the only feeling she could recognize was disappointment.

Quinn reached around her and opened

the wrought-iron gate. Together they walked up the narrow path to the porch.

CHAPTER 14

The black Packard came to a stop in front of the diner, its radiator hot from the long drive. The mid-afternoon sun poked briefly from among the rainy clouds, the light dazzling as it danced off the car's wet exterior. The respite in the damp day was brief; seconds later the sun was once again hidden from view, the day back to matching the gloomy mood of the Packard's driver.

Richard Pope glanced fitfully through the car's windshield as he peered up at the weathered sign above him. "Evans Diner," it read plainly. Nothing about the place merited notice. It had poor lighting, a long crack in one of the four windowpanes that fronted the main street, chipped and peeling paint around the door frame, and a tattered awning that would surely offer no protection from the rain. Grass and weeds grew in the cracks of the cement walk in front. Wearily, he got out of the car and headed for the front door.

"Damn rain," he muttered.

From the moment he had discovered Adrianna missing, he had been searching for her. He could only guess how many diners and gas stations he had entered up and down the roads that led from Shreveport. At first, he'd been full of hope and a sense of conviction that he would soon find his wayward bride-to-be. Now, after disappointment followed disappointment, every town had begun to look the same. Still, he continued on in the belief that she had to have stopped *somewhere* or that she had been seen by *someone.*

Pushing the door open, Richard stepped into the midst of the afternoon lunch crowd. Men in hats and overalls sat elbow-to-elbow at the long front counter, their shoulders hunched over their meals and the sounds of their gruff voices carrying over the din of forks striking plates. Several couples sat at the narrow booths near the windows, the women cackling like barnyard hens. The tangy smell of frying meats mixing with the odor of cigarette smoke assailed his nostrils.

"Just grab yerself a seat," a woman's voice said. Startled out of his disdain, Richard looked down to see a fat lump of a woman with an apron around her waist staring back at him. Her wisp of a smile showed a missing tooth and others that were soon destined to join their lost sibling. Absent-mindedly, she scratched behind her ear with a pencil.

"Excuse me?"

"Just find a place to park yer fanny, and I'll come get yer order." Without another look, she was off to tend to a waiting table, her gnarled mop of dirty brown hair bouncing behind her.

Finding the last empty booth back in the far corner, Richard trudged to his seat with contempt. It took every bit of self-restraint he had not to pull a cloth from his coat pocket and wipe the seat. *How could the inside of this place be as filthy as the outside?*

As he waited for the dumpling of a woman to return to take his order, his mind raced over the question that had haunted him from the moment he had found Adrianna gone. With her father dead, why hadn't she realized that he had given her a great honor asking her to be his wife? Frankly, the only course that offered her the same comforts she had become used to was with him as her husband.

What galled Pope the most was that Adrianna had run away from the comforts of Shreveport and rushed headlong into the ignorant masses of the Louisiana countryside. *Didn't she realize that nothing in her life had prepared her to cope with the working class people who were beneath her?* He had to fight to keep a sneer from crossing his lips as he looked out from his booth at the simpletons that filled the diner. As his harsh gaze went from face to face, one of the patrons at the counter, a stick of a man wearing greasy overalls, opened his mouth in a mask of laughter, and the soup he had been eating spilled out and ran down his chin. Absently, he wiped it with the back of his hand, his peal of laughter never wavering. Pope wanted to stand up on his seat and scream at these people, but he knew that his educated words would be lost on them.

Richard Pope's station in life was something that he was terribly proud of, and he intended to guard it. His father, a successful banker in his own right, had taken great pains to educate his only child about the importance of being a man of high standing. Private schools and harsh discipline had been his lot. Even after a banking crisis robbed the family of much of its wealth, as well as the health of the family patriarch, Richard had put his lessons to use. Through his relationship with Charles Moore, he'd rebuilt all that had been lost. His marriage to Adrianna would be the crown jewel of all he had strived for.

"What can I getcha?"

While he'd been viewing the diner with disdain, the waitress had sidled up to the table, an order ticket at the ready. Like a mindless cow, she nibbled on the pencil eraser.

"Just a cup of coffee," Richard muttered.

"Sure I can't interest ya in a slice a pie?" she pressed. Moving closer and giving a conspiratorial wink, she said, "I ain't one ta do much braggin', but we got the best darn pecan pie in the state of Louisiana."

"Not for me."

While the waitress went to fetch his order, Richard reached into his suit coat and pulled out a photograph. Sliding it faceup onto the table, he couldn't suppress a small smile as the beautiful face of Adrianna looked up at him. It was the same photo that had sat upon the mantel above the fireplace back in Shreveport. He had made a small alteration to it, cutting Charles Moore free from his daughter; the old man was dead and gone and no longer a part of his life. Where once this picture had been a cherished memento, it was now an instrument to be used. He'd sullied the photo by bringing it to innumerable diners and gas stations, hoping that someone would recognize her.

"Here ya go." The waitress interrupted his thoughts and placed the coffee mug on the table. A couple of drops of liquid sloshed out of the cup and landed near the photograph.

A sudden rage washed over Richard, and it took all of his composure to keep from screaming at her. Instead, he snatched the photograph from the table and said, "Thank you, my dear, but before you run off, I was wondering if I might ask you a question."

"Sure thing, honey."

He handed the portrait to the waitress. Inwardly he cringed at the thought of the woman's dirty fingers holding Adrianna's likeness, but he knew that there was no choice. "Have you ever seen this woman in here before?"

Without more than a cursory glance, the woman looked back at him, her eyes wide. When she spoke, her words were dipped in scandal with every syllable. "Did yer sweetie run away from ya?"

The lie that rolled over Richard's tongue was as well worn as an old shoe; he'd used it enough that if he himself had heard it, he would have believed it. "Nothing that exciting, I'm afraid. This woman is my cousin.

She was driving through these parts a couple of weeks ago on her way to Florida, and we haven't heard from her. I, being her closest relative, am looking for her."

The waitress seemed to ponder his explanation and then, with a shrug of her shoulders, turned her attention to the photograph. Her brow furrowed and knit tightly in concentration as she studied Adrianna's face. Momentarily, Richard's heart leapt with the hope that this would be the end of his search. However, the waitress looked up at him and frowned. "I ain't never seen her before."

"Are you sure?" he pressed.

"Yep."

As quickly as his heart had jumped with hope, it now sank with the realization that he had once again come up empty in his search. *How many more times will I have to go through this?* Before he could reach out and snatch the picture from the waitress's hand, she surprised him by speaking.

"It's just that . . ." she began but stopped.

"What?" he asked. "What were you going to say?"

"Well, it's just that I been gone from work for a bit," she explained. "I had me a touch of the sick and ain't been here. If she come in while's I was gone, I wouldn't a seen her."

"Who would have been here?" Richard took the picture from her hand and looked at her with disgust. "What about the other waitresses? One of them could have seen her."

"Maude woulda been here most of the days I was gone. If yer cousin done come in, she woulda seen her."

"Is she here today?"

"Yep."

"Then go ask her to come here!" Richard barked. A few heads turned at the sound of his voice but soon returned to their meals. The waitress, like the obedient dog he considered her, scurried off. Try as he might, he couldn't suppress the rise in his hopes.

Minutes later, the woman returned with the other waitress, the one she had called Maude. Unlike the first woman, Maude was stick-thin and tall, her gangly arms hanging limply at her sides. Together, they were almost comical, their shapes reminding Richard of a female version of the actors Stan Laurel and Oliver Hardy.

Once again Richard took the picture from his pocket. "Have you seen this woman?" he said and handed it to Maude.

She looked at it intently. Then, slowly at first but gaining in momentum, she began to nod her head. Richard could barely contain his excitement as Maude said, "Yeah. I seen her in here last week. I remember 'cause it was the day of that big storm, and there weren't too many folk come to the diner."

"Are you sure it was her?" Richard prodded.

"Yeah."

"You need to be certain!"

"Mister," Maude explained, one hand planted on her bony hip, "if there's one thing we get used to in this line a work, it's people's faces. Most of the folks around here ain't as stupid as city folks think we are. She's a face I'd be sure to remember."

Richard sighed heavily. All of the work he had done, all of the roads he had taken that had led to nothing but dead ends, had finally produced a result. He was on the right track. Finally, he knew which direction she'd taken.

He was feeling happy with himself, nearly giddy. All he needed to do was to keep following the road until he found her. To that end he asked, "What towns lie farther up the road to the east?"

"There's Vincent, Beauville, Lee's Point, and then Connelly on the way to the river," Maude explained.

Triumphantly, Richard said, "Ladies, I do believe I will have that piece of pie, after all!" As the two of them left to retrieve his food, Richard took another long look at the photograph of Adrianna. Even in the stench of the diner, he swore he could still remember the fragrance of her perfume. It wouldn't be long before they were reunited and then married. He smiled, and his lips trembled at the thought.

Soon . . . you will be mine!

CHAPTER 15

Standing on her tiptoes, Adrianna peered at the top of the armoire in the corner of the living room. She'd spent the bulk of the morning searching the house high and low for any books to use in teaching Jesse, but so far she had come up empty-handed. Even now, the armoire yielded nothing but more dirt and dust motes. *Was there anywhere in the whole house that Lola had actually cleaned?*

Disgruntled, Adrianna stood with her hands on her hips. With the ordeal of the previous night over, she'd hoped that the day would settle into a more normal routine. Sleep had come fitfully, her mind tossing and turning over the fight at the tavern. When she closed her eyes, all she could see was Reuben standing before her at the piano, his lips curled in an ugly sneer. Only by replaying the moment when Quinn's lips touched hers was she able to calm herself

209

enough for sleep to claim her.

When she'd wakened, Quinn had already left for the lumber camp. *When on earth did that man sleep?* After a quick bite of a hardly passable breakfast, she had visited Jesse in his room and told him of her intention to begin some rudimentary instruction until she or Quinn could talk to his teachers at the school. He'd grumbled, much as she'd expected him to, but reluctantly agreed to her plan. She'd happily set off in search of material. Now, over an hour later, she'd found nothing except discarded pulp magazines, and her initial elation had begun to wane.

So far, she had resisted the urge simply to ask Lola if there were any books in the house. The woman hadn't uttered a word during breakfast, nibbling away on a piece of toast like a determined mouse. Adrianna had watched her warily. Adding what Quinn had said about the housekeeper's relationship with Reuben to the way Lola had treated her from the moment she'd arrived at the Baxter home made Adrianna want as little to do with her as possible. Still, this wasn't about the bitterness between the two of them . . . this was about Jesse. It was also about what she had promised Quinn. With a deep breath and extra purposefulness in her step, Adrianna set off to find Lola.

She was standing near the windows, staring out the filthy glass at the day beyond. Yet again, Adrianna's mind raced over all of the things Lola *should* be doing, but she bit her tongue and came to a stop behind her. Slowly, as if she had just noticed that there was someone else in the room, Lola turned to face Adrianna, her face a mask of disdain.

"What do you want?" she snapped.

Swallowing the urge to snap back at the other woman, Adrianna explained, "I'm trying to find some books that will help Jesse with his lessons. Do you know if there are any here?"

"So there is something you don't know." Lola sneered and pushed her stringy brown hair from her face. "Must be hard for you to admit you don't know everything."

"Are there any books here or not?"

"Why the hell do you want to teach that boy anything?" Lola spat, the sugar-sweet voice she used when in Quinn's presence as absent as he was. "It ain't like he's gonna get out of that chair and go off to college. Even if he walks again, he'll still be stuck right here in Lee's Point. Ain't no amount of books is ever gonna change that."

Try as she might to retain her composure, Adrianna's patience was wearing thin. "He

211

is going to walk again, and when he does, he'll need to have finished his schooling if he has any intention of making a decent life for himself."

"Does Quinn know what you're doing?"

"Yes."

"You're lying," Lola spat. "Once him and me are married, we're gonna sell the Whipsaw so we'll have money. Then we can get down to what really matters . . . makin' babies!"

Adrianna's stomach churned at the very thought. She desperately wanted to lash out at the brash woman, to let her know that she was a servant here and until she and Quinn were married, that is all she would be, but Adrianna knew that her words would accomplish nothing except to make matters worse. She had to keep her personal feelings out of the situation for Jesse's sake.

"All I want is to know if there are any books in the house," she reiterated.

Lola sized her up for a moment, the scorn in her eyes speaking volumes of what she thought about the woman standing before her. With a shrug, she turned her attention back to the window.

For a moment, Adrianna thought that Lola intended to ignore her, but she said, "There's a box up in the attic, but I can't say for sure what's in it."

"Where is . . . ?"

". . . The attic? Even an idiot knows where an attic is."

"What I meant was, how do I get there —"

Lola cut her off. "At the end of the hallway there's a door."

Without a word of thanks, Adrianna turned on her heel and left the room. *Every word that comes out of that woman's mouth irritates me.* For the life of her, she couldn't fathom why Quinn employed her. Adrianna tried to tamp down her anger as she headed for the door leading to the attic.

As she passed by Jesse's room, she glanced in to see him lying on the bed reading one of his magazines. She went up the stairs, continuing down to the end of the hallway, and pulled open the door leading to the attic. Adrianna was instantly assaulted by a wave of stale, warm air. Before her, the narrow steep stairs extended upward into a murky darkness. She fumbled along either side of the doorway, feeling for a light switch but found none.

She muttered a seldom-used swear word to herself.

Leaving the door open behind her for some extra light, she grabbed on to a railing and began to make her way upward to the attic.

At the top of the stairs, Adrianna looked across the attic to the small window. She stood still, allowing her eyes to adjust to the scant light that came through the dirty pane.

Even before her eyes were able to make out any details, she felt the heat. The attic was an oven. Sweat instantly began to bead on her forehead and then run down her cheeks. Every breath she took seemed to weigh on her chest like a load of bricks. The heavy air was full of dust and mold. It must have been a long time since the attic had been aired, as even the small movements she made had stirred up the dust.

Finally, her eyes began to make out shapes. The pitched roof of the house ran along its entire length. Boxes of all shapes and sizes were piled here and there across the rough floor. A tailor's mannequin had tipped over and leaned precariously against a dilapidated dresser. The attic in Quinn's house was definitely a refuge for discarded items.

"Where shall I look first?" she said aloud.

Making her way cautiously around the stairs, she inched forward into the gloomy attic. Waves of heat washed over her as she moved. Her clothing began to stick to her as rivulets of sweat ran down between her breasts.

"Find the books and get the heck out of this place," she said to herself.

The first box that she came to held discarded clothing, as did the second. The third one she opened appeared to hold nothing but everyday trash, easier to toss up into the attic than to take where it belonged. If she were to make a wager, Adrianna would swear that this was Lola's doing. She'd not put anything past that lazy woman!

Suddenly, a movement out of the corner of her eye startled her. In that split second, she imagined rats running along the base of the attic's walls, making a beeline for the stairs in order to block her escape. Now the air, thick and hot, seemed to magnify in its intensity around her, smothering her as if it were a blanket.

Moments later, she found the source of the movement: herself. Pressed tightly against the roof's pitch stood a full-length mirror. Inside an ornate wooden frame, the mirror's glass had been broken vertically and half of it removed. In the strange, half-image before her, she had to squint in the gloom to make out any details. The face that looked back at her glistened with sweat; her hair hung in wet strings.

As she inched sideways to take a better look, her knee struck something hard.

"Ouch!" she yelped.

When she bent over to rub her wounded knee, Adrianna discovered a dark wood trunk lying next to the broken mirror. She hadn't been able to see it until she bumped into it.

"Maybe you're just what I'm looking for."

She knelt down in front of the trunk and turned to allow the light from the window to shine on it. Seizing the trunk's handle, she tugged and pulled with all of her might. Whatever was in the trunk weighed a lot! Grunting and groaning, her muscles aching from the strain, she kept on until she managed to drag the large box near the window. Now she would be able to see more clearly. As she struggled to open the trunk's latch, the light provided her with a sight that she would rather not have seen: A huge brown spider ambled over the trunk's lid a few scant inches from her hand.

"Oh!" she cried and fell back.

Calling on all her courage, Adrianna brushed her hand across the lid in the hope that it would drive the spider away and quickly undid the latch. Grasping the lid firmly with both hands, she pushed upward and threw it back.

She had struck the mother lode! The trunk was full of books, books, and more books! As she pulled them out, she looked at their titles in the light, her smile growing wider and wider. She found *Gulliver's Travels, Robinson Crusoe,* and *A Tale of Two Cities,* all of which were books that she had enjoyed reading with her father. There was even a copy of Horace Greeley's *The American Conflict,* which she could use to teach Jesse history. All of the grief, from Lola to the heat of the attic and the big spider, had been worth it!

"Jackpot!" she exclaimed.

As she was pulling out the last of the books, something in the trunk grabbed her attention. In the faint light she could see several photographs scattered across the bottom of the box as if they had been tossed there haphazardly. Tentatively, trying to ignore the possibility that more spiders lived in the trunk, she reached out to pick up the photos.

The first photograph was of the same two people who had been in the picture she'd seen upon first entering the house. She'd initially assumed that the two people had been Quinn's parents, and this new image seemed to prove it. It was another studio portrait, identical in many ways to the first, but the man and woman were much younger. Through the gloom of the attic and the graininess of the picture, Adrianna could see Quinn staring back out at her through his father's face; the same piercing eyes, the tight mouth that seemed to hold mischief at the corners. Jesse resembled his mother, with a rounder face that was not as sharp around the edges and a gaze that was inquisitive and maybe a touch sad.

The second photograph was another window into an earlier time. This was also a studio photograph, but much less formal than either of the other two she had seen. There, standing beside his parents, was Quinn and sitting on his mother's lap was Jesse. Both were much younger; she would have guessed Quinn's age at no more than fifteen, and he wore the annoyed look of young man who was being forced to take a photograph he did not want to pose for.

"You were ornery even then." She smiled as a drop of sweat rolled off her nose and landed on the dry wooden floor below. There was Jesse, with his mother, his whole life before him, with no idea that he would find himself unable to walk. There was Quinn, unaware that the burden of caring for his brother was about to be placed squarely upon his shoulders.

As if it were a lightning bolt from a clear sky, the realization struck Adrianna that she was much like the Baxter boys. Back home in Shreveport, she was certain that there were photographs of her and her parents, taken at ages at which she would have found the whole thing silly or a waste of time. All of them would have been smiling and full of joy. At those moments, she would have been incapable of understanding what was going to happen to her life, that she too would be left to fend for herself. As the thought roiled through her, Adrianna found herself fighting back tears.

Suddenly, the sound of a door slamming exploded across the attic, and the dim light that came up from the stairs was cut off. Momentarily unable to speak, Adrianna heard only the pounding of her own heart.

The attic door!

"Hello?" she said tentatively. "Is anyone there?" There was no answer.

She didn't know if she was imagining things, but Adrianna could have sworn that the temperature in the attic soared. In the near darkness her heart beat like a frightened rabbit's as the heat descended on her as if it were a net trying to ensnare its prey.

As steadily as she could, Adrianna rose to

219

her feet. What had happened? Had a gust of wind pulled the door shut? Now she needed to find her way back out of the attic. Trying to remember the location of each of the boxes she'd seen, Adrianna inched her way across the attic back in the direction of the steps. She tried to move slowly, confidently, but her fears picked at the corners of her thoughts. Her foot brushed against a box, and she moved to the side to avoid it.

"That's the way," she reassured herself. "Nice and slow."

She'd only taken one more step forward when a thought occurred to her. What if she were to step forward blindly and fall down into the stairwell? In this darkness, she couldn't be entirely sure she would see it until it was too late. She could break an arm or worse. With this new concern hanging over her, she got down on her hands and knees and felt her way.

As she slid along, dust rose from the floor and clouded in her face, forcing her to cough. All of the worries about spiders and other animals disappeared. Sweat poured from her face and coated her skin.

It is so damned hot. I need to get out of here!

She was beginning to panic when her hand caught the lip of the stairwell. Following it along its length, she was soon at the top of the steps that led down to the floor below. Still careful not to lose her balance, she took her time descending. A small sliver of light came from beneath the door, and she sighed as her hand found the knob.

Anticipating the feel of cooler air washing over her drenched body, she reached for the doorknob. The knob stayed firm in her hand, refusing to move.

The door refused to open!

CHAPTER 16

Adrianna continued to try to turn the doorknob. "Open, damn it!" It didn't occur to her that it was locked; she assumed it was only stuck.

Certain that it would finally open and free her from the confines of the scorching hot attic, she continued to turn the knob and push on the door. "Lola," she called. "Open the door."

She was momentarily shocked by the sound of her voice echoing around the stairwell. To her ear, it sounded distant, frail, and a bit frightened. Balling her fists, she pounded against the door. It shook on its hinges but refused to give way. When she spoke again, she heard the first tinges of irritation in her voice.

"Lola, this isn't funny. Open the door." There was no answer. Lola had locked her in and left the house.

Sweat poured down the sides of her face;

she felt as if she were in a steam bath. The heat was a palpable thing; she could have sworn that it was physical enough to touch. It was all around her, bearing down on her, making it hard to breathe. She wiped her brow, and it was again instantly beaded with perspiration. Still, the cold finger of fear played along her spine.

"I have to get out of here," she murmured, "or I'll faint from the heat."

Opening her mouth to once again yell for help, Adrianna stopped herself and fell silent. No one would be able to help her. Even if Jesse were to hear her, he would be unable to come up the steps to open the door.

Adrianna was sure that Lola had shut the door and locked it, leaving her in the hot attic. It was possible that the wind had closed the door, but that seemed unlikely. Even if Lola were to hear her shouts for help, Adrianna could only imagine that the cleaning woman would be pleased, a malicious smile plastered across her face. Shouting would do her no good. She would have to find another way out.

What am I going to do? It will be hours before Quinn comes home.

Climbing back up to the top of the stairs, Adrianna's eyes sought the dusty window at the far end of the attic. It was too high for her to reach, but she could throw something at it and break the pane.

Keeping that thought in mind, she peered back into the attic's interior and wondered what she might to find to help her. She hadn't searched all of the boxes. Surely there would be something that could be used to pry open the door!

Taking a tentative step, Adrianna was hit by a wave of dizziness that crashed into her head and wobbled her knees. She swayed unsteadily, one hand rushing to her temple while the other searched blindly for something to grab hold of. A fit of intense nausea roiled in her stomach. After what seemed like several long minutes, the wave rolled past her and was gone. Without any doubt, she knew that her enemy was the heat. With ruthless efficiency, it was bearing down on her and breaking apart her defenses. It would only be a matter of time before she succumbed to it.

She didn't want to die in this dusty attic.

With a new sense of urgency, Adrianna moved back into the depths of the attic. She tried to inch along cautiously, not wanting to invite another bout of dizziness or stumble blindly into a box. Soon she was back beside the broken mirror and the trunk that had held the books and photographs. Picking up some of the larger books, she quickly discarded the notion of using them to bang against the door in the hopes of dislodging it; none of them was heavy enough. She even entertained the idea of trying to use the mirror but feared that she would cut herself on the cracked glass. The idea of bleeding to death was even less appealing than dying from the heat.

What she wouldn't do for a tall glass of ice water.

Once again, a reflection in the half-mirror caught her attention. This time, rather than being frightened at some unknown animal, her heart leapt at the possibility of escape. There, right where she had seen it earlier, was the dressmaker's mannequin.

Grabbing it from where it leaned, Adrianna closely examined the peculiar object. While the covering around the top of the mannequin was little more than a limbless assembly of soft fabric, the pole on which it sat was an iron rod. The bottom was originally a three-pronged base, but one of the prongs had broken where it made contact with the pole, which must have been the reason it had been discarded in the first place. As she hefted it in her hands, the desperation in her heart began to be inched out by hope.

With the mannequin held in one sweat-soaked hand, Adrianna hurried back down toward the door. As the early-afternoon sun hammered down on the roof, the heat grew even more intense. If she could have seen clearly, she would have sworn that there was heat shimmering off the old wooden boards. As her mind raced over the joy she would receive from a tall glass of water, Adrianna took a step and found that the floor had disappeared beneath her.

Her fall was a short one. She hardly had time to gasp before her knee struck the stairs and her shoulder collided with the wall. The force of the blow knocked the air from her lungs and the mannequin from her hand, sending it clattering to rest below her. As she sucked in gasps of hot, humid air, pain flared through her shoulder and knee. In her hurry to return to the locked door with her prize, she had fallen partway down the stairs.

"Owww!" She winced as she rubbed her leg and said under her breath every curse word she had ever heard. The words that came from her mouth were words she had never spoken before.

Adrianna sat on the steps and let the tears run down her cheeks to mix with the sweat that coated her face. She realized that she had been lucky. If she had struck her head, she could have been knocked unconscious and would have lain there in the heat for hours. She could have died before Quinn found her. Gingerly making her way down the stairwell, she soon located the mannequin. She checked it by feel and found the rod that ran up the middle of it had fallen out. Now she could use it to break down the door.

Stepping away from the door and up one of the steps, she positioned the end of the steel rod so that it was a couple of inches above the lock. Then, with all of the strength she had left, she pulled it back and drove it forward into the door. The bang of the strike sent shivers up and down her arms. She'd instinctively closed her eyes before she'd swung and expected when she opened them to find the door open. Rearing back, Adrianna swung again. Then again. And yet again. Still, the door held.

It seemed to her that the attic door was as impregnable as the door on the vault of her father's bank.

Fatigue began to wear her down. Her arms throbbed and ached. The heat was nearly unbearable. Oddly, at that moment Adrianna thought of her father. The adversity he had faced would certainly have humbled a lesser man, but not Charles Moore. Even when things had seemed their worst, he had refused to give in to defeat, instead choosing to hold his head up and simply try harder. As his daughter, she could hardly expect less of herself.

She took a deep breath and steeled herself for another go at the door. Even in the near darkness, she tried to visualize hitting the lock cleanly. When she was certain she was ready, Adrianna swung. The end of the rod hit the metal lock with a resounding bang. Her hope that the door would fly open was dashed.

"Oh, shit!" she said in utter frustration.

How can I ever get out of this damned attic? Tears began to well at the corners of her eyes. The hope that had fueled her moments ago vanished. Before despair could sink into her too deeply, she reached out and felt the end of the pole and was surprised to find that it was tapered sharply.

Luckily the door was not a tight fit. There was a small space between the door and the frame. Without giving it another moment's thought, Adrianna jabbed the tapered end of metal into the gap. She remembered that when she came to the attic, the door had swung outward. If she could use the remaining length of the mannequin's pole as a type of lever, she might be able to force the door open.

Please let this work, she silently prayed.

Taking a moment to wipe the sweat and tears from her eyes and blot her hands on her blouse, Adrianna checked to see if the metal end was in place. It held firm against her efforts. As grim determination knotted her brow, she began to push.

Off in the distance she heard Cowboy barking. Lola had shut him outside and her in the attic. She wondered how she would explain that to Jesse.

At first, Adrianna was afraid her efforts would be in vain. No matter how hard she pushed and prodded, the door didn't give an inch. Then, imperceptibly at first, things began to change. With the muscles in her arms straining, Adrianna felt the lever move less than an inch, and then shift ever farther outward. The incessant pounding in her chest and ears was so great that she could barely hear the creaking and fussing of the door as it was forced outward.

A fearful thought rushed through her head: *What if the moaning and cracking was coming from the place where the metal met the wooden pole?* Ignoring such a possibility, Adrianna pushed on.

Much like the moment in which her car had struck against Quinn's in the storm, something suddenly stopped Adrianna from pushing on toward her intended path. It was probably the lock, stopping at the point at which it was not meant to pass. Sweat poured freely. The muscles in her shoulders quivered from the strain. *When I get out of here, Lola, I am going to pull every hair out of your ugly head. Even nice girls have their limits. You'll not think I'm so uppity when I get through with you, and I don't give a damn what you say to Quinn or what he thinks!*

Damn, damn, damn, everyone in this blasted town. It's time I show you what I'm really made of. You'll see I'm not the useless little rich girl you think I am. My grandfather settled this area, and he passed his grit on to me.

With a hiss of hot air through clenched teeth and determination in every line of her body, Adrianna threw her shoulders into the iron pole and strove forward with her last ounce of strength. At first the door held but this time it met with more force than it could resist and it broke from its hinges. With a loud rendering sound, the lock finally yielded, and the door flew out. As the resistance to her pushing disappeared, Adrianna fell against the wall with a thud before collapsing into a heap on the floor.

"Thank God, thank God!" she muttered.

Crawling out of the stairwell, Adrianna passed the door before falling face-first into the upstairs hallway. Blessed cooler air washed over her.

Slowly, Adrianna made her way down the stairs. When she passed Jesse's closed door, his radio was blasting. No wonder he hadn't heard her trying to batter the door down. In the bathroom she wet a cloth and ran it along the back of her head. Cool water trickled down her neck and ran beneath her blouse. The wetness chilled her skin but she hardly noticed it; after the blazing heat of the attic, she wondered if she would ever feel cool again.

Shutting off the faucet, she listened for any sounds coming from inside the house. Cowboy was still barking. *Why in the world isn't Jesse yelling for Lola to let him in?*

Adrianna took a long look at herself in the mirror. Strings of hair were plastered along her forehead and neck. Her eyes were bloodshot and distant. Her face was flushed such a crimson red that her cheeks resembled overripe tomatoes. However, the feature that she could not tear her eyes from was the furrows her tears had made down her dirty face.

When she'd finally managed to get to her feet, she had examined the door. Just as she'd suspected, it had been locked from the outside. She had been able to free herself because of the pressure provided by her makeshift lever. It had been no accident that she had become a prisoner in the attic. There was only one person who could have acted as her jailer.

"Lola!"

Tossing down the towel, Adrianna made for the kitchen, her anger rising with every step. As she neared, she could still feel the dizziness that floated around the back of her head but chose to ignore it. There was far too much to do for her to be ill. She passed Jesse's still closed door without a pause and made a beeline for where she had last seen the spiteful cleaning woman. She was just about to set foot in the room when a man's deep guttural laugh froze her in her tracks.

". . . ain't nothin' that bitch can do about it!"

The voice had come from just outside the door that led out of the kitchen and onto a small porch at the rear of the house. Where anger had just filled Adrianna's heart, it was now replaced with a chilling fear. The night before that same voice had threatened her.

Reuben!

Adrianna was frozen in place as if she were a rabbit trying to convince a fox that she wasn't there. At any moment, that beast of a man could step in the door, find her standing there, and finish the job he had promised. Try as she might to move, she was rooted to the floor.

"If you had just done what I told you, I wouldn't have to go to such trouble."

Lola's venomous voice came from the other side of the door. If there truly had been any doubt that the scheming woman had been behind the troubles at the Whipsaw, it was gone now. Somehow, the sound of her voice broke the spell holding Adrianna in place. Quickly, she scurried behind one of the pillars in the entryway, her head inclined to listen.

"I didn't know your lover boy was gonna stick his nose in," Reuben argued.

"Don't you talk bad about Quinn!"

"Why in the hell you gotta slave after that good-fer-nothin', anyhow?" the man snarled. Adrianna couldn't imagine how Lola was able to stand up against a man so terrifying, particularly when he was so irate. "He ain't never gonna marry you! The whole damn town knows it."

"You shut your mouth! Just shut up!" Lola

screeched. "Don't you ever say one bad thing about Quinn Baxter! He's more man than you'll ever be, you shitty bastard! I swear, if you ever say anything bad about him again, I'll never so much as give you the time of day!"

The ferocity of Lola's words sent a chill racing down Adrianna's spine. She was certain that Reuben would respond with a thunderous bellow of his own, but to her surprise, nothing came. When he did finally speak, his voice was shockingly timid and meek.

"Do you think she'll get out of the attic?"

"Probably," Lola answered matter-of-factly. "A damn child could get out of there. A good kick right on the doorknob would probably break that old thing in two. All I want is to scare her a bit," the housekeeper continued. "If she ain't smart enough to get out of there, she deserves to die. No . . . when the time comes, there ain't no way she's gonna escape."

"What about the kid?"

"Jesse?" Lola laughed. "What about him?"

"All I'm sayin' is it ain't his eyes and ears that are busted," Reuben explained. "If he catches wind of what yer plannin', he could tell the brother, and then you're shit outta luck."

"Do you think I'm a goddamn fool?" Lola shot accusingly.

"Lola . . . I didn't . . ."

"You think I just waltz around this place actin' just like I do when I'm with you?" She laughed mockingly. "You think I give them any reason to worry? There ain't nobody that knows what I'm really plannin'! Not even you! I've already tried it out and it works."

What is she planning? Adrianna's mind raced over the possibilities but found that they were all too difficult to digest. Was Lola after more than Quinn's hand in marriage? If she was acting while she was in the company of the Baxters, what was she really like? Adrianna was afraid she knew the answer to that last question; she was evil!

"But what about us?" Reuben asked.

"You and me?" Lola scoffed. "What with the way you bungled up last night and what you were saying about Quinn, I can't imagine how you could expect me to give a damn about you."

"I said I was —"

Lola cut him off. "If I was you," she began, holding the moment so long that Adrianna felt as if a knife were being held to her throat. "I'd start thinking of ways to make it up to me."

CHAPTER 17

The ceiling fans in Comstock Grocery turned lazily in the mid-afternoon hour, their blades doing little more than pushing the heat around. A folksy song crackled from a small radio, its faraway music tinny in the high-vaulted space. The only other sound came from the flies that hovered above the shelves, their buzzing an incessant background.

Adrianna had left the Baxter home as much to get away from Lola, as to pick up a few things at the mercantile. Her head still felt a touch fuzzy from her time in the attic, but her strength was returning. What she'd really needed was some time alone; besides the store owner, the only other customer was a woman examining the spools in the thread cabinet.

"What a day," Adrianna commented under her breath.

No matter how hard she tried, she could

not get the conversation between Lola and Reuben out of her mind. The single fact that Lola had intentionally locked her in the attic was bad enough without knowing it was only one of the vile woman's plans. With an ogre of a man like Reuben willing to help her, was there anything too low for her to do? *"There ain't nobody that knows what I'm really plannin.'"* Lola's words chilled her.

"Is there anything I can help you with, miss?" a voice behind her spoke, startling her.

Adrianna spun quickly to find that the store's clerk had come out from behind the counter. A portly man on whose bald head only small tufts of white hair remained near his ears, the clerk had a smile nearly as wide as his entire face. A pair of pincenez glasses balanced precariously on his bulbous nose. There was something about him that reminded Adrianna of a preacher; she supposed that there was certainly a touch of salesmanship in both professions. As he wiped his hands across his apron, he seemed to sense that he had startled her.

"I'm terribly sorry if I gave you a fright. It's very easy to get lost in thought in a store like this. Lord only knows how many days I've spent staring off into nothing," he explained. Extending one hand toward her, he said, "I'm Roger Comstock, the owner. If there is anything I can help you with, please don't hesitate to ask."

"My name is Adrianna Moore," she said, giving him as warm a greeting as he had given her. "I'm afraid that I've never been in your nice store before, and I was wondering where I might find the bath soap."

"Right this way."

Mr. Comstock led Adrianna to another aisle where he directed her to what she was looking for, before excusing himself and returning to the counter. Thanking him for his help, she looked halfheartedly amongst the various kinds of soap, her mind still racing over all that had befallen her.

It was enough that she had found herself in Lee's Point at all, let alone that she was faced with the possibility that an irate woman she hardly knew wanted to do her harm. The decision to run away from Richard Pope's advances had seemed like a wise idea at the time; but had she known all of the calamities that would befall her on her journey, she might have been a bit more cautious. Still, she'd run, and the situation she had found herself in was of her own making. Her life with her father in Shreveport seemed many years and thousands of miles away.

The question that gnawed at her the most was whether or not she should tell Quinn about what had happened with Lola. At first, she'd been angry enough to have spoken out. It would have been a simple matter to have shown Quinn that the door had been locked behind her. He would have had no choice but to fire Lola and get her out of the household.

But is it really that simple?

As more time had passed, doubt had begun to eat away at the strength of her resolve. What if there was even a single grain of truth to what Lola had said about her and Quinn's relationship? Would he just laugh away all accusations? After last night, when he had tenderly planted a kiss on her lips, she had great difficulty believing that he could be involved with someone like Lola.

But still . . .

Right then and there, in the middle of Comstock Grocery, she decided to hold her tongue, not out of a fear of Lola's reaction or even of a rejection by Quinn. Instead, it was because of a business lesson she had heard her father say he had learned: *Keep your friends close but keep your enemies closer.* Lola was dangerous, of that there was no doubt. But she would be undeniably *more* dangerous if she were out of sight. Adrianna decided that until she was certain, she would keep her tale to herself but keep both her eyes on Lola.

"Are you waiting for that bath soap to jump off the shelf?"

As she turned to the sound of the voice, Adrianna expected to find the clerk, Mr. Comstock, returning to make a small joke. Instead, a dapper-looking younger man in a well-tailored suit stood eyeing her mischievously. His blond hair was slicked back in a style she hadn't seen since she'd left Shreveport. The ceiling fans blew the scent of cologne to her nose as the man absently rubbed one thin hand along his jaw line.

"Excuse me?"

"The way that you were staring at all of these bars of soap," the man said, taking a step toward her while gesturing to all of the soap on the shelf, "made me think that you wanted them to make up your mind for you."

There was something about the sarcastic way in which the man spoke that made Adrianna uncomfortable. She'd had enough awkward meetings with strangers in the last several days to last her a lifetime! Turning on her heel, she meant to simply walk away and ignore the man, but when he spoke again, he stopped her in her tracks.

"You play piano at the Whipsaw, don't you, Miss Moore?"

"How do you know my name?" she challenged him.

"Well," the man said with a smirk, moving once again to narrow the distance between them, "it might have been that I simply overheard you introducing yourself to the clerk a few moments ago, but I'm afraid that would be a lie. The fact is, word of the mysterious new piano player at the Whipsaw has traveled across this little town as if it were the wind itself. You can hardly wonder how news could travel so fast, though. With so little to entertain themselves, the citizens of Lee's Point have become well-practiced gossips."

"Hopefully, they had good things to say."

"I have heard that your playing is excellent," he said evenly.

"You weren't there?" Adrianna asked, her tone a touch challenging. Images of the free-for-all that had occurred sprang back to mind.

"I wouldn't set foot in that rattrap dive unless it was a matter of utmost importance. From outward appearances," the man said, looking her up and down, "I would think that a cultured woman like yourself would feel the same."

The hairs on the back of Adrianna's neck suddenly stood up. This man had her at a distinct disadvantage; there were things he obviously knew about her although she wouldn't have known him from a bale of hay. That needed to change. "I'm afraid I did not catch your name."

"That would be because I have failed to mention it," the man said coolly, a smile faintly crossing his lips before fading. Stepping ever closer, he extended his hand. "My name is Fuller. Dewey Fuller."

Adrianna refused to take his greeting. "I'm afraid that I don't understand just why you have interrupted my shopping, Mr. Fuller. Surely you're not seeking piano lessons."

The man's laugh rose quickly, overpowering the other sounds in the store. The woman examining the thread looked up for a moment before returning to the spools in the cabinet. "That is quite a wit you have, Miss Moore." Dewey chuckled. "As much as I would like to take lessons from someone as pretty as you, I'm afraid I lack musical talent."

"As well as manners," she said firmly.

"You cut me to the quick!" He feigned pain, bringing both his hands to his heart. "I think that you've mistaken me for the type of common folk who attend taverns and sing-alongs. Actually, my reason for interrupting your shopping is that I have an . . . interest in you."

"What?"

"Maybe that isn't the way to put it, not exactly, anyhow," he tried to explain. "Maybe the better way to phrase it would be to say that I have an interest in your welfare."

As if she were back in the sweltering attic, Adrianna's stomach roiled. *Could this be another one of Lola's henchmen?* Without any hesitation or another word, she snatched the bar of soap off the shelf and hurried toward the counter.

"Did you find everything you needed?" Mr. Comstock asked as she dropped the soap on the counter with a loud thud. It came to rest next to a newspaper emblazoned with the headline "Babe Ruth Retires from Baseball." Adrianna hardly saw it, her mind was still a jumble.

"Yes. Thank you," she answered with a weak smile.

"That will be twelve cents."

As she dug the coins out of her purse, Adrianna threw a quick glance over her shoulder. Dewey was standing right where she had left him, his arms crossed over his chest, watching her every move. The look on his face wasn't one of anger, but of amusement.

She thanked the clerk, snatched up the sack, and headed for the front door. Choosing another aisle from the one that Dewey occupied, Adrianna hurried on her way. She never so much as glanced up at him, but as she passed him, she caught him moving beside her out of the corner of her eye.

He's following me!

Opening the mercantile door, its small bell jingling, she scooted through and began to hurry down the boardwalk when he once again said something that froze her in place.

"How well do you know Quinn Baxter?"

Rather than fear, it was anger that swelled in Adrianna's breast. From the moment her father had died, she had been tossed and turned through life as if she were nothing more than a ship lost at sea. From Richard Pope to Quinn Baxter to Lola and now to Dewey Fuller, it had all been the same. Everyone she met seemed to know the answers to the questions she didn't even know she should ask. *No more!*

"What are you saying?"

"I'm asking you how well you know the man in whose house you are now staying," Dewey explained as he once again approached her, but she was not afraid. Being out in public somehow made it easier for Adrianna to be around him. "It seems to me that you're being quite trusting of someone you know next to nothing about."

"He's been very much a gentleman to me," she said with some conviction.

"He's no saint."

"And I suppose you are?"

"I hardly think I would qualify." Dewey chuckled. "I'd like to fancy myself as more of a businessman than someone who would stand behind a pulpit and preach. But this isn't a discussion about me, is it? This is about Quinn."

"You'll have to pardon me, Mr. Fuller, but it seems that you like to speak in riddles," Adrianna said defiantly. Her first impression of the man had been wrong; it was Quinn he was interested in instead of her, although neither proposition made her very comfortable.

"The only riddle I can see is why a woman like you would involve herself with a man like Quinn."

"How do you know what kind of woman I am?"

"It's easy, you've got breeding written all over you."

I don't need to explain myself to this man!

245

Setting her back straight and holding her head high, she said simply, "I don't know you, and I resent your familiarity."

"And that, my dear Miss Moore," Dewey said syrup-sweet, a toothy grin spreading across his face, "is what makes you as different from Quinn Baxter as a queen is from a peon."

"What are you talking about?"

"What if I were to tell you that Quinn is on the verge of losing not only the Whipsaw but his father's beloved home as well? Would any of that truly surprise you?"

"That's Mr. Baxter's personal business and none of mine," Adrianna said sharply.

"It honestly doesn't shock me that he wouldn't tell you any of this," Dewey said with a dismissive wave of his hand. "Why would he? After all, a beautiful woman like you doesn't come into a man's life every day, especially in a pissant town like this one. He would certainly have been afraid that you would think less of him."

Adrianna's head reeled. It was as if the storm that had brought her to this town had been reborn around her, although instead of rain, wind, and lightning there were now the lives of Quinn, Jesse, Lola, and even Dewey Fuller buffeting her from all sides.

"From outward appearances, he certainly

has designs on you," Dewey continued. "He's taken a complete stranger into his house and given you a place to work. He's even got Delmar working on your automobile. Maybe I was wrong . . . maybe he is a saint after all."

The way that Dewey described what had happened made her angry. It was far more complicated than he made it seem. *Even if what the dapper man is saying about Quinn owing money is true, it is no business of mine.*

"Why are you concerned by any of this?"

"I'm concerned for your welfare, not Quinn's," he said, taking another step in her direction. He was right before her, his blue eyes staring down into her own. Even though his dress and speech were cultured, there was something about his eyes that was calculating. In that instant, she knew Dewey Fuller was not the type of man she would want for a friend. "If there is one thing that you should be aware of, Miss Moore, my family and I are very well respected in this town."

"What's the point of telling me?" she asked impatiently.

"Because generosity has its limits," he answered matter-of-factly. "My father and I don't think the Whipsaw is any place for a refined young lady."

"Your father?"

"Is the man who bought up Quinn's loan from the bank to keep that fleabag of a tavern open," Dewey said, providing the answer to her question. "I told him that he would regret the offer, but what's done is done. He was willing to look past the lateness of his repayment, but no longer."

"That's between Quinn and your father. It has nothing to do with me."

With that, Adrianna turned to walk away from Dewey Fuller. She'd had as much strife as she could stomach for one day. Before she could even take two steps, however, he grabbed her by the arm and spun her around. As her eyes met his, she was shocked by the venom in them. Clearly, he was a man who was rarely rejected.

"It would be best not to walk away from me again," he sneered.

"Let go of my arm," she demanded.

"You're mistaken if you think you have no role to play in all of this, my dear."

"Get away from me," she snapped.

"You are going to march back to Quinn, and tell him that you're not going to lower yourself any longer to playing the piano in the Whipsaw," Dewey ordered. His hold on her arm seemed to tighten with every word.

"Why do you care?"

"That's none of your business. Just do as I say."

With her face inches from Dewey's, her eyes were drawn to a thin, pink scar that ran down the left side of the man's face. With the anger flushing his face, the mark's tissue flushed a dark shade and appeared to leap out at her. Try as she might, she couldn't take her eyes off it.

"Take a good, long look," he ordered, seeing her gazing at the scar on his face.

Momentarily embarrassed, Adrianna stammered, "I'm sorry, I didn't mean . . . to stare."

"The next time you're with your vicious friend, Quinn Baxter, ask him how I came to have that scar," he spat. "Ask him about what he did to me . . . what can never be repaired! See if he's as generous with the truth as he is when he's in bed with you!"

A new wave of anger washed over her. What was he insinuating? What did he mean? Before she could retort, he released her arm and moved away. As he did, the sack of soap slid from her grasp and landed hard at her feet. Her arm throbbed and ached where his hand had held her tightly. She could only stare as the man stalked away.

CHAPTER 18

If Adrianna hadn't actually experienced all that had happened to her, she knew it would be difficult to believe it was real. All through dinner, she'd waited for the opportunity to tell Quinn that she'd been locked in the attic. He had been his normal self, joking about his day at the lumber mill with Jesse, not in the least aware of the turmoil that roiled within her. Lola's sickeningly sweet act returned during the meal, although Adrianna could see a coldness lying just beneath the surface. As for herself, she had been mostly silent, speaking only when spoken to.

"Quinn, I was locked in the attic today," she finally blurted out.

"Locked in the attic?" he said disbelievingly.

"Yes. Locked in the attic." Adrianna looked up from her plate. Quinn was leaning back in his chair, his arms crossed over his chest, the top two buttons of his shirt undone. He had a deep scowl on his face.

"Are you sure?"

"Yes, I'm sure," she said angrily. "I had to break down the door to get out. It was damned hot up there, as you well know," she said looking at Lola.

"Don't tell me about it. I had nothing to do with it."

"Then who did? It wasn't Jesse. He doesn't go upstairs."

Quinn was looking from one woman to the other. Adrianna's face was set in angry lines.

"The wind could have blown it shut." Color had crept up Lola's neck to cover her face.

"I suppose the wind could have locked it, too," Adrianna said sarcastically.

"Are you saying I shut you in there?" Lola demanded.

"Yes, I'm saying you shut me up there. You even put Cowboy out so he wouldn't hear me."

"Quinn," Lola said, her tone soft and gentle, "I don't know what she's talking about."

"I heard some banging on a door." Jesse had helped himself to jelly, which he spread on his bread. "I had the radio on, and I thought the sound was coming from it."

Quinn got to his feet. "Come out on the porch, Annie. I want to speak with you."

Lola gave her a triumphant look as she passed.

Adrianna stepped out the front door to stand on the long porch. From far away she heard the mournful sound of a train whistle. It was a beautiful night; stars twinkled brightly in the sky, a dog howled in the distance, and a gentle breeze cooled an otherwise humid atmosphere. Even with all of that to marvel at, she was glad the day was coming to an end.

Adrianna spoke softly: "This night reminds me of those I spent with my aunt."

"How so?"

"When my mother passed away, her sister — my aunt — came to stay with my father and me. It was a way to make the loss a little less painful for both of us," Adrianna explained. "One night, she took me out into the country to the south of the city so that I could look up at all the stars in the sky. Living in Shreveport, I'd never imagined there could be so many. She told me they were jewels twinkling only for me. I was just nine at the time, so I believed her."

"Your aunt sounds like a smart lady,"

Quinn said with a chuckle.

"She is," Adrianna agreed. "When I was still quite young, she told me that her love of the outdoors was the reason she left Louisiana and went to Mississippi. The man that she had fallen in love with was a lot like her. He had a small farm with horses, so even though it was a long way from home, she left to be with him."

"Mississippi, huh? Was that where you were headed?"

Adrianna could only nod.

It was hard to believe that it had only been a few short days since she had hurriedly packed her belongings and headed out at the break of dawn for her aunt's home and sanctuary. Never in her wildest imaginings would she have envisioned herself standing in Lee's Point in the company of a man like Quinn Baxter.

Adrianna waited anxiously for Quinn to tell her what he wanted to speak to her about.

"Care to join me?" he finally asked. Quinn had moved to the swing at the far end of the porch. Gently, he patted the seat beside him, beckoning her. A touch of shyness momentarily delayed her, but she overcame it and crossed the porch to join him. As she sat, her arm brushed against his, and a strange thrill rushed through her.

"Annie, could you be mistaken about Lola locking you in the attic?"

"Absolutely not."

"I hate to think that Lola would do such a thing," Quinn countered.

"You don't know her as well as you think you do."

"She's afraid you'll take her place here," Quinn said.

"She needn't worry about that."

"Annie, I'm sorry you had such a fright. I'm sure Lola didn't realize you were up there. I'll fix the attic door so it can't be locked."

They sat quietly while each was absorbed in thought. Adrianna wondered how Quinn could be so blind that he couldn't see what type of person Lola was.

"I know what it's like, you know," Quinn commented, changing the subject.

"What do you mean?"

"What it's like to lose your folks," he said, turning to face her. Even in the near-darkness, she swore that she could see his eyes racing over her face. "I know what it's like to feel like the only choice you have is to run away."

"You think that I'm imagining things?" she said, breaking eye contact.

"No, I don't think that for a minute. The way I see it, each one of us deals with grief in a different way," he soothed. "That doesn't mean that mine was any harder than yours or anyone else's, just different."

"How was yours different?"

He paused for a moment. "You really want to know?"

"I do."

"All right, then," he said, placing his hand on hers. His skin was so rough to the touch that it startled her. But beneath that roughness, there was warmth of a kind she had never felt before. "One of the hardest things for a man to do is to follow in the footsteps of a giant of a father. That's what John Henry Baxter was in these parts. A giant. Does that make any sense?"

"Yes, it does."

For the second time that very day, Adrianna was reminded of just how much she had in common with Quinn. She knew *exactly* what it was like to grow up in the shadow of a successful father. Charles Moore was a name spoken with reverence in Shreveport's business circles. As a woman, her following along behind him had never been an option. If she had been Charles Moore's *son,* she would certainly have had a different life.

"My father was a man who'd come up from nothing and was damn set that he wouldn't go through life that way," Quinn explained. "He built the Whipsaw with his own two hands, slaving day and night until it was ready for business. When it was finished, he did the same with this house, and several other business buildings, all the while running the tavern with only a couple of other fellas to help him. He worked himself to the bone. Needless to say, he wasn't around much."

"What about your mother?" Adrianna asked earnestly. The woman she'd seen in the photographs didn't look like the sort that would take too quietly to being ignored. "How did she manage without her husband around to give her a hand?"

"She didn't like it, not one bit." He chuckled. "But no matter how much she complained and cajoled, it didn't make any difference. My father would nod his head, make a few promises, and then head right back to the bar and the bottle."

"He drank?"

"Not as a regular thing, not like most of the men who are there every single night, but he liked to take a knock here and there. But the booze never changed him. He was still the same old hardworking bastard he'd always been. He was the way he was. The problems between him and me didn't really start until he made it clear he expected me to follow his lead."

"Because you wanted to do something else," she said, filling in the gaps.

"Yep."

"So what happened when you told him?"

"An awful lot of yelling and cussing." Quinn smiled uneasily. "The problem wasn't so much that I told him I didn't want to follow him to the Whipsaw, it was that I told him I wanted to be a logger. He'd seen so many of the men use themselves up at the mill that he didn't want me to end up the same way."

"He was just looking out for you."

"I can see that now, but at the time . . ." Quinn stopped in mid-sentence. They sat in silence for a moment, Adrianna unwilling to ask questions. Obviously, what had occurred between Quinn and his father had been painful, the wounds still raw after all the time that had passed.

Finally, she said, "You don't have to talk about it if you don't want to."

"But I do," he said, determination in his voice. "I want you to know." He took a deep breath, looked to the stars, and said, "At the time, I told him that I thought he'd wasted his life. He just stood there, silent, looking at me. Then I said that he could go to hell, packed my things, and moved out of the house. I never saw him again. He died of a heart attack before I could come to my senses and tell him I was sorry."

"Oh, Quinn! I'm so sorry," she exclaimed. This time, it was her turn to put her hand on his. He took her offer and held her fingers tightly. "I don't know what to say!"

"There's nothing to say," he explained. "What's done is done."

"I'm sorry," she repeated, unable to come up with anything else.

"It wasn't long after that that my mother died in an accident, and then Jesse was in the school bus crash," he continued, painting a family history of tragedy that had forever altered his life. "Even though they had more than their share of difficulties, my mother loved my father very much, and his death had been a hard blow. The day of her accident, it had been raining like the dickens. She should have been watching the road, but her mind was probably on John Henry when the crash occurred. Her car hit a truck and then rolled. She was already gone when the first person reached her."

From the moment she had first met Quinn Baxter, Adrianna had wondered why he had been so angry at her for causing the accident that had injured Gabe and broken the tavern's liquor bottles. Now she knew, her pity for him swelling and overflowing her heart.

"I suppose Jesse was lucky," he said. "Even if he is in that damn chair."

"What he's lucky for is to have a brother like you," she argued, squeezing his hand with all of her might. She looked at him, willing him to look at her, but he kept his gaze away.

"Once things had settled down a bit after the accident and we realized that he was going to have problems, people said that I'd never stay here to take care of him. He would be a burden."

"Jesse is *no* burden!"

"Oh, I know," he said with a defensive tone. "But people talk, and in a small town like this, it's hard not to listen. I just chose not to believe what I was hearing. Caring for your family, for your brother, is something that you do out of love, not because it's an obligation. It became something of a crusade for me; the belief that he would walk again was with me night and day, and I couldn't shake it. I knew it was true with all my heart."

Hearing Quinn's words, Adrianna knew

that this belief was as much to sustain him as it was for Jesse's need to walk. Losing both of his parents in such a short time had been a vicious blow. Instead of running away from his problems as she had, Quinn had chosen to run *toward* them.

"Doc Bordeaux and I have gone around and around on this."

"That's because she doesn't want you to be disappointed if he never manages to walk again," she said softly. "You need to listen to what she's telling you. That's why she's the doctor."

"I just want it so damn bad!"

"Now it's my turn to tell you that I know what you're talking about." She smiled warmly. "When my father first found himself in a wheelchair, I hoped upon hope that he would walk again. He'd been such a robust man, picking me up and throwing me in the air when I was a little girl, that I couldn't imagine him any other way."

"What happened to him?"

"Polio. It cut him down so quickly that it was almost as if I had blinked and he'd changed." As she spoke, the sadness crept into her voice. "It was too difficult to bear."

"How did you get over it?"

"I don't know if I ever completely recovered," she said honestly. "But it was because of my father's strength that I managed to cope. You see, he took what had made him a successful businessman, honesty and integrity, and applied it to his illness. He struggled and fought, complained and cursed, but he refused to let himself give in to self-pity. He always used to say that a wheelchair couldn't make him unhappy unless he let it."

"I don't know if Jesse has that kind of strength."

"Maybe not, but you do."

Quinn shook his head. "I don't think so."

"Don't be stupid!" she said sternly, turning in the porch swing until she was facing him. "Look at all that you've done. You run from your job at the mill to the Whipsaw, working yourself to the bone to provide for yourself and Jesse. You've put food on the table, clothes on his back, and a roof over his head and even hired someone to look after him during the day. What is that if not strength?"

He looked up at her sheepishly, his eyes telling volumes that his voice wasn't willing to speak. Before he spoke, he looked away. "I don't know if you can really understand."

Instantly, Adrianna thought of the words Dewey Fuller had spoken to her earlier in the day at the mercantile. *Was what he said the truth?* Had Quinn been forced to borrow from Dewey's father in order to keep the Whipsaw afloat, only now to find himself deep in debt, on the verge of losing everything that he had fought so hard to keep? A weight pressed down on her chest as she thought about asking Quinn for the truth, yet she held her tongue. After all that he had shared with her, she couldn't ask for more.

"I suppose not," she murmured.

"I'm always trying to put a good face on things for Jesse." Quinn sighed. "The last thing he needs is to see me dragging my ass in the door all worn out. Compared to what he's going through in that chair, I've got the easy life."

"What's it like there?"

"At the mill?"

"Yes," she answered. "I have to admit that when you all are talking about it, I don't have the slightest idea what is being said. I don't really understand what it is you do there."

"Then you'll have to come and visit," Quinn exclaimed, his eyes lighting up as if he were a boy getting his first look at what Santa Claus had brought him. "I'll have Gabe drive you over so you can see it."

262

"I don't want to be a bother," she protested.

"You won't be."

Adrianna had to admit that the idea of seeing where Quinn worked intrigued her. His job at the lumber mill was another part of his life that she wasn't familiar with, and she found herself wanting to know more. *Why is it so important to me?* she thought. *What am I feeling?*

"Thank you." Quinn's voice whispered in her ear. She turned her head to find his face only inches in front of her own, his features bright in the starlight. She made to move to back away from him, a touch of happiness spreading over her to have him so near. Her eyes drank him in.

"Why are you thanking me?"

"For listening to me," he explained. His fingers slid up from her hand and touched the soft skin of her arm. "Talking about my folks isn't the easiest thing. I hope you don't mind me burdening you."

"It's no burden," she reassured him. As his fingers played across the soft hairs on her arms, chills ran up and down her spine. "I'm happy you felt you could talk to me."

"I've never met anyone like you before."

"Neither have . . ."

Before she could utter another word,

Quinn leaned forward and placed his lips against hers. Even though she had been enjoying his hand against her skin, she was momentarily startled by his advances. Still, rather than pulling away from the kiss, she found herself embracing it, and allowed herself to let go. She closed her eyes, not wanting anything to interfere with the moment. Sensing her agreement, Quinn's mouth became more passionate, the warmth and wetness of the kiss making her feel as if she were dreaming. She'd been kissed before, but nothing had ever felt like this!

Her hand circled his forearm and squeezed it tightly. Their mouths melted into one, and suddenly all the things that had bothered her drifted away: Richard Pope, the car crash, Lola's machinations, and even Dewey Fuller's accusations against Quinn. It was as if she had been set free, a balloon allowed to float gently on a summer breeze.

"Why did you do that?" she asked when Quinn moved his mouth from hers. Adrianna lingered in the space they had shared, her heart not wanting to let go. When she finally looked at him again, his smile could have lit up the darkest of nights.

"Why did you kiss me back?" he replied.

"I . . . didn't."

"Yes, you did."

"I . . . was taken by surprise."

"I can't say I've ever kissed someone like that before." His face was close to hers. She could feel his warm breath on her lips and his eyes on her face.

"Me either," she admitted with a blush.

"I kissed you because I wanted to."

"It must be nice to be so big you can take what you want."

"It wasn't like that and you know it."

"I don't kiss men who are engaged to other women."

"What are you talking about?"

"You're engaged to be married, aren't you?"

"If I am, no one told me about it."

Quinn continued to look at her, his hand found hers and held tightly, the electricity still jumping between them. In that scant minute, Adrianna's mind spoke eloquently, pleading a new case.

Maybe it isn't so bad that I'm here in Lee's Point. Maybe all of the things that have befallen me since my father's death have had some hidden meaning I couldn't understand until now.

Maybe . . .

Gently letting go of her hand, Quinn stood. "I need to check on Jesse . . . make

265

sure he's settled for the night. He was looking for his new pulp magazine."

"All right," Adrianna answered. "I think I'll sit for a moment longer."

He nodded. It looked as if he wanted to say more, but he held his tongue. Even though she couldn't see him clearly, she would have sworn that he gave her a wink before he turned and went into the house.

Returning her gaze to the stars above, one thought raced through her mind.

Adrianna Moore, you brazen hussy. You kissed that man . . . and you liked it.

CHAPTER 19

The next morning, Gabe parked his battered truck in front of the house. The sun shone brightly, the start of another hot day in the making. As he walked, he whistled, "On the Sunny Side of the Street," a popular tune that had recently caught on at the Whipsaw.

Adrianna had accepted Quinn's offer to come visit the lumber mill and, one quick phone call later, plans had been made for Gabe to pick her up in time to arrive at the mill by the lunch hour. She'd risen early to prepare a picnic basket and was waiting anxiously when the Cajun arrived.

"It's a beautiful mornin', *n'est-ce pas?*" Gabe greeted her warmly.

"It most certainly is."

"Then let us be on our way, *mademoiselle,*" he said with a flourish.

The Montville Lumber Company's mill was located some five miles to the north of

Lee's Point. As Gabe steered the truck in that direction, Adrianna looked out of the open window, the breeze blowing through her hair, and watched as the town quickly melted away into a glorious countryside.

They drove past a few farming plots that clung to the outskirts of the small town, but soon they were passing large swatches of tall pine and oak trees that reached for the sky. Sunlight filtered haphazardly through the high branches, lighting a spot here and there on the needle-carpeted forest floor. Wildflowers sprang up in bunches alongside the road, bright yellows, whites, and reds vying for her attention. Adrianna breathed in deeply, the rich smell of pine filling her senses.

As the trees and flowers sped by in a blur, the truck's tires crunching over the rough road, Adrianna thought about the choices made by her aunt Madeline in Mississippi. Looking at all that nature had to offer, it was easy to understand why she had forsaken the city life to live out in the country with a man she loved. Maybe she was more like the older woman than she realized.

"Some of these trees are more than two hundred years old," Gabe said.

"Really?" Adrianna exclaimed. "That's amazing!"

"I imagine that many of them were here long before the pirate, Jean Lafitte, roamed here, or even before the Indians who once lived in these parts," he said as his eyes scanned deeply into the woods. "Many of them will certainly be here long after we are gone, *c'est la vérité.*"

"They have more right to be here than we do."

As Adrianna looked over at the Cajun's rough profile, she wondered if she should ask him about Quinn's supposed money troubles. Gabe struck her as a wise man, smart in the ways of the world. Surely, he knew about what was happening at the Whipsaw? Before she could open her mouth to ask, a voice in the back of her head cautioned her. Whatever was wrong, *if* anything was wrong, it was Quinn's business, not hers. For the next several miles, they rode in silence.

Slowly, signs of the mill began to come into sight. A couple of men stood next to a small truck, one of them looking into surveying equipment. Gabe said they were using a level and a target rod, but she had trouble figuring out what was what. He explained that they were probably either measuring the growth of timber or constructing topographical maps, but he couldn't be certain which it was.

Soon, a railroad line came out of a break in the woods and ran parallel to the road, running ramrod straight as far as her eye could see.

"We'll follow that all the way to the mill," Gabe explained.

With every passing mile, more and more logging activity was visible. Groups of surveyors abounded, many of them looking at maps and pointing in one direction or another. They were now joined by men wielding axes and saws of many shapes and sizes. Other men sat about in clusters, laughing and joking as they ate their lunches. Several waved at Adrianna as the truck passed. Farther on, an enormous log loader stood beside the tracks, its tall crane loading felled trees into a railroad car's bed as black smoke billowed from its stack.

They had barely passed the loader when a strange sight caught Adrianna's attention; there was a small clearing where tiny trees had been planted. They were all uniformly spaced; it reminded her of a garden, well tended by a patient hand to yield a large crop. The miniature trees looked strange next to their towering brethren beside them.

"What are those over there?" she asked with a point.

"Those are seedlings."

"Seedlings?" she echoed.

"They plant these seedlings to take the place of the trees that have been cut down," Gabe explained. "Too often in the past, loggers have done nothin' more than taken from the forests. They haven't given a thought to what they've left behind. That ain't the case here. It's taken very seriously in these parts. *Les hommes* that work for the forest service go around makin' sure that what is taken is replenished."

For the rest of the drive, Adrianna couldn't get the principle behind reforestation out of her head. Life was really no different; when people are taken, her or Quinn's parents for example, they leave behind something that will grow in their stead. They were different yet the same; she was honest and true like her father, while Quinn was hard-working like John Henry Baxter before him. The thought made her smile.

Finally, the Montville Lumber Company camp came into view. The road opened wider to reveal several buildings all grouped together. However, one stood out above the others: the mill. It was a large two-story barn with a ramp that led from the ground to an opening on the second floor. Logs

271

were being pulled by a chain through a mechanism that washed them, the force of the water blasting off the bark. One log after another moved up the ramp as if they were in a hurry to be cut into pieces.

"We'll have to park here and walk," Gabe said, pulling into a spot.

As Adrianna got out of the truck, she was overwhelmed by the bustle. People and machines were everywhere! All the activity she had seen on the drive eventually ended here at the camp. The train tracks came to a clearing not far from the ramp, and teams of men with levers rolled the logs from the car beds onto the ground with thunderous crashes. From another road, large trucks, their frames straining from the weight of the logs they carried, came steadily. There were even a couple of men using oxen to move logs in preparation for their trip up to the saws. The smell of cut wood was everywhere.

"C'est magnifique, non?" Gabe commented as he wiped his brow.

"I've never seen anything like it," Adrianna admitted. All of the fevered work made it hard to follow each step in the process. She wondered how Quinn managed. "What is it that Quinn does?"

"He is at the top of the bull chain," Gabe

said, pointing up at the point where the ramp entered the second floor of the mill. "Each of the logs must pass by him before it makes its way to the saws to be cut. He checks to be sure that each one has been washed properly."

"Why does it have to be washed?"

"In order to get any bark, leaves, or other debris off," Gabe answered. "You need to have the wood as clean as it can be so there aren't any errors with the cuttin'."

Gabe led the way toward steps up the side of the mill, Adrianna following wide-eyed behind him, picnic basket in hand. The camp was made up entirely of men; she couldn't spot another woman as far as she could see. Every face she encountered, whether young or old, looked like it had somehow been marked by the hardness of working as a logger. Deep lines of fatigue, rough-looking skin, and grit and grime were written on everyone she saw. Still, smiles abounded, and more than one man tipped his hat to her as she walked past.

At the top of the steps, Gabe stopped and pointed to the rear of the mill below. Adrianna looked down to see many more men loading long planks of cut wood onto railway cars. As they watched, a locomotive blew its piercing whistle and began to roll slowly down the tracks, headed for some unknown destination. She wondered how many homes or businesses originally came from this very spot.

When they entered the mill, Quinn was conferring with a man near the ramp. He was talking animatedly, pointing at one of the logs that had just entered the building. As she looked at him, Adrianna felt a wave of emotion wash over her. Her thoughts raced back to the night before, when their lips had touched, and the strange feelings returned. Just then, Quinn looked over and saw her, and a grin crossed his rugged features. Slapping the other man on the shoulder, he hurried over to join them.

"I was wondering if you were ever going to make it," he said with a smile.

"What are you talkin' about, *mon ami?*" Gabe said with a grin of his own. He pointed at his watch as he added, "We are perfectly on time. It is you that are late, *c'est la vérité!*"

"If you'd like," Adrianna added, "we could just take this lovely picnic I've prepared and head back to Lee's Point. We wouldn't want to put you out, after all."

"No, no!" Quinn said, raising his palms in defeat. "I'm hungry enough to eat a bear. I swear . . . if I hadn't gotten a break for chow soon I would've started gnawing on one of these logs!"

Quinn led the way back down the steps, across the railroad tracks, and along a short path that opened into a clearing sparsely populated by medium-sized pine trees. Adrianna spread the blanket she had brought and laid out the food she had prepared, and they all dug in hungrily.

As she ate, Adrianna looked at her surroundings. Through a break in the trees, she could see row after row of large white tents set up in a large clearing. There were a few men milling about, some of them working over small stoves set out in front of their tents.

"What are those tents for?" she asked Quinn.

"They're set up by the company for the men who traveled for the job."

"I don't understand," she said. "Those men aren't from around here?"

"Times have been tough around these parts, *ma chérie*," Gabe explained. "It can be hard work for a man to find a job that lets him care for his family. Some of these men have traveled hundreds of miles for this work. Men from Florida, Georgia, Oklahoma, and other places all come here."

"It's good pay," Quinn added. "It's hard,

backbreaking work, but it gives these men enough money to send some home and put food on the tables of their families. The company understands that, and they do what they can to make it easier."

"But eventually they all find their way to the Whipsaw," Gabe laughed. "And give a little of that money back!"

As the two men enjoyed Gabe's joke, Adrianna's heart sank ever so slightly at the realization that she had no idea what most of these men were going through, including her two lunch companions. Even during the worst of the depression, her father had managed to keep them living in relative luxury, and they had wanted for nothing. Truthfully, she hadn't worked for an honest day's pay her entire life. Seeing the lengths that Quinn had to go to, working two jobs for the long hours that went with them, was humbling. That he was sacrificing so much for Jesse proved to her that he was blessed with great strength.

"While most of these men do this work because they have to," Gabe said, slapping Quinn playfully on the back, "*mon ami* works here because he has it in his blood, too."

"Is that true?" Adrianna asked looking up at Quinn.

"I suppose there's some truth to it," he conceded. He picked a small pinecone off the ground and juggled it in his hand. "I was just a little boy the first time by father brought me out here to see the mill. From the moment I laid eyes on the place, there was something inside me that wanted to be part of it. I guess I saw it as some kind of an adventure . . . being out in nature, working with other men, feeling like I'd accomplished something. After my first day, there was no going back. Once John Henry knew my intentions, I think he regretted ever bringing me to this place."

"How long have you been working here?" Adrianna asked.

"I started here when I was about eighteen," Quinn answered.

"C'est la vérité!"

"Do you think you'll ever give it up?" Adrianna asked, a part of her instantly regretting asking the question.

Quinn looked at her long and hard for a moment, his eyes searching. When he spoke, his voice was calm but confident. "I can see myself giving up being a logger someday, sure."

"Really?" Gabe exclaimed.

"If there's one thing I've learned about life from what happened to Jesse, it's that you never know what lies around the bend in the road." His choice of words was shocking to Adrianna, and she was sure it showed on her face, but Quinn continued without seeming to notice. "Once I'm able to hand the Whipsaw over to Jesse, things will be different. Then I'll walk away from this, maybe settle down and start a family."

At that, Adrianna flushed a deep shade of red.

The rest of the picnic went quickly, and soon it was time for Quinn to return to work. They were walking back across the road toward the mill when he asked Adrianna about playing the piano.

"Do you feel like playing at the sing-along tonight?"

It had only been a couple of days since her confrontation with Reuben and the brawl that had come from it. There was still a fear nagging at her chest but she pushed it down. If what Dewey Fuller had said was true, Quinn needed all of the help he could get, even hers. With a nod of her head, she said, "I can do it."

"Great!" Quinn exclaimed. "The way I see it, if we can —"

Suddenly, the panicked shouts of men split the afternoon sky. Looking up, Adrianna was horrified to see one of the giant logs that had been lying on the bed of a rail car break free from the control of the men with the levers and come bounding off the car too soon. As if in slow motion, the log struck the ground with a thunderous noise, bounced once, then twice, before slamming into a man, crushing him beneath its tremendous weight. It had all happened so quickly that the man hadn't had time to move an inch.

"Oh my God!" she screamed.

Before she could draw another breath, Quinn raced away from her, sprinting to where the fallen man lay. As she and Gabe hurried to catch up, she could see Quinn and several other men straining against the log, marshalling all of their strength to push it off its victim. All around her, voices shouted.

"Get a winch!"

"Push 'em free!"

"Somebody go and grab the doc!"

When she was close enough to see what had happened, Adrianna gasped at the sight of the man lying beneath the log. He screamed in pain to the heavens above as the log pinned both of his legs to the ground, but still, she couldn't look away. Quinn strained mightily, the veins on his arms and neck standing out. Agonizing moments followed one after another as the men pushed and prodded. Finally, the large log rolled free enough to allow two men to scoop the wounded man from where he had been trapped and whisk him away for medical attention. Without a word, Quinn followed them. Adrianna arose to follow, but Gabe's hand held her fast.

"He must do his job."

As she watched him retreat, she marveled at the way Quinn confronted danger. It was more powerful than the way he had sought to protect Jesse and to keep the Whipsaw alive. It was in his nature to jump in to fight Reuben or to leap to help the pinned man. *Quinn Baxter is the type of man who is instinctively drawn to doing what is right!* Even if he was in financial peril or if his own well-being was threatened, he strove to overcome what was in front of him, danger be damned!

"He's one of a kind," she muttered.

"Oui, mademoiselle," Gabe agreed.

CHAPTER 20

Adrianna spent the rest of the afternoon with Jesse. He seemed to enjoy exercising with the bar Quinn had hung over his bed. He joked about being the man on the flying trapeze and said his aim was to sling his feet over the bar. Adrianna had laughed and said he'd better learn how to swing his feet off the bed first.

She was growing quite fond of the boy. On one occasion when he had told her that he might fall in love with her, she had kissed him on the forehead and told him she would consider waiting for him to grow up. The time she spent with him was the most pleasant part of the day.

After Quinn had kissed her the night before, she'd lain awake for hours thinking about it. Her stupid heart pounded at the thought that he might really be falling in love with her. But logic told her that he was being kind and reassuring, as if she were about the same age as Jesse. If that alone had been true, would he have kissed her? She both looked forward to and dreaded seeing him at the dinner table. She heard him when he came in and heard Lola's voice asking him about his day as if she were his wife.

When the call came that supper was ready, she was in Jesse's room, and the two of them went together to the table. Adrianna darted a glance at Quinn. His dark eyes met hers and held them. After their talk on the porch and the kiss that followed, she felt shy with him, and he seemed to be aware of it. Holding her gaze he winked at her and color flooded her face. During the meal, she said nothing, giving Jesse the opportunity to talk to his brother.

When Lola wasn't giving her full attention to Quinn, she watched Adrianna.

Goddamn stupid little bitch! Lola stared over the top of the water glass, her eyes shooting daggers into the woman sitting across from her. She had come into her life and was trying to ruin everything! Dinner had been served and they had all sat down to eat, but the thought of food made her stomach churn; the hatred she felt was strong enough to even keep her hunger at bay.

"It won't be any trouble at all," Quinn

explained to Jesse. "Whenever there's any kind of ruckus down at the Whipsaw, things are always calm for a week or so afterward. It seems that those who wanted to fight got it out of their craw."

"I hope you're right," Adrianna said, her gaze darting across the table to sneak a peek at Lola. "It's hard enough for me to play in front of strangers. If I had to worry about another fight breaking out, I don't know if my fingers would stop shaking long enough for me to hit the keys."

"Don't worry about it. Gabe and I will see that you're not bothered."

What in the world does Quinn see in this woman? Lola was thinking, her mind half on what was being said. This was the question that had roiled around in her mind from the moment she'd first noticed that Quinn might have a soft spot for Miss Adrianna Moore. A blind woman could have seen his interest! But why?! She was certainly no stunning beauty, her breasts were not even a good handful compared to hers. But the worst thing about her was the way she seemed to think she was so superior. *She walks around with her snooty nose in the air like I was just a mere servant here.*

"Some potatoes please, Lola?" Quinn asked, breaking her thoughts.

"Of course," she said sweetly, plopping a large spoonful down on the plate he held out. She'd hoped that her smiles would get a response, but he had already turned his attention back to the *bitch* without even giving her so much as a word of thanks! In her heart, she knew that her beloved Quinn wasn't blameless, but she couldn't bring herself to blame him for it. He was enchanted with the bitch — for now. Lord only knew it was easy enough to entice a man; she had led Reuben around as if he were a dog on a short leash, eager to please, hoping for a little petting. Quinn was a man, after all. He could be steered around by his pecker just like all of the rest of the men she knew. The problem was that she wasn't the one doing the steering!

From the moment she had been hired to help tend to Jesse and to clean the Baxter house, Lola had had a plan. It had been a simple one, to hitch herself to Quinn by hook or by crook, and everything had been going according to plan. It would only have been a matter of time before Quinn would have realized that he couldn't live without her and declared his feelings. But now the plan was in danger of running off the tracks!

Man-stealing little slut!

Lola wasn't so generous with her feelings

284

for the younger Baxter boy. Taking care of Jesse was a chore, one that she grew more tired of with each passing day. *Who gives a damn if the little shit ever gets out of that chair?* She sure as hell didn't! All along, her intentions had been to ship him off to some home as soon as she'd landed Quinn, but it was possible she had been shortsighted. Maybe she needed to get rid of him sooner. Who knows, maybe the added grief of losing his brother would drive Quinn right into her arms? Maybe if she —

"— I want potatoes, too!"

Lola looked up to see Jesse holding his plate toward her, the look on his face demanding. She felt the edges of her mouth begin to curl into a sneer but quickly fought the expression down. As she was about to demurely do as she had been told, a voice spoke from across the table.

"You should ask politely, Jesse," Quinn scolded.

Properly chastised, Jesse nodded and asked again with exaggerated politeness. "May I please have some more potatoes?"

"You certainly may, dear," Lola answered warmly, dishing up the food. Even though the little shit's legs didn't work, it was still possible for him to be led by his pecker, too! Outwardly, she remained as pleasant as an angel but her insides roiled with fury.

She imagined leaping across the table and stabbing the slut's eyes out with a fork, the fantasy giving her a temporary moment of glee, but it was fleeting. If she were to do so, all that she had painstakingly worked for would be ruined. No, this required something different.

When she had realized that Adrianna Moore wasn't the type to be frightened away, when even Reuben had failed to motivate her to leave Lee's Point, she had begun to think differently. She needed to be ruthless and unforgiving. To that end she had come up with a different plan, one that had been set in motion that very night. When it bore fruit, no one would be any the wiser. Then everything would be back to the way it was. The way it should be. *It's only a matter of time, bitch! Only a matter of time.*

"That gator was twice as long as the boat itself! I leaned over and took me a long look see and just then that critter done opened his mouth as wide as he could! There was more teeth than there is keys in that there piano, I done do swear!"

Adrianna smiled politely. She hadn't found the story as funny as Roy Long had.

He was busy slapping his knee with one gnarled hand as he threw back his head in a hearty laugh, but she'd always had a gift for patience.

When she and Quinn had arrived at the Whipsaw minutes earlier, he had made a beeline to the bar where he'd begun to talk business with Gabe. She'd only been a step behind, but it hadn't been enough; she'd immediately been cornered by the crusty old man who'd proceeded to talk her ear off.

"That sounds like it was frightening," she commented politely.

"Darlin'," Roy crowed, smacking his worn lips together, "I done seen enough in my years here on this earth to put any of them movie fellas to shame. I ever told ya about the time me and my cousin Huey done hitched us a ride down to New Orleans with them there bank robbers?"

"No, you haven't," she admitted reluctantly.

As Roy continued talking, Adrianna's eyes stayed fixed on Quinn. With each passing day, she found that there was much more to the logger than met the eye. Each discovery she made caused her skin to tingle as if it were charged with electricity. She had begun to feel drawn to him, to feel a connection building, and she wanted to know every part of him.

"Fella showed me his gun. It was as big as his arm, I done do swear!"

It was the kiss they had shared that had truly turned her world upside down. The memory of his lips against hers was a treasured one. Even though they came from such different worlds, she from the luxury she had known in Shreveport and he from the rougher, rural world of Lee's Point, she felt an attraction to Quinn Baxter that she'd never experienced before, that she had never even dreamed of.

"Huey just looked him in the eye and said he didn't take no shit!"

Again, Adrianna's mind drifted away from what Roy was saying. Ever since she had spoken to Dewey Fuller, she had wondered if what the dapper man had said about Quinn's money troubles was true. Why else would the man have spoken to her? At first, she'd tried to convince herself that it was none of her business and that by asking Quinn about it, she'd only be interfering.

"Should have seen 'em standin' there when we stole their car!"

She'd wanted to tell Quinn at the picnic earlier in the day that Dewey Fuller had talked to her about his finances, but the time had not been right. She just needed to find the appropriate moment.

Her thoughts were interrupted by a sharp pain that suddenly arced across her stomach like a bolt of lightning, each of its many tendrils burning brightly. It ached so intensely that her hands involuntarily went to her midsection and she winced in agony.

"Ouch," she said under her breath.

Roy stopped telling his story and reached out to her, steadying her with his rough hands. "What's the matter there, darlin'? You went as white as a sheet, I done do swear!"

It took a few moments for the wave of pain to pass, but Adrianna finally found some relief. As she tried to compose herself, she felt momentarily dizzy and had to use the support the old man offered until she regained her balance. "I think I might have been in the heat for too long," she explained, the memory of being in the scorchingly hot attic still fresh in her mind. "But I feel better now. Thank you for your hand."

"Weren't nothin'. Y'er probably still a might touched about the other day, that's the way I see it."

"The other day?"

"What with all the fightin' and all," Roy explained. "But ya ain't got no reason to be worried. If'n another starts up, I'll come to yer rescue just like ol' Quinn did, I done do swear!"

Adrianna smiled warmly. She was just about to thank Roy for his offer when she noticed Quinn walk from behind the bar and head across the tavern toward the office. This was her chance! Behind that door, she'd be able to ask him about Dewey in privacy.

"I'm sorry, Mr. Long," she said quickly, trying to excuse herself, "I've enjoyed your company very much, but I need talk to Quinn for a moment before I begin playing."

"Don't worry your pretty little head none, sweetheart," he cackled. "Way I sees it, this done give me another chance to belly on up to that bar and have myself a drink or two!"

Weaving amongst the Whipsaw's tables and customers, Adrianna arrived at the office door seconds after Quinn had entered, closing the door behind him. As she raised her hand to knock, she was suddenly racked by doubts. Would he appreciate knowing that Dewey Fuller wanted her to stop playing the piano on sing-along nights?

"You can't run from everything," she muttered.

Screwing up her courage, taking a deep

breath, and straightening her back, Adrianna knocked firmly on the door, then entered without waiting for a response. Quinn looked up from where he sat behind his desk, a momentarily surprised look crossing his face, and gave her a warm smile. Several sheets of paper were spread out before him; he quickly brushed them together into a pile before speaking.

"There you are," he said. "I was just going to come rescue you from Roy."

"He's quite the talker," she admitted.

"If there's one story in these parts that he doesn't know, I sure as hell can't imagine what it would be. It'll be worse later in the night. The more drinks he has in him, the more his tongue wags."

As she stood on the other side of the desk, Adrianna had the sudden urge to just blurt out her concerns, but her tongue had abandoned her. Instead, she could only stare at him, her hands growing sweaty. It was as if the walls of the small office were closing in. He looked back at her curiously, his head cocked to one side.

"Nervous about playing?" he asked.

"Not really," she honestly answered. "After what happened the last time, I doubt there is anything that could possibly happen tonight which could be worse."

"Let's hope not. The only thing I can think of that would be worse would be if the old girl burned to the ground. After all the trouble Gabe and I've gone to, it'd be nothing short of a damn shame," Quinn joked. He held the papers up in a pile and smacked his hand against them before adding, "But at least these damn bills would burn, too."

There it was! Her opening! Cautiously, Adrianna asked the question that had been tickling her thoughts for days. "Is there something the matter with the business?"

"What makes you ask?" he asked with a dismissive wave of his hand. "This is 1935. We're in this depression Roosevelt was going to get us out of. Business is rough all over."

"The New Deal hasn't helped, huh?"

"Not one damn bit. One week business is good, but then the next it's bad," Quinn explained. "Folks around here are having a hard time keeping food on the table and shoes on their kids. They never have had a lot of money. Whatever they manage to scrape together has to go for food, clothes, and a roof over their head. Whatever we manage to get is the part that's left over."

"I want to ask you something," she said hesitantly. "If I wasn't here to play the piano, would your business fall off to the extent that you would have to close down?"

"No, of course not. I don't want you to worry about it."

In that moment, Adrianna knew she faced a choice; she could either hold her tongue or tell Quinn about her conversation with Dewey Fuller. She'd hoped that if he were facing money troubles, he would have been forthcoming, but she couldn't tell if he had been telling the truth or not. For the sake of what she hoped was growing between them, she realized that she had no choice.

"I met a man at the mercantile the other day," she began slowly, the words tripping their way out of her mouth. She paused before plunging forward, knowing full well that she could never take back what she was about to say.

"He introduced himself as Dewey Fuller."

At those final two words, Quinn stood and angrily crumpled the papers in his hand. Outrage and confusion were written across his face in equal parts.

"Fuller!" he spat between clenched teeth. "What in the hell were you doing talking to Fuller?"

"He came up to me. He knew who I was," she explained defensively. "He said that he knew I was playing the piano at the bar and asked how I had gotten involved with you."

"That dirty son of a bitch!"

"He wanted me to quit playing the piano here."

"Damn it to hell!" Quinn cursed.

Adrianna pushed on. "He said that you owed his father a lot of money."

Quick as a flash, Quinn was out from behind the desk and standing before her. His brow knit in anger. "Now listen to me and listen to me good. Dewey Fuller is nothing but a goddamn snake in the grass! Every other word out of his mouth is a lie. He's the type of bastard who'll say anything if he thinks it will put him ahead of the game."

"Why was he telling me to quit playing here then?" Adrianna asked.

"He came to you because he thought he could intimidate you and you'd stop play-ing, which in turn would cause me to lose business," he explained, trying to hold on to his temper. "He and that father of his would like nothing more than to see me ruined, no matter how they got the job done!"

"Quinn, please," she soothed, reaching out and placing a trembling hand on his arm. She'd had no idea he would become so angry; if she had, she was certain that she would never have mentioned the encounter.

For a moment, she thought her touch was calming him, but she was wrong; he moved away from her and headed for the door.

"Excuse me, sweetheart," his hand was warm on her shoulder, "I'd better see to business."

As Adrianna moved to follow him, his words echoed in her ears. *He called me sweetheart. Did he really mean it?* Before she could think further about it, the pain once again dug into her vitals. It was so intense that it stopped her in her tracks. Biting her lower lip, she could do nothing but wait as the seconds ticked by, hoping it would end. What was happening? Finally, the ache subsided enough for her to move. When she looked up, Quinn was gone.

Adrianna's fingers flowed over the piano keys as if they were walking in a dream. Her eyes followed the notes as they danced across the sheet music, but her mind was somewhere far away. Distantly, she could hear the notes she was playing and the voices singing loudly and off key.

She paused when she finished the song and looked around for Quinn. He was not behind the bar. Gabe walked over. When she asked him where Quinn had gone, he only shrugged his shoulders and said that he must have had something to take care of. "It is time for *la musique, mademoiselle*," he said, pointing at the clock.

She had wanted to ask the Cajun more about why Quinn was so upset at the mention of Dewey Fuller. Instead she looked out over the crowd and saw the expectant faces staring back at her, knowing that most of those who'd come to the Whipsaw that night had done so for the music, to hear her play the piano.

Now, sitting on the small wooden stool, she stole glances out into the crowd in the hope that she would see Quinn come back inside. Through the light and the curtain of tobacco smoke, she searched and stared but didn't find him. *Why did I tell him about Fuller?* she asked herself. *Oh, I wish I hadn't.*

Through her misery, she heard voices singing:

"Let me call you sweetheart,
I'm in love with you,
Let me hear you whisper
That you love me too."

The song's lyrics weighed down on her. She bowed her head, and a lone tear slid down her cheek and fell onto the piano keys. Everything around her seemed to be breaking apart. The only bright spot was that Quinn had kissed her and called her sweetheart.

For the first time in days she wanted to cry, cry for the father she had lost, the home she'd had to leave, the strain of staying out of Richard's clutches, and the stress of living in a house where the housekeeper despised her and who she feared would harm her.

CHAPTER 21

Richard Pope was bone tired. He stifled a yawn as the Packard's headlights cut a swath across the dark and dusty road before him. He had been driving all day, and with the onset of night had come fatigue. If he didn't manage to find what could pass for a hotel, he might be forced to spend the night sleeping in the cramped confines of the car. It was that sober thought that kept his eyes open and fixed on the road; that was an experience he *never* wanted to repeat.

It had been days since the waitress had identified Adrianna as a customer in the decrepit diner. That spark, that meager piece of information, had consumed him. Now, days removed from the hope he'd initially felt, he was burnt out. All that remained of his physical stamina was a pile of embers. Failure had met failure; he was just as unsuccessful as he had been on his initial forays outside of Shreveport. Regardless, onward he drove.

Darkness surrounded the automobile as he maneuvered around corner after corner. He had the windows down in the sweltering heat of the summer night; the smell of the woods was strong and pungent. A rumble of thunder rolled over him from somewhere in the distance. It might have been foolish for him to push on from Beauville, but he felt as if something unseen in the distance was calling to him, prodding him to move on. He was nearly certain that it was nothing more than the ravings of a sleep-deprived mind.

But still . . .

From around a tight corner, the road straightened. Richard wasn't sure how many miles had passed since he'd left the last town in his search, but it had been enough time for him to suspect that this was his destination. In the distance, he could see a sprinkling of lights. Slowly, the car's headlights brought a weathered roadside sign into view. Peering intently ahead, he was finally able to make out the faint writing.

"Lee's Point," he said aloud.

In a few minutes he passed from the first scatter of houses on the outskirts of town to the center of the main street. Nothing about Lee's Point set it apart from the dozens of other small towns he had been forced to visit. Simple businesses offered the barest of necessities, drastically different from the abundance of a city like Shreveport.

As he inched his way down the deserted street, Richard could not suppress a sneer of disdain. *These people and their pathetic lives are beneath me.* They toiled away at their insignificant jobs, returned to their hovels, and bred child after child who would aspire to more of the same. Simply being among them made his skin crawl. He needed to find Adrianna as quickly as he could so that the two of them could return to their true station in life.

"Now to find a fleabag of a hotel," he muttered.

He traveled the entire length of the main street searching for a place to spend the night but was discouraged to find nothing. Turning around at the church, he made his way back in the direction he had come from in the hope that he'd simply missed what passed for lodgings, but still came up empty. *Was this place so pathetic as not even to have a hotel?*

As the thought of sleeping in the Packard sent a shiver of disgust down his spine, Richard began to drive down the main street yet again. This time, instead of continuing on until the street ended, he turned at one of the few intersections, hoping there would be something tucked away off the thoroughfare. However, one turn after another revealed nothing more than closed storefronts and darkened homes.

"Damn," he swore through clenched teeth.

As he was about to give up hope, he turned another corner and suddenly, right before him, was a business awash with light, with a handful of dented and dirty vehicles out front. He couldn't read the weather-beaten sign clearly, but seeing the man who stumbled out the door, it took Richard only a split second to realize he had come across a tavern. It figured that the only place of business still in operation at that late hour would be a place of spirit and sin. *Who wouldn't want to drown their sorrows living in a place like this!*

Richard hesitated. Surely there would be someone inside who knew where he might find a bed for the night. But just as surely he might find trouble; liquor did little to assuage the savagery of the simple folk, and a mere slip of the tongue might light the fuse. As if to weigh his options, he looked over his shoulder into the Packard's backseat.

"So what is it going to be?" he asked himself.

He parked the car down the street and walked back to the tavern. Staring up at the sign, he made out the name "Whipsaw."

How quaint, he thought sarcastically.

Upon opening the door, the first thing that assaulted him was the noise. Nearly every patron in the place was singing at the top of his lungs to some rather plebian plinking on the piano. He didn't recognize the tune, and their caterwauling made his ears hurt. He couldn't really blame them; these fools wouldn't know real music if it bit them!

The smell of tobacco and stale beer burned his nose. Stifling the urge to pull his handkerchief out and press it to his face, he decided to simply ask where he might find a bed for the night and then leave; the quicker the better. Weaving amongst a handful of outlying tables and a tipsy couple, he made his way over to the long mahogany bar. He was just about to flag down the bartender, a thin, rustic-looking character, when a glimpse of something out of the corner of his eye nearly stopped his heart.

Richard could not believe his eyes. For a moment, he wondered if he were imagining it, if he had spent too many hours on the road and fatigue was playing tricks on him, but when he blinked, the sight was still there. Slowly, a grin spread from ear to ear across his long face. After all of his hard work, after all of his diligence, he had finally found his love.

Adrianna!

As Adrianna played the final notes of the song, loud clapping and whistles broke out across the Whipsaw. Even though her head was still full of thoughts about Quinn, she felt her chest swell with pride. Her playing had brought joy to the men in the tavern at Lee's Point and nothing, not even a misunderstanding with Quinn, could change that.

Smiling, she looked up from the sheet music and scanned the faces in the crowd. Everyone seemed to be having a good time. She was about to turn her attention to the bar where she knew Gabe would be looking on appreciatively, when someone stepped before her, blocking her view. A chill ran down her spine as she thought of Reuben.

"Hello, Adrianna," a voice said.

Before she even looked at the speaker's face, she knew who it was. Fear coursed through Adrianna's veins. It was so palpable, so real, that she felt as if someone were holding a knife to her throat. When she finally brought her eyes to meet his, her heart jumped so hard that she wondered if it was trying to leap out of her chest.

"Ri . . . ri . . . chard," she managed to say.

Richard Pope beamed down at her with the look of the cat that had just cornered the canary. "Oh, my dear," he gloated. "You didn't actually think you would get away from me, did you?"

Even though she was incapable of speech at that moment, Adrianna knew the answer to his question; she had thought she would escape him. With every passing day in Lee's Point, with every moment she spent *away* from Richard and *with* Quinn, thoughts of the nightmare that awaited her in Shreveport retreated to the shadows. While her fear of being found by Richard had never disappeared, it had lessened. She knew she'd let her guard down, but she'd never imagined he'd find her . . . not here!

"How . . . how did . . ." was all that she could say.

"You could never have gone far enough away," he explained, inching closer. "There isn't a corner of this earth that I would not have been willing to search. I would have found you anywhere because we are supposed to be together. You will always be mine!"

As she had when Richard had first declared his intentions, Adrianna felt the strong urge to escape. Even though she was largely paralyzed by fear, she still managed to push herself away from the piano and to her feet so fast she stumbled. She grabbed hold of the piano to steady herself.

"St . . . stay away!" She meant for the words to sound like a scream, but it more resembled a whimper.

"Don't you understand, sweet Adrianna," Richard said, moving around the piano stool to once again tower over her. His eyes were wild, dancing in their sockets as he stared at her intently. "I'm willing to forgive your folly. You made a mistake in leaving before our wedding, but I've found you now. All will be as it was intended."

As if in slow motion, every moment from when she left her father's house began to play itself out before her eyes. One image followed another: packing her belongings, the storm raging, the force of the automobile striking the pickup truck, and waking up in Dr. Bordeaux's office; and through it all there was Quinn. She was instantly aware of how it felt to be touched by him, to feel his lips against hers, to hear his voice and his laughter. Somewhere beneath the fear that quaked through her body, Adrianna was aware that there was anger as well, anger at Richard for trespassing on what she had found in Lee's Point, anger at his having inserted himself into her time with Quinn.

"Ne . . . never!" she protested. Pushing herself backward, Adrianna kept her eyes locked on Richard. If he were to make a move, she wanted to see it coming. *Oh, Lord, I've got to get away. I've got to get away!*

Without warning, another spasm of pain shot through her body. This time it was different, stronger, making what had come before seem like mere pinpricks in comparison. It was as if her entire world were turned upside down and shaken, all the individual pieces of her life going willy-nilly, this way and that. The pain struck with such force that it seemed to freeze her in place, making all her limbs useless. Through the haze that drifted over her eyes, she made out Richard as he bent toward her, his hand extended to her, his fingers inches from her skin. She wanted to scream, but when she opened her mouth, no sound came out.

"Hey there. What'n the hell ya think yer doin'?"

Richard turned toward the sound of the voice and visibly recoiled at the sight of the man. Roy Long had ambled over from his usual perch on the bar and now stood before him, a drink still clutched in his bony hand.

"Back away, fool!" Richard barked. "This doesn't concern you."

"It sure do," Roy contradicted him. With a quickness that was surprising, he swatted Richard's hand away from Adrianna while using the other hand to take a drink. "Ain't got no idea where it be ya come from, but in't 'round here, and we ain't a gonna take too kindly to ya bother'n the lady. Besides, I done told this here young lady that I was a gonna watch out for her and that's what I'm a gonna do!"

Anger flashed across Richard's face like lightning, and a sneer curled his lips. Still roiling in pain, Adrianna couldn't be certain if it was due to Roy's disagreeing with him or the fact that the shabby-looking man had touched him. "How dare you!" Richard roared. "Just who do you think you are?"

"Name's Roy Long," the older man said, straightening his back with pride. Stepping closer to Richard, he added, "Don't ya ever forget it."

While the two men argued, Adrianna saw her chance. Pain still rolled through her in wave after unrelenting wave, but she somehow found that she could move her feet. With all the willpower she could muster, she managed to place one foot in front of the other. Salty, hot tears began to slide down her cheeks as she hurried toward the door.

"You'll not escape me again, Adrianna!" Richard roared from behind her.

"Ya done leave her be!" Roy yelled.

Adrianna was only barely aware of what was happening behind her. Her head swam as she stumbled forward, desperate to escape Richard Pope once again. Before her, bodies seemed to part, eager to get out of her way. She weaved among the tables and chairs, colliding with more than she missed, moving ever closer to the front door. A sharp wave of agony chose that moment to strike, but somehow she managed to retain her balance.

"Ma chérie," Gabe called as he stepped out from behind the bar. "What is happening?"

Adrianna ignored him. She knew that he was concerned, just as Roy Long had been when he had interceded with Richard, but she didn't want to involve others in her plight. No one besides her knew what kind of a man Richard truly was; no one knew what lengths he would go to in order to get what he wanted.

Step after agonizing step finally brought her to the door. She crashed into it, fumbled with the knob, and somehow managed to get through it, stumbling out into the summer night. Above her, the moon looked down accusingly, as if it were watching her every move.

"Oh, my God!" she cried.

Her legs as weak as a sailor's on his first voyage to sea, Adrianna moved out from between the cars parked in front of the Whipsaw and into the street. The pain that filled her grew in intensity by the second but she would not give in to it, would not relent to being caught once again.

As her vision spun wildly before her, Adrianna became aware of a shape moving quickly toward her from across the street. She could no more make out the stranger's face than she could count the stars in the sky, but before she could react, the man was upon her, clutching her in his arms.

"No! No!" she shrieked into the night. "Let me go!"

In that split second, when the pair of arms latched on to her tightly, refusing to let go no matter how hard she struggled, Adrianna's mind careened over the horrible possibility that Richard had somehow managed to get ahead of her, utterly relentless in his pursuit.

"Annie! It's me! It's me! Stop it!"

The sound of Quinn's voice broke through the haze that threatened to overtake her. As she looked up, her vision cleared long enough for her to make out his rough face, his eyes touching her with concern. Sobs began to rack her body, and she quivered in his arms.

"What is it, sweetheart?" he asked intently. "Don't be afraid, I'm here. If it's Reuben, I'll beat the hell out of him."

Try as she might, Adrianna couldn't control the emotion that was coursing through her. The pain that had plagued her that night seemed to work itself into a fever pitch, the agony pouring into her like water from a well. Her legs buckled, and the only thing that kept her from falling to the ground was the strength of Quinn's arms.

"Tell me!" Quinn prodded her. "You need to tell me what's wrong."

"It's . . . it's . . . it's Richard!"

Before she could utter another sound, the front door to the Whipsaw banged open, and Richard Pope barreled out into the street. As his eyes locked on to Adrianna in another man's arms, rage consumed him. He strode toward them with purpose, his hand reaching to jerk Adrianna away.

"Get away from her!" he bellowed. "Get away from her this instant!"

The lids of Adrianna's eyes felt as heavy as the logs cut at the lumberyard. Her breath came ragged and thick, her heart pounding a furious beat. Sweat mixed with tears to wet her skin.

"Who the hell are you?" Quinn demanded.

"I'm her husband!" Richard retorted.

With those words, Adrianna's knees buckled. Only Quinn's arms kept her from falling.

CHAPTER 22

The words had not registered yet in Quinn's mind when he scooped up Adrianna in his arms and started down the sidewalk toward the doctor's house.

Adrianna groaned and struggled in his arms.

"Be still, honey, I'm taking you to the doctor."

"Rich — ard don't let him —"

"Don't let him what?"

"Take — me." Adrianna clung to Quinn. "Quinn, don't let him take me."

"He said he's your husband."

"He lied," Adrianna said breathlessly. "He lied, Quinn. He lied."

"We'll get that straightened out, but first, I've got to get you to Dr. Bordeaux. So be still." Quinn continued walking down the sidewalk, carrying her as if she weighed no more than a child.

"Where is he?"

"Don't worry about him. I won't let him take you, if you don't want to go."

"How did he find me?" she murmured.

"What did you say, honey?"

"Oh, oh, oh." Another pain sliced through Adrianna's stomach, and she stiffened in his arms. "It hurts, it hurts so much."

"Where, honey, where does it hurt?"

"My stomach. Terrible pains." Her head dropped against his shoulder, and she took deep breaths.

"We're almost there," he said close to her ear.

"I can walk," she gasped although she knew she couldn't.

"Be quiet, we're almost there," he repeated.

Fear mixed with pain consumed Adrianna. What she had feared most had happened. Richard had found her, and at a time when she was unable to run from him. Her hand clutched Quinn's arm. She had to warn him about Richard, that he was utterly ruthless when it came to something he wanted. He would ruin Quinn without batting an eye. Oh Lord, she had gotten him into this. It would be better if she just went away with Richard than to have his wrath come down on Quinn and Jesse.

When they arrived at doctor's door, Richard was close behind. Quinn kicked on the door with his booted foot. A minute later, the doctor opened the door.

"Quinn!" Her eyes went to Adrianna. "What's wrong with her?"

"Annie's got terrible pains in her stomach."

She threw the door open wide. "Bring her in." Richard barged in behind Quinn. "Who are you?" the doctor said and turned her back to lead the way across the reception area and into the hall.

"I'm her husband, or soon will be," Richard retorted belligerently.

"Annie said he's lying." Quinn turned the corner into the doctor's examination room. He gently placed Adrianna on the table but stood close beside her, holding her hand. "Get the hell out of here," he said to Richard.

"I don't think you know who you're dealing with. Adrianna is my responsibility. Her father gave me written consent to take care of her. Stand in my way, and I'll see to it that you wish you had never set eyes on her."

"Get out of the way so the doctor can tend to her."

Richard stood his ground. "If anyone leaves, it will be you. She's mine."

"She doesn't belong to either one of you.

She's of age. She is a person within her own right," the doctor said angrily.

"She's right, *mon ami.*" Gabe stood in the doorway. "Need any help here, Sarah?"

"They're fighting over her like two dogs over a bone. Get both of them out of here."

Gabe stepped into the room and motioned for Quinn and Richard to leave.

"Not until he goes," Quinn said and gave Richard a push toward the door.

"Keep your hands off me, you ruffian!" Richard stomped out ahead of Quinn but first he said to Dr. Bordeaux, "Do what you have to do. I'm taking her home in the morning."

"Like hell you are," Quinn snarled. "You're not taking her anywhere if she doesn't want to go."

"Stand in my way, and you'll regret it until your dying day. I have influence in this state, and I'll use every bit of it to ruin you. I'll send you to prison for holding her against her will."

"You can try."

"I'll take you to court."

"I doubt you'll make much of a showing with a broken nose and no teeth."

"What's this all about?" Gabe asked.

"Adrianna Moore is under my protection," Richard explained looking directly at Gabe.

"Why does she need your protection?" Gabe asked. "What are you protecting her from?"

"Men like you, who would steal her fortune."

"What fortune?" Quinn asked.

"I'm not surprised that she didn't tell you about it. She would be leery of telling men of your caliber that she is rich."

"Shut your damn mouth!" Quinn slammed Richard Pope into the wall with all his might, the force of the blow rattling a picture frame. Rage held him in its grip, refusing to let go. Pinning the older man with his muscular forearm, he cocked his fist ready to knock his head through the wall. Through it all, Richard stared back at him impassively, his eyes utterly devoid of fear.

Quinn's fist literally trembled, so strong was his desire to strike. However, before he lost control and slammed his fist into the smug bastard's fat nose, rough hands grabbed him from behind, desperately trying to pull him away. Gabe knew that a blow from his friend's fist could shatter the bones in the man's soft face.

"It is not worth it, *mon ami,*" Gabe argued

as he tried to hold Quinn still.

"The hell it isn't!"

"You would be wise to listen to your backwoods friend," Richard sneered as he straightened the lapels of his suit coat. As he shot his cuffs, he added, "Even in this poor excuse for a town, I believe the law wouldn't take very kindly to your striking a man of my social position."

"I don't give a goddamn about your position." Quinn's curse echoed off of the walls. The space wasn't much, with a rickety old table, a pile of thumb-worn magazines, and three mismatched chairs, and it made him feel caged. His forced nearness to the stranger from Shreveport had been fraying his nerves. *Hell! I disliked the man from the moment I first laid eyes on him.*

After Adrianna had collapsed limply in his arms, confusion and fear had filled Quinn's head. When Richard had run toward him, demanding that he hand over the semiconscious woman, his first instinct had been to slug him. Instead, his concern for Adrianna had taken precedence, and he had scooped her up and made a beeline for the doctor's office. The overbearing ass had trailed along behind. Once they had managed to wake Dr. Bordeaux, she'd shooed them into the waiting room and taken Adrianna to the examination room. Now, after listening to Richard describe himself as Adrianna's husband-to-be for the last ten minutes, Quinn had finally had enough.

"You have no business putting your hands on me like that," Richard spat.

"I'll do whatever the hell I want with you," Quinn barked, pointing an accusing finger at the cocky bastard. "You come to this town throwing your weight around and spewing your lies, you'll be lucky if all you get is a fat lip!"

"Lies?" Richard echoed incredulously. "What would you know of the *truth?* What do you know of her life in Shreveport? Haven't you been listening to a word I've said? Adrianna is to be my wife, and there is nothing you can do about it."

"I think there is."

"She is ill," Richard snapped, taking a step toward the bar owner as if he were daring him to react. "Her father, the man who had cared for her all of her life, has recently passed, and the emotion of her loss has overwhelmed her. She has always been a frail young woman, and I am all the greater fool for having taken my eyes off her long enough for her to abscond. It is a mistake I will not repeat. As her future husband, it will be my duty to be ever vigilant. Not yours!"

Quinn stared at him with malice. His fists and jaw clenched and unclenched. As much as he detested the high-brow tone with which Richard spoke, it pained him to admit that there was a grain of truth to what the man was saying. He knew that Adrianna had recently lost her father. He'd suspected that she'd come from a family of means in Shreveport; she certainly comported herself differently than any other woman he had ever met. *Is it possible that some of what this no-good son of a bitch is saying is true?*

"I can understand that you might have fallen for her, I really can. She is a charming woman," Richard continued. "But do you really believe that she could be happy living in this backwoods town with a man such as yourself? Your station in life is simply too far beneath her."

"That is enough, *monsieur*," Gabe interjected, trying to stave off an attack by Quinn.

Richard's eyes never left Quinn's, and he paid no heed to the Cajun's words. He stepped ever closer to his adversary. When he finally spoke he was mere inches from Quinn's face.

"This isn't the end of it. You'll see."

Never in his life had Quinn wanted to strike another man more than he did at that very moment. His muscles coiled to attack, his hand clenching into a tight fist. However, before he could so much as move, something stopped him. Instantly he knew what it was.

With a deep breath, Quinn allowed the tension to leave his body, his hands falling easily to his sides. His gaze held Richard's for a moment longer, the fire of hatred still burning in his gut. Finally, he turned on his heel, threw the front door open and stepped outside.

The early morning light showed in the east. Above him, thin wispy clouds covered the sky like gauze, and a few birds wakened from their night's sleep floated on the soft breeze. All in all, it was another day much like the one before it. He wouldn't have been able to count how many mornings exactly like this one he had seen in Lee's Point, but something about *this* morning was different. He realized that if what Richard was saying proved to be true, if Adrianna was to be taken from him, his life would be different from that day forward. He had not realized how deeply he had fallen in love with her until now. The thought that she could leave him cut him to the quick. She had become so deeply embedded in his heart that it was hard to believe she had come into his life less than a week before. He remembered his mother saying that God made a woman for every man, and if you were lucky enough to meet her, you should never let her slip away.

"Do not pay him any mind, *mon ami.* Wait and hear what Adrianna has to say." Gabe came out of the doctor's office to join him. He stood beside Quinn, and they both stared up at the sky as it slowly turned crimson. "It's intended only to get a rise out of you. That man is nothing but a *trou du cul.*"

"He might be an asshole," Quinn admitted, "but that doesn't mean that what he's saying isn't partially true."

"What do you mean?"

Quinn turned to look his friend right in the eye. "We don't know anything about her life before she slammed into the pickup."

"That's not the way I see it," the Cajun said, shaking his head. "I cannot tell you how many people have stood on the other side of my bar, *c'est la vérité,* but if there is anything I have learned over the years, it's how to judge someone. Now that *petite fille,* the only thing I can see she has in common with *Monsieur* Pope is that they both come from Shreveport."

"But what abou —"

"But, nothing," Gabe cut him off. "You have seen the way she is with a man such as Roy Long, a man who's own mother might have trouble giving him the time of day. She also has had no reservations caring for Jesse. Tell me, *mon ami,* is she anything like Richard Pope?"

Quinn knew there was truth in what Gabe was saying. In the short time she had been staying in the Baxter home, he'd noticed a change in Jesse; a small change, but he was different nonetheless. In Adrianna's own way, regardless of whether she was talking about his legs or his education, she was eager for him to get better. Her compassion was real. From what he had seen of Pope, Quinn doubted that the man had *ever* felt a moment of compassion in his entire life. Still, he didn't know the entire story. He had to wait and hear what Adrianna had to say.

"He could be telling the truth," he said reluctantly.

"There is only one person who can tell you what the truth is," Gabe said as he placed a hand on his friend's shoulder. "All you have to do is go and ask her."

■ ■ ■ ■

Adrianna woke from a fitful rest, a dream about sunflowers drifting away from her as if they were smoke. She blinked slowly, her vision still clouded around the edges. For a brief moment, she thought about staying at the Baxter house, playing the piano at the Whipsaw, and even the sweet, tender kiss she had received from Quinn. All of this had happened in just a few short days. Her life had changed forever.

Richard Pope has come to Lee's Point!

"We're making a habit of this."

Adrianna turned her head slowly, a tremor of dizziness passing behind her eyes, to see Dr. Bordeaux where she had been on her first visit, right at the side of her bed. The woman looked tired, there were dark circles under her eyes, but she smiled warmly.

"What . . . what happened?" Adrianna spoke, her mouth dry.

"You fell ill at the Whipsaw and were brought here," the doctor explained. "You've awakened from time to time with stomach cramps and had to vomit, but you have been sleeping soundly for a couple of hours now."

"What's the matter with me?" Adrianna

started to sit up but fell back against the pillows.

"What have you been eating? Something that you ate didn't agree with you. It could have been anything. Either way, let's hope it's run its course. In any case, you'll need to spend some time in bed."

Adrianna took in all that the doctor had to say. She had to admit that she felt as weak as a newborn kitten. Her stomach still rolled and reeled, but it now felt more like a spring shower than a summer gale. Whatever had struck her, the worst seemed to have past.

"Is . . . is Quinn here?" she asked cautiously.

Dr. Bordeaux nodded. "He hasn't left since he brought you here. He's out in the other room with Gabe." She paused for a moment, throwing a glance to the door, before adding, "There's . . . another man with them."

"Oh, no!" she moaned.

"He's been rather insistent that he should be let in here with you," the doctor explained, "but I haven't allowed it. It really doesn't matter if you are going to marry him or not, you need your rest."

Dr. Bordeaux's words cut into Adrianna's mind. "He . . . he . . . said that he was my future husband?" she finally sputtered.

"That he was engaged to you, yes," the other woman said, the look on her face one of obvious confusion. "I have to admit that it was a bit surprising to hear since you said you were not married. Is this the man you were telling me about when you were here after the accident?"

"Yes. He's the man I was running away from."

Slowly, Adrianna's hand made its way to her mouth, which was still agape with horror. *It was a nightmare!* Richard hadn't only pursued her, he'd spread his horrible version of events amongst the acquaintances she'd made in Lee's Point. If she didn't put her foot down, if she didn't offer her side of the story, his lies could be believed!

"Is something the matter?" the doctor asked.

"He's lying," Adrianna answered, her voice strong.

"Why is he saying this?" the other woman asked.

Drawing up all of the strength that she had left, Adrianna sat up in the bed and looked at Dr. Bordeaux with plaintive eyes. "Quinn," she said with conviction. "I need to speak with Quinn, right now!"

Dr. Bordeaux brought Quinn back to the

room where Adrianna was resting. She'd needed to shoo Richard away from the door over his loud protest. Even now, with the door closed, Adrianna could hear him bellowing about the injustice of being kept away from his fiancée. The sound of his voice made her skin crawl.

For several long moments, Quinn and Adrianna stared silently at one another. As she looked at him, she was amazed at how much had changed between them from the first time they had been in that very room. On that occasion, he had been loud and aggressive, belligerent to the point of frightening her. Now, all she could think was how handsome and strong he was.

"Annie," he began, finally breaking the silence, "I don't know what's going on between you and that man —"

"Please, Quinn," she cut him off. "Let me say what I need to first."

He stared at her intently before giving a slight nod.

Taking a deep breath, she began. "I don't know what Richard told you about his relationship with me, but I can assure you that most of it is not true. His professed love, his infatuation with me, he's not lying about that, but I can assure you that his feelings are not returned."

"He says that you are engaged to be married."

"That is his intention, but it isn't mine!" she defended herself. The thought that Quinn believed the lies that had come from Richard's mouth both horrified her and made her angry. She couldn't allow the charade to last even a moment longer. "He came to me after my father's funeral and simply told me that we would be married. He never asked for my hand but, even if he had, I would *never* have accepted it!"

"But, then —"

"He's a lying conniver, Quinn," she continued, cutting him off again. "I believe he coerced my father into signing papers that gave him control of my inheritance. He thinks it gave him control of me too. I wouldn't marry him if he was the last man on earth." The words flew out of her mouth quickly, as if she were pleading a life-or-death case. "That's why I was on the road the day that I struck your truck. I was running away from Shreveport, from Richard and the life that he had picked out for me. I had to get away!"

"Why didn't you tell me this before?"

"I . . . I . . . didn't see any reason to," she sputtered. As if the dam had been released on a raging river, hot tears began to slide

327

down her cheeks. "All I wanted to do was get away from Richard."

"Then you should have just told that stubborn son of a bitch that your answer was 'no'!" Quinn barked. "Tell him how you feel and that you want another kind of life."

"Richard Pope isn't the type of man who takes rejection well," she protested. "He's in charge of everything I have. I don't even have a home." Her tears turned into sobs that racked her whole body. She tried to wipe the wetness from her eyes but did little to stop their flow. "He'll never leave me alone! He'll keep following me, pestering me, trying to wear me down until I give in. I would rather die than marry him!"

Slowly, Quinn made his way over to her. He sat down gently on the bed beside her, taking her trembling hand in his own, his skin warm to the touch. "I think I might have a solution."

"What?"

He waited until she looked in his eyes before saying, "You could marry me instead. Then I'd have the right to keep him away from you."

The power of his words hit her with so much force that it was as if she had been struck by the truck all over again. She couldn't breathe, and the only sound she could hear was the thunderous pounding of her heart. She searched his face for some sign that he was joking but couldn't find any. "Are . . . are . . . you serious?" she stammered.

"Absolutely," he said simply.

"Oh, but I couldn't let you do that. Marriage is forever."

"I know that."

"You might find someone you really like. You'd be tied to me."

It was as if she were struck with another bout of the illness that had brought her there, her world turned upside down. But this time, rather than pain, the cause of her malady was confusion. Finally, she managed to say, "I could only marry a man that I loved and who loved me."

"Do you think I could marry a woman I didn't love?" Quinn's dark brows were drawn together in a fierce frown. "Did Lola tell you that there was something between her and me?"

"More than once."

"I swear to you, Annie, I am not interested in Lola or anyone else but you, if you'll have me. I have no feelings for Lola but pity. She comes from a dirt poor family with a house full of kids. I gave her the job to help her out. She was real good . . . at first." Quinn studied Adrianna intently for a long moment, thinking how pretty she was and how he would spend his life taking care of her if she let him. Suddenly he asked, "Do you love Richard?"

"No," she blurted out venomously. "I detest him!"

"Could you learn to love me?"

His words set Adrianna's hand trembling but Quinn held her steady, his eyes locked onto her own as he searched the depths for her answer. The forwardness of his words shocked her. She tried to speak, but it was as if her mouth had been stuffed with cotton.

Suddenly, the door to the room flew open and the doctor entered, slamming it shut behind her with a crash, Richard's voice shrill behind her. She appeared flustered, her cheeks a bright crimson.

"That man is insufferable!" she complained, pulling an unruly strand of dark hair behind her ear. "I swear, if he isn't allowed into this room soon, he's going to try to break the door down. He's threatening to get the sheriff. He even says he has influence with the attorney general."

"I won't see him!" Adrianna protested. "I just can't!"

"You don't have to," Quinn said calmly.

He held her hand in both of his. Turning to Dr. Bordeaux, he asked, "Hey, Doc. You still have that stretcher we used to move Jesse from the car?"

"Of course. Why do you ask?"

The corners of Quinn's mouth rose. "I've got an idea."

CHAPTER 23

" '. . . and then Sheriff Wayne slid his brilliantly polished silver pistol into his holster, patted his trusty steed Shylock on his dusty flank, and rode off into the setting sun, turning his back forever on the poor souls of Tombstone. His work, as always, was done.' "

Jesse closed the pulp magazine and leaned back in his chair, a broad smile crossing his youthful face. His eyes danced. "So what do you think?" he asked.

"It was . . . interesting," Adrianna offered.

"That's all you've got to say? Interesting?" Jesse was incredulous. "You must not have been paying any attention! What about the part where Sheriff Wayne shot that train robber in the saloon? Or when he beat up that city slicker for tryin' to cheat him at cards? Or when that lady kissed him to reward him for protectin' her honor? That just has to be the best Sheriff

Wayne story ever!"

From where she lay in her bed, Adrianna laughed heartily at Jesse's enthusiasm. In the three days since Quinn had brought her back from the doctor's office, Jesse had come to read to her nightly. The choice of material, his favorite tales from his pulp magazine collection, might not have been her cup of tea, but she was always grateful for his company.

Quinn's idea had been a sound one. He and Gabe had borrowed Dr. Bordeaux's stretcher and, after gently loading Adrianna onto it, had made their way out the back door of the office. While the doctor went out to try to handle Richard, they'd hurried their charge across town and back into her room at the Baxter home. From that moment, her life had been relatively peaceful. She'd had several visitors; Gabe, in particular, had made several stops. The doctor had also come to check in on her regularly. To her great relief, Lola had kept her distance. But her greatest joy was reserved for the fact that there was no way Richard could get to her now.

Much to Lola's chagrin, Quinn had been attentive to Adrianna through it all. He had spent every minute with her when he wasn't working. He'd brought her her evening meals, looked in on her at all hours during the night. They'd talked for hours, but the subject of his proposal and whether or not she could love him hadn't come up again. *At least not yet,* she thought to herself, as she lay looking out the window.

"I hope you found that book by Ralph Waldo Emerson just as exciting," Adrianna said to Jesse, alluding to the reading she had given him the day before as part of his schoolwork.

"Aww, jeez, Annie," Jesse whined. "Readin' that stuff was about as much fun as bustin' rocks!"

"You still need to read it." She sighed. "Schoolwork is something you must take seriously if you want to graduate. You should try to make the most of this."

"Then why does it have to be so darn boring? I don't have the slightest idea what it is I'm supposed to be learnin' when I'm readin' stuff about walkin' around in the woods and all that," he complained. He slapped one hand against the pulp magazine and added, "These are the only things that give me any hope of ever gettin' out of this damn chair."

"What do you mean?"

"Well," he began as he straightened himself in the wheelchair, "when I read these stories, I can travel to the Sargasso Sea, plunge down into a diamond mine in Africa, or get into a shootout in the Old West. All of those places sound so much more exciting than Lee's Point that I just want to start walkin' again so I can get the hell outta this town."

"You want to leave Lee's Point?" Adrianna asked in surprise.

"Hell, yeah, I want to!" Jesse crowed. "I know you haven't been here too long, but you can't help but notice that there isn't a lot that goes on here. I'm not gonna spend my whole life livin' in the same place just because I was born here."

"But what about the Whipsaw?" she asked. "Quinn said that he was taking care of it so you could take over when you were older. He said it would be your legacy."

"Did he ever ask me if it was what I wanted?" Jesse said loudly, his voice nearly rising to a shout. "Ever since I found myself in this damn chair, all I've heard is how as soon as I'm able, I'll get to run that bar. That's what Quinn wants! Can you imagine what it's like not being able to make your own choices? Would you want someone always tellin' you what to do?"

Once again, Adrianna was reminded just how much she had in common with each of the Baxter boys. Like Jesse, her life was often laid out before her regardless of whether she agreed with its direction or not. Richard's declaration of love and marriage certainly didn't take her own views into account. If she were to find herself in Jesse's position, she realized she would react with the same anger and resentment.

"No," she admitted. "I wouldn't like it at all."

"So what am I supposed to do about it? If I told Quinn that I didn't want that old bar, he'd be disappointed."

Somewhere deep in her mind, an idea occurred to Adrianna. Maybe there was something she could do that would help *both* of their situations. A thin smile formed on her lips. "You just worry about finishing your schoolwork," she assured him. "Leave the rest to me."

That evening, Quinn knocked lightly on Adrianna's door before entering. He was carrying a makeshift tray on which he had balanced a steaming bowl of vegetable soup, several slices of bread, an apple, and a tall glass of milk. Placing it gently on the bed beside her, he stepped back to smile approvingly.

"Dinner is served."

"Soup again?" Adrianna needled him playfully. "Doesn't this make three days in a row?"

"It seems to be all that sits well in your stomach," he said. "If you don't want it, I'll run downstairs and tell Lola to whip you up some eggs."

Jesse had told Adrianna that Lola had said, in no uncertain terms, that she wasn't going to wait on her, cook for her, or do anything else for her. According to Jesse, Quinn and Lola had a big ruckus, and Quinn had told Lola to do as she was told and to stay away from Adrianna or he would fire her. Jesse said Lola had cried and said she was sorry, and begged him not to fire her. Quinn gave in.

Quinn sat silently as Adrianna ate. Slowly, her appetite was returning to the point where she was eating a little more. It would be only a matter of days before she had her strength back. After she had finished her dinner, he removed the tray, then reseated himself by her bed.

Adrianna held his eyes playfully for a moment, but that was all it took for the darkness that had tainted her life in Lee's Point to start coloring the edges of her thoughts. Somewhere out there was a living, breathing nightmare who was waiting for her. Her voice was barely a whisper when she asked, "He's still out there, isn't he?"

"I'm afraid so," Quinn said matter-of-factly. "Gabe said he's got a room over at the Bellevue Hotel and spends his days tramping over to the telephone office and back. It's plain that he's up to something. Lord only knows what."

Even though Adrianna had felt secure in the safety that the Baxter house provided, the thought of Richard close by unsettled even her happiest moments. She'd been awakened the night before by the sound of tapping at her window. She'd been paralyzed with fear, absolutely certain that Richard was trying to break in and snatch her out into the night, until she had realized that it was merely the branches of the elm tree tapping on the window. Sooner or later, she would have to settle things with Richard Pope; she couldn't stay bedridden for the rest of her life.

"Whatever am I going to do about him?" she asked nervously. "He's never going to simply give up and go back to Shreveport. If he's staying in town, that means he's still set on taking me with him."

Quinn took her hand in his own as gently as if he were cradling an egg. "Hush now about all that business," he soothed. "Right now, that man is the last thing you should be worrying about. The important thing is how you're feeling. Have you had any more pains?"

"A few. Not as bad as before."

"Listen to what I'm telling you," he scolded her. "I may not be as smart as the doc when it comes to this medical stuff, but on this I'm certain I'm right. You have to stay in bed until you're recovered to the doctor's satisfaction."

"I suppose you're right."

"Darn tootin'!" He grinned, cradling her small chin between his thumb and forefinger. As she stared into the depths of his gray eyes, Adrianna realized how easy it would be to become lost in them. Embarrassed by her own thoughts, she looked away, her face flushing.

"I really do feel better," she said quickly. "Between the doctor's visits, Jesse's wild stories, and the soup, I'll be dancing on top of a table at the Whipsaw before you know it!"

"I would like to see that." His grin was endearing.

"You just might be surprised. I took tap dancing lessons when I was a child."

Quinn paused for a moment, his eyes lingering on her face. He took a deep breath, squeezed her hand, and said, "Do you feel up to having a more serious talk?"

"Serious talk?" she echoed.

"I wanted to wait until you were better before I mentioned this particular subject again," he said sheepishly. "The last time we talked about it, we never really got a chance to finish it properly."

Adrianna's breath caught in her chest. Her heart pounded so loudly that it rang in her ears. She knew Quinn was talking about their discussion at the doctor's office and his marriage proposal. Much like her thoughts of Richard Pope, the events of that particular morning had stayed with her, picking at her whenever she let her guard down. She still wasn't certain if the offer had been genuine.

You're not sure of your answer, either, she thought, and held her breath waiting for him to speak.

"I want to tell you the truth about the loan I took in order to keep the Whipsaw afloat," he said solemnly. "You need to know why Dewey Fuller is trying to use you to get to me."

Slowly, Quinn got up and moved to where he could stare out the window. For a moment, he stood silently, his strong profile reflected in the glass. When he finally spoke,

Adrianna hung on every word.

"When my father passed away," he said, his voice strong and steady, "I didn't give the Whipsaw much thought. I was going to sell the damn thing. Looking back, I suppose the last thing I wanted to do was to follow in John Henry's footsteps. The way I saw it, he spent his life slaving over that bar, so why would I do the same?" He paused for a moment before adding, "All of that changed when my mother died and Jesse was hurt."

At that moment, Quinn turned to face Adrianna. She swore that she could see a wetness in his gaze. She wanted to soothe him, to reach out to him and give him comfort, but she bit her lower lip and let him continue.

"By the time I gave a damn about that bar, a lot of damage had been done," he explained. "The fella that helped my father had been a no good son of a bitch who drank as much as he poured. Even after I got rid of him, one look at the books told me it was only a matter of time before I'd have to lock it up and put the place up for sale."

"Why didn't you?" Adrianna asked, unable to hold her tongue any longer.

"Because of Jesse," he said evenly. "Even

if I'd been able to find a buyer, there would scarcely have been enough to cover what was owed. Nothing would have been left over to provide him with a start. I'd made my own way in life, even if I'd gone against my father's wishes, but Jesse wasn't old enough to make his own choices. I wanted to be able to give him something. I wanted him to have the means to provide for himself once he got out of that chair and started walking again."

As Quinn spoke, all that Adrianna could hear were the words Jesse had spoken to her earlier in the evening. Unbeknownst to Quinn, even as he poured all his heart and soul into providing his brother with a legacy he could use to support himself, his gift had already been rejected. She wanted to tell Quinn what Jesse had told her, but she couldn't speak the words.

"I tried everything I could think of to raise the money without putting the house up for collateral. But finally I had to and then the worst thing happened. Old man Fuller bought up the bank loans," Quinn went on. "I swear I went to every damn bank in the whole county, but no one would give me a dime without the house. Times were tough all over, so I can't say I blame the bank."

"You've had trouble making the payments?"

Rejoining Adrianna at the side of the bed, Quinn looked into her eyes. In the piercing gray of his she could see his despair and his embarrassment. "Yeah. Now I'm at the point where I could lose the house. All that Fuller would have to do is take the contract to court, and we'd be out on our ears."

"That's awful!"

"I don't have anyone to blame but myself," Quinn sighed.

"It had to have been difficult," she offered.

"I was just a young kid who didn't know any better. I figured that we'd get the Whipsaw up on its feet and be making money hand over fist. But I'd let things go too long. Fuller even let me slide on a payment or two, but now he's ready to foreclose. That's why Dewey came sniffing around the bar the other day. That's also why he talked to you."

"What does he think I can do?"

Quinn shrugged. "Quit playing at the bar. I suppose he figures that if you do, I'll lose business and fall further behind on my payments. He'll have a better reason to foreclose."

As Adrianna watched Quinn bare his secrets, she was again reminded of how different her life had been while she lived in

Shreveport. She had never gone without, had never known what it meant to have to struggle to come up with money, and she knew that she had been spoiled by her luxury. Even now that she had lost her father's money, she still didn't *really* know what it meant to go without. The thought of what Quinn had gone through, was still going through, pierced her heart. Before she was even aware of it, her hand moved up his arm and she hugged it to her.

Gently, he pushed a couple of stray strands of hair from her face and planted a soft kiss on her lips. As if he had brought a flame to dry kindling, a blaze erupted in Adrianna's heart and she leaned into him, needing to feel his body against hers.

As she had the night she had sat beside him on the porch, Adrianna felt her heart pounding and her breath coming in gasps. Even though there were many ways in which their lives were different, there were others in which they were close, ways that pulled her toward him with a strength and intensity that shocked her.

"Quinn, I . . ." she began, but that was all she could say before he kissed her again. Deeply.

The touch of his lips against hers stirred up a torrent of feeling inside of her. Tentatively, her mouth explored his before opening into fevered passion. Distantly, she was aware of her hand moving to caress the side of his face as she strove to meet him, her body melting into his own. She was poised on the brink of giving in, of giving herself to Quinn completely, when he suddenly lifted his head.

As he moved his face away from hers, she could see the slightest curl of a smile at the corners of his mouth. His gaze was penetrating; if she were to get lost in those eyes, she might never find her way out.

"Remember this moment," he said softly. "When you're back on your feet, when the doc gives you a clean bill of health, I'm going to kiss you as much as I want to. Don't forget."

Not for my whole life, she thought.

CHAPTER 24

Damn! Damn her!

Lola rubbed the dishcloth roughly over a plate as she tried to dislodge a particularly stubborn piece of food. Its tenacity angered her, and she rubbed ever harder. Her muscles ached and her brow furrowed, but her mind was elsewhere.

Somewhere in the upstairs room, the whore rested. If that wasn't bad enough, matters were made even worse by the fact that Quinn was undoubtedly waiting on her hand and foot. Lola had last seen him an hour earlier when he'd left to take Adrianna a tray of food; every tick of the clock marking his absence was like a blow to her face. The very thought of the attention being paid to that little bitch made her sick to her stomach. Still, she didn't try to push the pain away; it was something that was to be hoarded and treasured. She would need it later.

"Goddamn hussy!" she hissed under her breath.

Absolutely nothing had gone according to plan!

Testing the potency of the method she had chosen to use, she'd tried the poison leaves out on Jesse's mangy mutt. Then she'd tainted Adrianna's food with what she had thought would be enough to make her sick and in constant pain until it was the right time to give her the final dose. The thought of the harlot writhing in sickness before she died had made Lola tingle with excitement. But her fantasy had been dashed. By some ironic miracle, the slut had not grown as sick as she had hoped. Even worse, Quinn had leapt to her aid like an angel, remaining ever vigilant at her side. At this rate, there would never be another chance. Who knew what was going on behind that door? With her imagination running rampant, her mind provided all of the sordid details; a smile here, a touch there, a glance turning into a kiss . . .

"Shit!"

Angrily, Lola dropped a plate onto the counter with a clatter. For an instant, she dreamed of taking all of the dishes and hurling them against the closed doors above until the floor was littered with debris. Of

347

course, she was too smart for such a reckless plan of attack, but the thought gave her comfort. Still, she had to close her mind to such thinking. She would need to have a clear head with which to come up with a new way to keep Quinn away from that slut!

What bothered Lola the most was the knowledge that she was being slowly eased out. From the moment she'd come to work for Quinn Baxter, she'd done everything she could to weasel herself into his good graces, to ensure that she would never have to go back to the meager, pathetic life she had been born into. She waited on that broken excuse of a boy as if he were a king. She put up with that mutt's barking and growling, and she had done it all with a smile. Now it looked like it would all be for naught. If things went the way they were headed, she would eventually be asked to leave, and that bitch would have everything that *she* had worked for.

As the soft sound of laughter rolled down the stairway and into the kitchen, Lola winced. They were having the time of their lives. The noise wormed its way into her chest and grated on her nerves. It was more than she could bear. Whirling on her heel, she wiped her dishwater-soaked hands on her skirt and headed for the rear porch.

Outside, the summer air was heavy with humidity. Only the tops of the trees held the colors of the sunset; darkness had begun to win out for the day. Cicadas called loudly from the trees, their incessant humming keeping time with the angry pounding of Lola's heart. In the near blackness, nothing stirred, and that was just the way she liked it.

Certain that no one was watching her, Lola made a beeline for a rusted pot that lay haphazardly in the far corner of the porch. There, tucked securely into the corner, was a pack of cigarettes and a box of matches. She didn't want Quinn to see her smoking, but it was an indulgence she wasn't entirely willing to give up, even for him. Striking a match, she lit the tobacco and inhaled deeply, the acrid smoke burning down her throat but calming her just the same. As she smoked, the amber glow of the cigarette's end smoldered menacingly, reflecting its fiery nature in her eyes.

Certainly, something had to be done and done soon. She'd been confident that Reuben would scare the bitch off, but the attempt had failed. Her belief in his strength and loyalty to her had been misplaced, and it had cost her. As her tramp of a mother had once said to her, *If you want something done right, do it yourself.*

She would have to be quick and she would have to be brutal. Hesitation was not an option. There would only be one chance to do it right, so she couldn't afford to make a mistake. An image of Quinn sitting beside the slut's bed flashed across her mind, and she realized she would have to be patient. Now was not the time. But soon . . .

Of course, Quinn would grieve over his loss, but that could easily be taken care of. In her experience, a man was easily soothed, even from the greatest tragedy, with the right woman in his bed. All it would take would be a kind word here, a touch there, and then she'd part her legs and let his animal urges do the rest. If you could lead them by their dicks, you could heal them the same way. After that, the slut from Shreveport would be a distant memory, an episode best forgotten.

Taking one last long drag on her cigarette, Lola dropped the butt onto the porch at her feet. The end burned defiantly before she angrily crushed it out with the toe of her shoe. When she removed her foot, all that remained was a crumpled husk of what had been.

"You're next, bitch!" she hissed. "You're next."

■ ■ ■ ■

Richard Pope was angry and frustrated.

As he stood in what passed for the lobby of the Bellevue Hotel, he marveled at what the simpletons of Lee's Point accepted as adequate accommodations for guests in their town. Grime-streaked wallpaper, some of it tattered and peeling in long strips, covered the walls. An ancient lamp hung limply from the ceiling, looking much like a man hanging from the gallows, two of its bulbs burned out. Even the beams that supported the entryway sagged as if they were as depressed with their surroundings as he was.

His room was no better. He could only hazard a guess at the multitude of sins that had taken place in his squeaky bed. Worst of all, upon entering the night before, he had been surprised to see a cockroach half the size of his fist scurry across the floor on its diseased legs before disappearing under the bed.

"Stayin' another night?" a voice asked from behind him.

Richard turned to glare at the Bellevue Hotel's proprietor. He was a wisp of a man; his clothes hung loosely on his skeletal frame, and his bushy mustache covered stained, chipped teeth. Richard could only imagine how many years he had managed to prop himself up behind his rickety counter, smiling his repulsive grin.

"I'm afraid so." Richard sighed.

"Well, then, I'll go on up and make sure your room is clean." As the man spoke, he absently ran one hand over his whiskers. To Richard's eyes, he looked like an old dog scratching at fleas.

"Fine."

Without waiting for another word, Richard headed for the front door. He'd pushed through, stepping out into the sweltering heat of another summer day, when he heard the hotel owner call out from behind him. "Make sure an' tell all your friends back in Shreveport about the Bellevue! Tell 'em they're welcome to stay any time! They can . . ." The man's grating voice finally fell silent when the door shut behind him.

"Stupid bastard," Richard spat.

Outside the sun shone brightly in the sky, its gaze searing everything it could touch. It stood straight overhead, blazing down accusingly. Not even the slightest kiss of a breeze had dared to show itself, instead letting the sun rule the day with its heat. Richard shielded his eyes with his hand and stalked off down the street, grumbling to himself.

In the short time he had spent in Lee's Point, he had come to loathe the town. It was as if he had stepped back in time to a simpler era, where people made do with far less in the way of basic amenities. He was half surprised that they even had running water or electricity. There was nothing even remotely comparable to the comfortable life he lived back in Shreveport. Every day he spent in the town was worse than the one before. How Adrianna had survived here for as long as she had was a mystery to him.

The very thought of Adrianna caused a welling in his chest and a tightness in his throat. It was as if he had been pierced by a lightning bolt of emotion, striking him flush in the heart. If he were a weaker man, he might have grown upset. "Oh, my darling, Adrianna," he muttered.

His relationship with her was another problem that continued to gnaw at the edges of his mind. He had gone from the elation of finding her behind the piano in that decrepit tavern to the horror of seeing her out on the street in another man's arms, the image of her limp body jarring him. Even though he had told them all the facts at the doctor's office, those who had come into contact with her in the short time she had been in town had conspired to keep them apart. Although he had explained that he and Adrianna were engaged, they hadn't even allowed him to be in the same room as his betrothed. Before he knew what was happening, his sweet Adrianna had been whisked away!

When he'd found out where she had been taken, he had been livid. The very thought of her living under the same roof as that barbarian who had laid hands on him at the doctor's office caused his blood pressure to rise. When he had marched up to the door and demanded entry, he had been turned away. He had even been threatened with physical violence if he chose to return. Leaving had been one of the most difficult moments of his life.

When he had gone to the sheriff's office to demand that Adrianna be handed over to his custody, he had been rebuked. That fat ass of a lawman had explained that since he and Adrianna were not legally married, there was nothing that he could do. Richard had begun to give the man a piece of his mind but had stopped when the sheriff became visibly annoyed, jangling the key ring that hung from his belt as a threat. Richard had nearly taken the man up on his offer; a night on a jail cot could not possibly have been worse than another night in that fleabag hotel!

"Afternoon," an older man offered Richard as he passed on the boardwalk, but he ignored him and walked on; he would have as little to do with these people as possible.

He stopped at the telegraph office but had no messages waiting. He had kept the wires between Lee's Point and Shreveport busy with messages being sent to and received from his business. Even though he was out of the city, money waited for no man and he was no exception. There were matters that he needed to tend to in order to ensure that the lifestyle he and Adrianna deserved was waiting for them upon their return.

Rounding the corner next to the auto mechanic's shop, Richard proceeded to the town's lone diner. "EAT" was the only visible signage. He had taken all his meals there since he'd arrived in town and, while the food was hardly passable, he knew that he needed to keep his strength. Pushing the door open, he found the diner nearly empty. A scattering of patrons sat at the tables, the faint sound of voices and the occasional clink of silverware rising to mix with the whirr of the ceiling fans. A radio chirped in the distance, an old-timey tune breezing around the diner, carried on the wafting smells of the greasy kitchen. Walking past a heavy-set woman in a floral print dress and a farmer puffing furiously on a corncob pipe, he took a seat at a booth near the window that afforded him a view of the hardware store across the street.

"What can I do ya for?" the waitress asked when she finally sidled up to the table. To Richard's eyes, all waitresses were cut from the same cloth; fat and homely. This one was no exception.

"What's the special?" he asked curtly.

"Corned beef and hash."

"Fine," he snorted. "That's fine."

"Whatever works for ya, darlin'," she said as she left to place the order.

As he waited for his meal, Richard's mind raced over what he was to do next. He would accept nothing less than Adrianna accompanying him back to Shreveport. But while she was confined to bed, he had little choice but to remain in Lee's Point and bide his time until he could make his move. *But what should that move be?* The man who opposed him was, in his own way, formidable; Quinn Baxter struck him as the sort who would fight for what he wanted. Still, Richard had faced many men who believed in brawn over brains, and he had triumphed

356

over them all on his way to success.

The problem was that he was out of his element. Things out in the sticks didn't work the same way they did in a board room back in civilization. What he needed was to find an advantage, something that he could use against his enemy to pry his beloved free. *But what?*

As if in answer to his unspoken question, a voice spoke from beside him. "Richard Pope, I'm to understand?"

Richard turned to look upon a dapper young man wearing a suit that, while a good year removed from the styles of Shreveport, was far more fashionable than anything he had seen in Lee's Point since arriving in this one-horse town. A bowler hat sat tilted across heavily pomaded hair as the man's eyes regarded him.

"That's right," Richard replied. "Who the hell are you?"

"The name's Dewey Fuller," the man said, extending his hand in greeting. He grinned broadly as he added, "And I just might be the man you're looking for."

"What do you mean?" Richard motioned for him to take a seat opposite him in the booth.

"I heard that Quinn has your fiancée and refuses to let you see her," Dewey began.

"That's right. But how did you know?"

"News travels fast in this little town."

"I'm going to ruin that ignorant clod. He won't think he's so smart when I get through with him."

"I know just how you can do it," Dewey said confidently.

The two men talked in low tones while Richard ate his meal. When he finished, Fuller picked up his hat to leave, extended his hand and said, "Good luck, friend."

"You're sure about this?"

"It will work. I guarantee it."

"Hmmm," Richard said to himself as he left the eatery, "I hadn't thought of that."

CHAPTER 25

"And the first ten articles of the Constitution are called?"

Jesse stared at Adrianna intently, his thumb tapping rhythmically against the tabletop. His face was twisted tightly in concentration, his mind racing to find the elusive answer.

"The Bill of Rights?" he asked with little confidence in his solution.

"Correct!"

"Crackers!" he exclaimed with obvious pride. "I can't believe I actually remembered that!"

Late afternoon sunlight streamed through the west-facing windows, inching its way across the wooden floor. Through the open sashes, birds and insects called out to elusive companions, signaling an end to one day and the beginning of another. Summer flowers suffused the air with their sweet aroma. A week had passed since Adrianna had collapsed outside of the Whipsaw. In the time she had been convalescing at the Baxter house, she had slowly regained her strength to the point where she had been out of bed for part of the day. Once she was able, she'd insisted on restarting Jesse's school lessons, beginning early in the day to make up for lost time. She was happy to help Jesse with his schooling. It kept her mind off the possibility that Richard could use his influence with a judge and she would have to return with him.

"I'm so proud of you." Adrianna beamed. "You've taken to one subject right after the other. I'm certain that all of these things will count toward your being able to graduate from high school."

"Maybe I'm not such a big dummy after all," he allowed.

Adrianna had been surprised by Jesse's aptitude. Once they had received the books from the school and a list of the lessons, he had taken to his studies like a fish to water. One subject after another had been explored; literature, history, mathematics, and even science had proven to be little challenge to the boy's sharp wit. But what had impressed her the most was his attitude. He had never complained, instead choosing to sit with nearly rapt attention as she had explained one lesson after another. As she saw his pride in his own work, so she felt pride in hers.

"In the future, you'll be glad you learned all of this," she explained.

Something in Jesse's expression hardened at her words. He looked her in the eyes for a second before breaking away, his gaze drifting across the table and down into his lap. "My future," he said absently.

"Of course," Adrianna added. "When you're ready for a career."

"I don't know how it's gonna help me standing behind a bar."

A wave of pity washed over Adrianna at the boy's words. Once again, Jesse had spoken harshly about the life Quinn was struggling to provide for him. He strove for more than his brother hoped for him but was unable to tell him his worries, to tell him that he wanted more. Jesse felt as if his life were being planned for him without regard to what he wanted. Adrianna understood; it was not very different from her own experience.

"That's up to you," she soothed.

"Is it?"

"Sure it is," she explained. "Everyone makes their own choices in life as it relates to their future. Others in our lives, family included, might have ideas that are different. We listen to them, but the final decision is ours. Things will work out for you, Jesse."

"Oh yeah?" he disagreed. "I'm stuck in this damn chair!"

"Well, if Roosevelt can become president of the United States while being confined to a wheelchair, you can go to college and be whatever you want. You've got as much courage as he has."

"I knew he had polio. But I didn't know that he was stuck in a chair."

"A friend of my father's worked in the White House. He told us about the president being in a chair."

"Well, he's rich, so he doesn't have to worry about making a living for himself."

"I have confidence that you are going to be all right. You're smart, Jesse. You'll get through school, and you've got something else going for you. You've got horse sense."

He looked at her and grinned.

"I mean it, Jesse. Some people have a lot of book learning but no common sense to go with it."

While Adrianna was spending her time helping Jesse with his mind, she'd pushed Quinn to help with the boy's body. He was using the bar Quinn had hung over his bed to lift himself out of his bed and into the chair. The goal was not only to make him more independent but to strengthen his weakened limbs.

"That chair will hold you back only if you let it," she chided.

"Yes, it will. I'm not like you!"

Confused by his statement, Adrianna asked, "What do you mean by that?"

"Once you've paid your debt to Quinn, you're free to pack up your things and head on down the road," he explained. When he looked at her, she could see that his eyes were bleak. "You can go on and do anything you want! I don't have that choice!"

The strength of Jesse's words took Adrianna aback. Most of what he said was indeed true; as soon as she had repaid Quinn for the damages she had caused in the automobile accident, she would be free to leave. Richard Pope's being in town certainly complicated things, but the end result was the same; she would have the option of leaving for good.

But was that what she wanted? In the short time she had been in Lee's Point, she realized there was more to Quinn Baxter than her first impression of him had suggested. It was evident that he dearly loved his brother and was willing to do anything to help him, even sacrifice his own future by running a tavern that he hated.

Thinking back, after the crash his tone had been aggressive, even a touch frightening. But now, when he walked into a room, she found herself short of breath, her heart hammering wildly in her chest. She'd never felt this way before, and it both excited and unnerved her. What scared her even more was the thought that he might not feel the same about her. His offer of marriage might only be a ploy to save her from Richard.

"Jesse, think about it. You have lots of choices," she said.

"Like what?"

"For one, you don't have to work at the Whipsaw just because Quinn wants you to. That's your choice and no one else's. If you want to leave Lee's Point and go off to college, that's your choice as well. All you have to do is set a goal and work toward it."

"Set a goal?" he echoed.

As Jesse thought over her words, the stark realization struck Adrianna that she needed to follow her own advice as well. She had decisions to make about a lot of things: Richard, Shreveport, and the life she had begun in Lee's Point. Most important, she had to make a decision about Quinn. And stick to it.

■ ■ ■ ■

After the evening meal, Adrianna retired to her room and settled down to read. She looked up from her book when Quinn came and leaned in her doorway. He was dressed as he had been at supper, a clean shirt tucked into his work pants. His dark hair was hanging loosely over his forehead. He'd shaved that morning, but now there was a slight stubble of whiskers on his face. Her heart started to beat faster at the mere sight of him.

"What are you reading?" Quinn asked with a warm smile.

She shut the book and laid it on the table beside her. "I was just going over some material for Jesse's lesson tomorrow. He's a fast learner. I thought he would be interested in *The Last of the Mohicans*. It's a good view of the French and Indian War."

"I'm proud of how he's taken to home-schooling," Quinn said stepping into the room. "Jesse's smart, I can say that much for him. You've made the lessons interesting."

"I don't know about that." She blushed. "I think I've learned about as much as he has."

"You've done an amazing job getting him to help himself. He's getting out of the bed and into his chair on his own, which is more than he could do a few weeks ago."

Adrianna took in her ability to teach Jesse, but there was another matter that she wanted to discuss. "Quinn," she began, the words sticking in her throat. "About Jesse . . ."

"Yes, what about him?"

"Have you ever wondered . . ." Even though she had imagined talking to Quinn about Jesse's reluctance to work at the Whipsaw many times, she found it hard to give voice to the words that had come so easily to her mind. Her brow furrowed at her failure.

"Ever wondered what?" Quinn prodded.

"Have you thought about whether Jesse actually wants to take over the Whipsaw?" she finally managed to say. "What if he wants to do something else?"

"What, for instance?"

"He's smart, Quinn. He could go to college and be whatever he wants, a lawyer or a teacher."

Quinn looked at her for a moment with an odd expression on his face. She braced herself for another explosion like the one in the Whipsaw office, but it never came.

Finally, the clouds broke, and he beamed at her with a broad smile. "He finally told you, huh?"

"Wh-what?!"

"I'm guessing he told you that he doesn't want to work at the Whipsaw." Adrianna could do little more than stare. There was Quinn before her, telling her the very thing that she had dreaded speaking to him about, with a look on his face that was far more amused than disappointed.

"How . . . how did you know?" she stammered.

"He's never actually told me as much himself, but I can read him about as easily as you can read one of those schoolbooks," Quinn explained. "I've known for a while now. It's not like I just fell off the turnip truck, you know! I'd have to be a blind, deaf fool not to see that Jesse's not exactly thrilled by the idea of standing behind a bar."

"Then why are you so insistent about it?"

Quinn fixed her with a hard stare and took a deep breath before closing the door and crossing the room to stand directly before her. Gently, he took her hands in his own.

"I'm trying to prepare him for life. Real life. The life that exists outside of this house and off the pages of those pulps he's always reading."

"But he told me —"

Quinn cut her off. "He needs an income even while he's going to school and he needs to be able to take care of himself should something happen to me." Softly, he took her chin in his fingers and turned her face toward his, his eyes boring down into hers. "Life is full of hard knocks. A fellow has to follow his head and not his heart."

Adrianna was certain that Quinn wasn't talking about Jesse; he was talking about himself. What he was telling her at that moment was that he wanted to be with her, but because of who they were and their different lifestyles they couldn't be together. As each searched the other's face, many thoughts were exchanged without words; one asked, the other pleaded, and then their roles were reversed.

Adrianna couldn't find the phrases to say what was in her heart. On impulse she stood on her tiptoes and pressed her lips to his in a kiss. At first, he seemed surprised by her actions, but no more surprised than she was, but he soon pulled her to him, his lips tenderly touching hers. It began gently enough but soon grew in intensity, as if they were both starving and needed the other in order to live. Sparks and passion passed between them. When they broke the kiss, they stood for long moments locked tightly together. Adrianna had never felt so alive in her life. When she felt a tug on her hand, she followed, knowing that she would follow him to the ends of the earth if he wanted her. He led her to the bed. As they passed the light, he reached over and extinguished it.

Even as the light that had filled the room disappeared, it was replaced by the faint glow afforded by the moon and stars that shone through the window. She could see the emotion play across his face like a dance, equal parts desire and confusion.

"Annie," he started. "If you don't want . . ."

She hushed him with a finger pressed firmly to his lips. "Shhh."

In truth, she had never wanted anything more in her life than to lie with this man. As she sat down on the bed, Quinn sliding effortlessly beside her, no action she had ever taken in her entire life had seemed so right. Her skin felt as if it were on fire, and her body began to tremble with want. When she once again placed her lips to his, her fingers ran wildly through his hair. As their kisses grew in intensity, Quinn's fingers slowly undid the buttons on her blouse; with every snap that freed another button, waves threatened to crest the barriers of Adrianna's heart. Soon they were all undone, and his rough fingers ran lightly over her alabaster skin.

"Oh, Quinn," she moaned into his open mouth.

"Annie," he answered breathlessly.

His hands searched her body as if he were looking for treasure. He cupped one of her breasts with a delicacy that made her suck the summer night air through clenched teeth. Passionately, yet teasingly, he ran one of his thumbs over her nipple, sending shock waves of pleasure roiling throughout her body. She arched her back to meet his hands. Suddenly she wanted to touch him in much the same way he was touching her. With none of the deliberation he had showed, she tugged at the buttons of his shirt, tearing them free with a fierce insistence. Soon her hands were tangled in his thick chest hair, the taut workman's muscles hard beneath her touch.

Never had she touched a man in this way. She'd always wondered what it would feel like to lie with a man, to share in the carnal pleasures that came from two whose bodies burned one for the other. But this was different, somehow even greater than she could have ever dreamed possible. This was the most natural act that a man and a woman could undertake with each other.

The next few moments went by as a blur; the movement of a hip here, a deep probing kiss there, an item of clothing tossed blindly into the darkness. They lay naked on the bed, completely exposed each to the other's touch.

Adrianna felt no embarrassment; her state of undress with this man was what she wanted, what she desired. As his hands roamed across her flesh, touching her soft parts and exploring her wetness, she knew that there were no more secrets, no more words left unsaid, but only an honesty she would never share with another.

In the same way, she felt no flush of awkwardness letting her fingers explore Quinn's body. Tentatively, she took his manhood into her hands, surprised by both its velvety softness and its hardness. It seemed to pulse in time with the beating of her own heart. The heat that it created was also surprising, and she clung to it as if it were a fireplace on a chilly January morning. As she moved her hands up and down its length, she was startled to hear Quinn groan.

"Am I hurting you?" she asked tentatively.

"On the contrary," he gasped. Even though she looked up into darkness at the sound of his voice, Adrianna was certain that he was grinning down at her, and it filled her with joy. There was a shifting on the bed, and then Quinn loomed above her, his muscular arms holding him aloft. She was open before him, ready to take him inside of her and become a woman. The thought set her limbs to trembling, her legs quivering not with fear but with anticipation.

"Quinn. I've never . . ." she stammered.

"I know. I know. Hush, my sweet Annie." His whisper came out of the darkness. "Everything will be all right. I swear it."

The tenderness of his words rolled over her like a wave. Never in her life had she ever felt so treasured and safe. Raising her hand to touch the side of his face, she whispered what she had longed to say her whole life. "I love you."

"And I love you, Annie."

With that declaration, Quinn eased himself forward and was suddenly inside her. There was a sharp twinge of pain at the beginning but it soon disappeared as if it had been blown away by a soft summer breeze. In its place was pleasure the likes of which she could never have imagined! As

Quinn began to move, tentatively at first but soon with more determination, passion began to explode across Adrianna's body and she melted into him, desperate to be joined to him forever.

"Darling, Quinn," she cried into his ear.

As he moved into her, Adrianna clutched at his broad shoulders, digging her hands into his hard flesh. It was as if the rest of the world had suddenly vanished, leaving the two of them and their senses as the only living things under the sky. She could feel him radiating inside of her, smell the musky odor of his body, taste the salty sweat of his skin, and hear the deep breaths that rose and fell with his movements. As his hand ran the length of her bare thigh to slide beneath her, pulling her upward to meet his thrusts, she was aware of it all, and it only heightened her arousal.

None of the problems that had plagued her since her father's death could find her at that moment. Instead, snippets of her time with Quinn flooded her mind: the night that he had kissed her on the porch, his easy smile as he watched her play the piano at the Whipsaw, the way that he spoke to Jesse, and even the hardness that had been written on his face the first time she had laid eyes on him. All of it had led to this very moment, and for that she treasured each and every one of them.

"Quinn!" she moaned.

Suddenly, his body shook as if seized by a deep tremor, his taut muscles growing harder. Even though she could not see him in the room's inky darkness, she knew that he was staring at her, and she looked back with the intensity of the stars above. She clung to him tenaciously, as if he were the only thing keeping her afloat in a roiling and raging sea of emotion. Quinn shuddered once more, and she was filled with a warmth that seemed to pass through her entire body, sating her in every way.

Quinn collapsed on top of her, the sweat of one body mingling with that of the other. Adrianna's hands held him tightly. As she was wrapped in his body, so too was she wrapped in happiness and love.

"Oh, Quinn!" she finally managed. "It was so wonderful."

"My Annie," he whispered.

As they peppered each other's faces with kisses, Adrianna knew with certainty that she had made a decision. She had finally refused to allow others to dictate the direction of her life; she had chosen her own path.

She had turned her back on Shreveport,

on the life she had led with her father, and on Richard Pope.

My life from this night forward will be with Quinn Baxter, if he will have me.

CHAPTER 26

As the early afternoon sun beat down, Quinn walked the streets of Lee's Point with his head held high. Everything around him, from the sound of the birds calling lazily from the trees to the color of his neighbors' houses, seemed somehow different, more vivid. There was a spring in his step that carried him along as if he were being pushed by a breeze. He knew that it was all because of one very special woman.

It was because of Adrianna Moore!

He had played every second of the night before in his head time and time again, savoring each detail. If he closed his eyes, he could still feel her skin beneath him, experience the desire of her searching kiss, and even inhale the smell of her hair as he had lain upon her, spent and exhausted. It was as if it were a dream . . . a dream come true.

When he had wakened beside her, he had

lain as still as he could, content only to watch her chest rise and fall as she slept. In the early morning sun bright and golden, her long hair had framed her face, haloing it to make her look like an angel. If it had all been a dream, then he'd certainly never want to wake. At that very moment, Quinn had known that he would do anything to keep her forevermore in his bed and at his side.

He hadn't wanted to leave her, but there were matters at the Whipsaw that required his attention. Thankfully, he had been able to take a leave from his logging job because of an oversupply of logs. Since Adrianna's collapse, he had spent so much time at her side that he had put off his other duties, a neglect that needed correcting. Still, it had pained him to leave. As he had bounded down the steps of the porch, he had looked back to see her peering out the window at him, watching him go. It was that sight that he carried with him now, a snapshot of a time he couldn't wait to return to.

Making a quick stop at Delmar's garage, he checked on the repairs to Adrianna's damaged car. Delmar assured him that it would only be a matter of days before the car would be drivable again. After Quinn thanked him and walked on, the first storm clouds formed over his cheery mood.

In the bliss of the previous night and the afterglow of the morning, he had steadfastly tried to push all thoughts of the future from his head; reality somehow seemed less sweet than the bliss of their union. For the scant bit of time they had in which to vent the feelings that had all but overwhelmed them, he had chosen to bask in the now with no regard for later. But there were matters he could not escape, no matter how hard he tried.

Adrianna's life had been so very different from his. He was from the country, a laborer, a man who worked with his hands and fought a constant battle to pay his bills. She was a woman of refinement; her manners and clothes spoke volumes, while he was a man of very simple tastes. She possessed a quick mind and an education the likes of which he could never have dreamed. The differences between them were as many as they were profound.

"But still . . ." he muttered.

Never in his life could he have imagined meeting a woman like Adrianna. He had had his share of flirtations and crushes, but none of them had ever made him dream of a life as a husband. This was *different!* The thought of her leaving Lee's Point and never returning was nearly more than he could bear. But at that moment, what he could do about it, he didn't know.

Rounding a corner, Quinn came to a stop in front of the Whipsaw and stared up at its battered sign. He sighed heavily. So many of the ills of his life were tied to this place: his father's ruined life, his meager hopes for Jesse's future, and the large sum of money that he owed Dewey Fuller's father. Still, if it had not been for the rickety old bar, he wouldn't have been on the road that day and wouldn't have been struck by a certain automobile.

"I guess I owe you that much." He smiled at the sign.

Inside, Quinn moved easily past the tables and chairs in the afternoon gloom. He flipped on the lights behind the bar. He was early. It would be a couple of hours before Gabe and the cleaning woman arrived to get the place ready for the evening business. In the meantime, he'd take an inventory of their liquor and make a list of what they needed. He'd been at it for only five minutes when there was a knock on the door.

Quinn looked up in time to see the door swing slowly inward and a well-dressed man step inside. With the bright day behind him, Quinn had to strain to learn his visitor's identity. At first glance, he'd thought it was Dewey Fuller, come to try to collect on his debt; but as his eyes adjusted to the brightness, his stomach curled as tightly as his fists.

It was Richard Pope.

"I hope I'm not interrupting," the city man said stiffly.

"What the hell do you want?" Quinn shot back. He moved slowly from behind the bar, his hands clenching tightly into fists he had no fear of using to pummel the man who had done Adrianna so much harm.

"If not a drink, then maybe a bit of conversation," Richard supplied, moving toward Quinn with his hands before him, palms upraised. "I only want a minute of your time. Regardless of what you might think of me, I certainly didn't come here to engage in fisticuffs."

"You shouldn't have come at all."

"I can certainly understand why you might see it that way," he said, nodding. As he came to a stop before Quinn, his jowls hung heavy in the summer heat. Sweat beaded on his bulbous nose and wrinkled forehead, running down to stain the starched high-collar shirt he wore beneath his suit coat. "After all, if I were in your position, I would see before me a man who had come to take something that I had come to treasure. I might even see a threat. Just as you do now, I would likely be too blind to see what I truly represent."

"All I see is a two-bit, big-city son of a bitch who thinks he can just waltz into town and start making demands," Quinn snarled. "This isn't Shreveport. You can't make the rules here."

"That is where you are wrong," Richard said matter-of-factly. "What you are failing to see is that I am your opportunity to a better life. Well, certainly a better life than this one."

"The only way you're gonna make my life better is to get the hell out of Lee's Point and leave Adrianna be."

"That is because you're speaking with emotion," Richard admonished him. "You're not allowing yourself to think clearly, to think with your head. You might be using too much of your heart . . . and your prick."

Quinn bristled at the man's tone. Briefly, he thought about just giving in to his emotions and thrashing the older man to within an inch of his life, leaving him with just enough breath to limp back to Shreveport. But before he could take a single step, something stopped him. Maybe it was the thought of Adrianna's gentle heart or simply a desire to let the man ramble, but he stayed his hand, content only to glare.

Richard took Quinn's silence as his cue to continue. The older man stepped over to the bar, retrieved two small glasses and a bottle of bourbon, and poured two fingers worth of the amber liquid into each. He slid one toward Quinn before downing his own in a gulp. Quinn never moved an inch.

"Despite outward appearances," Richard began, "you and I are cut from much the same cloth. We are both businessmen and, as such, we have certain responsibilities that the common rabble that stand on the other side of our counters can never truly understand. We must account for employees, product, and even such trivialities as graft in order to make our way. Each and every one of these things comes with a cost."

Quinn remained silent, his teeth grinding with suppressed anger.

"Sometimes these costs can become a burden that cannot be overcome," the older man continued calmly, his tone almost sympathetic. "In the direst cases, a businessman can have no choice but to seek out others from whom he can borrow the funds to keep his door open. Paying back such a loan can be like swimming upstream in a flood.

Many fail, drowning in the mess they themselves have made."

As if an electric current had been thrown open, Quinn instantly understood the reason for Richard Pope's visit, and the blood ran cold in his veins. Anger raged within him with an intensity that frightened him. When he finally composed himself enough to speak, the name that he gave voice to exploded from between clenched teeth. "Dewey Fuller!"

"That is correct," Richard said evenly.

"What in the hell did that bastard tell you?"

"He told me everything, Mr. Baxter. He explained every sordid detail dating all the way back to when your father, John Henry, opened this fine establishment." Richard paused, pouring himself another shot of alcohol as he let the sting of his words settle in. "Once Mr. Fuller explained how much you had sacrificed in order to keep this tavern open, all for the sake of your injured brother, well, I have to admit that I saw you in a new light. I dare say that I even felt a bit sorry for you."

"I don't want your pity," Quinn spat.

"I could give you all of the pity in the world, and it still wouldn't pay your debts, now would it?"

Once again, Quinn was forced to squelch the urge to let his fists settle their differences. It was a struggle, but he was finally able to overcome his impulses, instead saying, "Fuller seems to want to tell every new face in town of my problems. But what's the point of him telling you all of this?"

"Isn't it obvious, my dear boy," Richard said, his eyes wide with surprise. "I was told because I am the answer to your dilemma. I am the one who can make this whole sordid mess go away."

"What are you talking about?"

"Think about it," Richard said excitedly, stepping closer to Quinn. The lazy ceiling fans blew a whiff of the older man's cologne to Quinn's nose. "With but a quick signature on a piece of paper, I can make all of these debts float off as if they were so much smoke! No more visits from the Fullers! No more hardships! No more nights lying awake, trying to figure your way out of this mess!"

"You'd do all of that?" Quinn asked.

"Certainly! With the money that I have amassed, it would be but a trifling thing!" Richard exclaimed, his mood growing as bright as the flush on his cheeks. "Of course, there would be a cost to you involved. After all, there is something given for everything that is received. It's the cornerstone to any good business transaction."

"In this case, that cost would be . . . ?" Quinn asked, letting the question hang.

"You would have to give Adrianna to me," Richard said quickly, the words tumbling out of his mouth like broken teeth. Hurriedly, he added, "Before you grow angry, you have to look at this for what it is . . . a business decision. It's truly no different than selling any other goods."

"What are you saying?" Quinn asked incredulously. "That Adrianna is nothing more than merchandise to me?"

"In many ways, yes," the older man said, nodding. "She hasn't been in your possession for very long, so you shouldn't have been able to develop much of an attachment to her. Your connection to this tavern is much greater. Why shouldn't you be able to hand one over for the sake of the other? Quite frankly, it is the only responsible thing to do."

Like the storm that had brought him and Adrianna together, emotion washed over Quinn with flashes of anger streaking across his mood as if they were lightning. That this pathetic excuse of a man could even say such things galled him! To someone such as

Richard Pope, people's lives were just playthings that could be maneuvered. To him, Adrianna wasn't a woman but a possession, something to be dangled from his chest like a medallion.

Where before, thoughts of the woman who had come to define his life had stayed his hand, they now flamed his rage. Images of Adrianna lying beneath of him flashed before his eyes, the tenderness of their lovemaking rubbing raw against his hatred of the man standing before him. Instead of struggling to remain calm, he allowed himself to lose control. The dikes that had held the floodwaters of his wrath broke, and the flood overwhelmed him.

Richard never saw the blow coming. Quinn moved with the speed and strength of a wildcat, his fist plowing into the softness of the older man's belly. All the air flew out of his lungs in a whoosh, sending him crashing to the floor in a heap.

"Ohhh!" Richard wheezed.

Quinn stood over the fallen man triumphantly, his fists still clenched. He wanted to do more damage, to rain more furious blows or kicks on the man as he lay prostrate on the floor, but watching him writhe in agony was good enough.

"Get every last thought of Adrianna

Moore out of your head!" Quinn raged. "Because if you ever bother her again, if you so much as present your face to her, send her so much as a letter, the beating you just got is going to seem like a picnic compared to what I'll do to you!"

Richard could only groan in response.

"You crawl out of here, get yourself back to your room, pack your bags, slide behind the wheel of that fancy car, and don't look back until you've arrived in Shreveport," Quinn continued, his finger jabbing the air before him angrily.

"Unhh . . ." Richard managed.

"She doesn't want to be with you. She's never wanted it. The sooner you get that through your thick skull, the better. If you don't, I'm the next person you're gonna see! Do you understand me?"

Richard rose shakily on quivering arms. He tried to hold himself up on his hands and knees, but his hands gave way and he fell back to the hardwood floor with a thud.

"Good enough," Quinn snorted and went back to counting the bottles.

Richard Pope stood on shaky legs, leaning against the corner of the building. He sucked air hungrily into his pained chest, the spot where Quinn had struck him still raw and tender to the touch. He couldn't remember the last time someone had laid hands upon him in such a way, but he was certain that it was an experience he didn't wish to repeat.

A few people drifted along the hot streets, giving him a look of curiosity and concern, but none of them bothered to stop. *Let them walk on,* he thought. *I wouldn't take their help if it was offered!* Besides, there was only one thing that would salve his wounds.

"I'll get even with you, you lowlife bastard," he muttered, his voice raspy.

He had truly entered that pisspot of a tavern with the best of intentions: to offer to cover Quinn Baxter's debt to the Fullers in full, to wipe the slate clean so that he could get on with his life in this miserable little town. All that he had asked in return was for him to hand over Adrianna; a mere bauble to a ruffian such as the bar owner but a treasured jewel to a cultured man like himself. But he had been denied. Even worse, he had been struck and then threatened with even further violence. This was an affront that would not stand!

Richard was not certain how matters of dispute were settled in a place such as this, but he wasn't about to run out of town with his tail between his legs! He had made the offer in good faith, but it was not the only means at his disposal to solve his problems. Far from it, he had many more to choose from. Many more.

Standing as tall as he could, Richard Pope straightened the lapels of his jacket and brushed a speck of dirt from the sleeve of his coat. He ran a hand across his sweaty brow and through his hair.

There was no time left for discussion.

CHAPTER 27

"Sure is a pretty night, *n'est-ce pas?*"

"It really is."

Adrianna walked comfortably beside Gabe down the streets of Lee's Point. It was after midnight, and most of the town slumbered quietly beneath the many stars above. A light breeze stirred the treetops gently, carrying with it the fresh smell of a rain shower that had fallen earlier in the night.

After a week of bed rest, Adrianna had felt much improved. While Quinn had been adamant that she get another couple of days of rehabilitation, she had insisted that she was well enough to resume her duties at the Whipsaw's piano. In the end, he had relented. Even though she had spent much of the evening with one eye peeled for Richard Pope, the session had gone without a hitch. Now, the day weighing heavily on her shoulders, she was escorted home by Gabe as Quinn stayed behind to close down the tavern.

"I bet it feels right nice to be out of the house," he commented.

"I'll say," she agreed. "While I truly appreciated everything that Quinn and Jesse did for me, I was tired of that room."

"C'est la vérité!" Gabe laughed.

They turned the corner and headed up the street toward the Baxter house. As they walked, the only sounds that could be heard above that of their footfalls were the calls of crickets. All around them was darkness, and Gabe and Adrianna made their way more by familiarity than by sight.

When they reached the house, Gabe pulled the wrought-iron gate open and led the way up the short walk. Halfway to the steps, Adrianna suddenly halted and stared up at the tall windows that lined the long porch. The only light she could see was the scant amount shed by the streetlamp blocks away.

"That's strange," she commented.

"What is?" Gabe asked.

"Normally when we come home, there's at least one light left on," Adrianna explained. "Quinn makes sure that Lola leaves one lit so that we won't make too much of a commotion when we come home and wake Jesse."

"She must have forgotten."

Adrianna's brow furrowed, but she nodded and said, "That must be it."

Even though she had agreed with Gabe's observation, something gnawed at Adrianna's nerves, leaving her edgy. Knowing Richard was in the area, she found herself waiting for the worst in every situation, expecting calamity to follow disaster at each turn. She found herself constantly looking over her shoulder. *That's no way to live your life,* she admonished herself. Taking a deep breath and trying to unclench her fists, she went up the steps to the porch behind Gabe.

The Cajun opened the door and she followed him inside. As Adrianna shut the door behind them, the click of the lock echoed around the foyer. All around them was silence. She peered intently into the inky darkness but, try as she might, her eyes refused to adjust and she stumbled blindly forward as she attempted to stay close to Gabe when he moved farther into the house.

"I don't like this," she whispered.

"There's nothing to worry about, *mademoiselle,*" he reassured her. "After all that you have been through, you are seeing things that are not there. This is nothing more than the Bax —"

Adrianna saw it coming far too late. Out

of the corner of her eye, she looked on in horror as the metal blade of a shovel caught enough light through the open windows to gleam for a scant second before it continued downward. Time seemed to stand still, the scream that she desperately wanted to give voice to caught silently in her throat. The only sound she heard was the hard clang of the metal striking Gabe's head.

"No!" she managed to gasp.

Gabe fell to the hardwood floor like a sack of potatoes. Even though she could not see him in the darkness, she knew that he lay still, certainly injured and possibly dead.

"Goddamn stupid son of a bitch!" a gravelly voice spat.

From out of the shadows that led into the living room stepped a dark form. His hulking shoulders seemed to completely fill the entryway, the shovel clasped in his hands as if it were a child's toy. Reuben! He moved toward her and stopped directly in a beam of light that somehow penetrated into the house from outside. In it, she could see him smiling insanely, his eyes dancing in anticipation of the violence that was sure to come.

"Shoulda kept his nose outta this here business!" he snarled in a loud voice.

Fear threatened to drown Adrianna. Even though she felt too scared to move, somehow she was aware of her feet taking tentative steps away from the vicious man; it was as if her body were acting without her control, her sense of self-preservation trumping her terror. Over it all, she heard Cowboy's frantic barking.

"St-stay . . . away . . . from me!" she gasped.

"I don't think so, bitch! You ain't gonna give my Lola no more trouble."

With a speed that startled Adrianna, Reuben's hand shot out and grabbed her arm. His grip was like an iron vise! No matter how hard she struggled, he dragged her toward him until she was inches from him. As he stared down at her, his hot breath washed over her face, smelling of tobacco and alcohol. This close, the fear became a real thing, and she trembled at the thought of what was to come.

"After all that there trouble you done caused me at that bar, I think you owe me a bit a fun!" Reuben paused, his bloated tongue licking his sandpaper lips. "A city lady like you are, ya ain't spent enough time on your back. It's time for that to change!"

Sheer horror raced through Adrianna's veins as she realized that Reuben intended to rape her. Instantly, his hands were all over her, roughly squeezing her breasts and shaking her so hard that she felt as if her head would come free from her shoulders. Then, he tore the fabric of her blouse as if it were nothing more than paper.

"No! Dear God, no!" she shrieked but no one answered.

Suddenly, a vision of Quinn leapt to her mind. In it, she saw him springing out from behind the Whipsaw's bar, ready to fight. She saw him running to aid the man felled by the runaway log, concern and determination etched on his face. She saw the way he fought to give Jesse a future, even if it wasn't necessarily what the boy wanted. While it would be easier to surrender to Reuben's rough hands, at that moment she knew that she would fight until her last breath.

With all the strength she could muster, she began to scratch and claw at her assailant, her nails searching for any soft spot where she could hurt the man, but try as she might, her actions seemed only to amuse him.

"That's right, bitch!" He laughed robustly. "Now yer startin' to get into it! I like it when a woman gets all fiery!"

Desperation grabbed Adrianna and refused to let go. She had to get free! An idea struck her, and she acted on it. As Reuben brought a hand near her face, she grasped him by the wrist and pulled his hand toward her. Like a ferocious animal, she sank her teeth into the side of his hand. Even when the man tried to jerk free, she refused to let go. Although the bitter iron taste of blood flooded her mouth, she clung to him tenaciously, as if her very life depended on it, which it most certainly did.

"Oww! Ya goddamn whore!" he roared. Finally, just before Adrianna could carve a hunk of flesh from the man's hand, Reuben shook free, hurled her to the floor and grasped at his bloody hand.

Adrianna shot to her knees, alert for her slim chance at escape. Her eyes had become better adjusted to the house's gloom, but what she could make out caused her heart to sink; from where she had fallen, Reuben stood between her and the front door. Her only chance away from the beastly man was to retreat deeper into the house. As silently and as quickly as she could, she slid out of the room, got to her feet, and hurried away.

She darted through the dining room and into the kitchen. She nearly shouted with glee; from here it would be an easy matter to slip out the rear door, onto the porch, and out into the street where she could find help for herself and the doctor for Gabe. In her hurry, she didn't see the edge of a chair.

Her knee slammed into it, and pain shot up her leg.

Don't make a sound! she ordered herself, clamping a hand to her mouth.

Limping to the door, Adrianna turned the knob but found that it wouldn't open. She jiggled it quickly, certain that it was simply stuck but it remained steadfastly closed. Panic began to color the edges of her thoughts as her hand searched frantically for the unseen lock or latch that was keeping her shut inside with Reuben. Her fingers roamed quickly but found nothing.

God help me! she silently prayed.

"Goddamn cock teaser!" a roar came from deeper in the house.

Adrianna knew she didn't have much time. If even a minute passed without her being able to open the door, the brutish man would be on top of her. After what she had done to him, his vengeance would be swift and it would be severe. Sweat beaded on her brow and her fingers shook but she still couldn't find her way to freedom. It was as if a grandfather clock stood before her, every tick bringing her one step closer to death!

Finally, reason won over her fear. As quietly as she could, Adrianna backed away from the door and slid into the shadows near the dry sink. It pained her to give up trying to escape, but as if to underscore how wise a choice she had made, at that very instant, Reuben burst into the room like a mad bull, his chest heaving and his voice deafening.

"Where in the hell are you hidin', ya blasted splittail!" he shouted. His face whipped from one corner to another, scanning for any sight of his prey. Unsettled and irritable, he waited for some sign, any movement that would allow him to unleash his rage. "You sure as hell ain't gonna get away from me! If there's one thing I can promise you, it's that!"

Adrianna remained stock-still. Her heart pounded loudly in her ears but she reminded herself that it was a sound that only she could hear. Her leg throbbed where she had struck the chair; though she desperately wanted to rub it, she didn't dare for fear she would alert Reuben.

"I'll find ya!" the man bellowed.

Adrianna thought of Jesse. Where was he? Had Reuben come to the house earlier and done something horrible to the boy? Just the thought of some harm befalling Jesse brought the first welling of tears to her eyes. For now, she just had to hope that he was safe.

One person whose safety she wasn't concerned about was Lola. Even though she had yet to show her face, Adrianna had no doubt that Lola was responsible for Reuben's presence. Lola had sent Reuben after her at the Whipsaw, and it was almost certain that she'd let him into the house to hurt her now. Once her rival was out of the way, Lola would go about trying to sink her hooks into Quinn. *I hate to disappoint you, Lola, but I'm not going to be that easy to get rid of!*

"Ya sure as hell ain't makin' it light on yoreself by hidin', ya slut," Reuben snarled, his heavy footfalls echoing off the kitchen walls. From where she hid, Adrianna watched as he tentatively made his way across the far side of the kitchen. In the scant light afforded to her, she could see a glistening wetness on one on his hands; she must have drawn quite a bit of blood.

"It'd be best just to show yoreself and get it over with." In moments, he would turn from the icebox and, passing in front of the dry sink, he'd be on top of her. Even in the near total darkness, she didn't like her chances of evading his gaze. If she were going to run, it would have to be soon.

"Come out! If'n ya don't, I'm gonna hurt ya . . . bad." Adrianna didn't doubt the truth of the man's words, but she did doubt if it made any difference at all as to when he got his hands on her.

"Goddamn bitch!" he swore again, his voice full of venom.

As Reuben reached the icebox, Adrianna's heart threatened to burst from her chest. He was close enough to her that she could have reached out and touched him. When he turned, his foot raised to take a step, she summoned every ounce of courage she could and lit out of her hiding place as if she were a rabbit bursting from her hole, a fox fast on her tail.

"There you are!" Reuben shouted.

She'd hoped that she'd be able to get a step or two away before he noticed her, but she hadn't managed to surprise the large man. His arm shot out to grab hold of her again, but instead only ended up with another fistful of her torn blouse. Adrianna stumbled slightly but refused to lose her footing. As soon as she was past him, she began to run as fast as her legs would carry her.

"Get back here!" he bellowed.

With every step, pain shot through her leg, but she paid it no mind; there would be time to hurt later. Whipping past the small table on which she had eaten many meals in Quinn and Jesse's company, she burst into the hallway at a sprint.

She was going to escape, and nothing would stop her!

Though she had only just left him in the kitchen, she could hear the sound of Reuben's footfalls behind her. For a man his size, he moved incredibly fast. It would only be a matter of moments before he caught up to her. If he ever got hold of her again, she was certain that she wouldn't be able to break free.

"I see ya!" he taunted her.

She headed deeper into the house. Ahead, she could see the staircase that led to the second floor. Bounding onto the lower steps, she began to move up them two at a time. If she could only make it to the upstairs bedrooms, she could lock a door behind her! She could yell out from one of the windows!

Suddenly, bright light filled the room as an electric switch was thrown. The unexpected brilliance caught Adrianna by complete surprise. In her shock, she stumbled on the stairs, and suddenly what was once up was now down. With a crash, she slammed down onto the stairs, the air nearly driven from her lungs. Dazed, she expected Reuben's large hands to grab hold of her, but nothing happened. Instead, the only sign of him was a deep roll of laughter from the bottom of the stairs. The next sound that Adrianna heard caused her blood to freeze.

"Well, well, well! What do we have here?"

Adrianna looked to the top of the stairs, to the place from which the voice had emanated. Standing there, a long knife in her hand, its blade shining in the sudden light, was Lola.

CHAPTER 28

"Bitch! Did you think I was just gonna sit back and let you waltz in and take my man!" Lola shouted. Spittle formed at the corners of her mouth, and her eyes danced maniacally. The knife flashed menacingly in her hand.

"Quinn's not your man!" Adrianna answered as Lola made her way down the stairs.

"Since the day you first showed your ugly, snooty face, I've watched as you picked here and there at all I've tried to do! You've strutted around here like you were the Queen of England, flashing a smile and shaking your titties in Quinn's face!" the wild-haired woman screeched. "I've had enough, you hear? I've had enough!"

Without question, Adrianna knew her life was in danger. Tentatively, she took a quick glance behind her at Reuben. Her heart sank as she realized he was too close for her to even try to run. Before she could manage to scramble to her feet, he would have been upon her.

"Don't look at him," Lola barked. "He ain't gonna help you!"

"You ain't just a shittin'," Reuben grunted.

"You shut your mouth!" Lola suddenly shouted at her accomplice.

"Now, honey bun," Reuben said in a placating tone.

"Don't honey bun me! Just shut up!" she yelled. Adrianna realized Lola wanted all the attention to be on her, to be the one in charge.

Adrianna tried to think. If she didn't do something, she'd be dead in a matter of minutes. It seemed unlikely that she had any chance of overpowering or escaping her attacker's grasp. Her only hope was to bide her time until help could arrive.

Hurry, Quinn! Please hurry!

With the way Lola was yelling, there was the possibility, no matter how small, that someone might hear. Then there was Gabe. If she could only keep them talking long enough for him to come to, then he could help her. *But what if he is dead?* She quickly pushed the thought out of her head; it was more dreadful than she could bear to think about.

"You'll not get away with this," Adrianna declared as defiantly as she could. *Oh, Lord. If they kill me, they would surely go after Jesse and . . . have they already hurt him?*

"Ain't no one ever gonna be any the wiser," Lola chuckled, the knife passing from one hand to the other, as she taunted. "Oh, sure, there'll be questions asked, but folks will figure you ran back to Shreveport. Maybe it'll be that you just left town to get away from that older fella that chased you here. Either way, it won't make no difference. You ain't never gonna be found. There's plenty of hungry gators in the swamp," Lola said with an evil smile on her face.

A shiver of dread raced down the length of Adrianna's spine. Fear grasped her so tightly that she had to force her jaw to work against its will. "Quinn will look for me."

"It'll be too late," Lola said flippantly. "It didn't have to be this way, you know. If Reuben had done what he was told to do, you'd have been brained at the Whipsaw, accidentally of course, and that would have been the end of it. Or, if you'd just have died in the attic, all my problems woulda been over."

"You deliberately locked me in," Adrianna stated, her ire rising. Memories flashed back to the excruciating heat of the attic. She thought of how she had struggled to free herself and nearly lost her life in the process.

"Of course I did." Lola sneered. "You've been walking around here with your nose held so high in the air that you couldn't see what was right before your eyes. Hell, you didn't even realize that the reason you got so gut sick was because I put oleander leaves in your soup!"

Adrianna was certain that all the color drained from her face. She could scarcely believe what she had heard. Lola had tried to kill her with poison! She had suffered, pain roiling throughout her body, keeping her in bed for a week with Quinn and Jesse worrying about her. All because of this jealous woman!

"I wish to God I'd used more than I did," Lola continued, a look of disappointment crossing her face. "It would have been so much easier. No one would have asked any questions."

"Quinn would have. He'd have found out what happened."

"Don't you so much as even speak his name!" Lola snarled. She reacted so violently that it was as if she suddenly had gone berserk. "I won't stand for you to say my husband's name! You aren't worthy of saying it! It sounds filthy coming out of your mouth!"

With that, any doubts that Adrianna had about Lola's sanity were erased. Somehow, she had wrapped herself inside a fantasy life from which she could not escape, from which she didn't *want* to escape. Even though none of it was real, she believed it to be the truth. Because of that, she saw Adrianna as a threat. *A threat that had to be eliminated!*

Instead of frightening her, the realization emboldened Adrianna. "He doesn't love you," she taunted. The fear that had run coldly through her veins began to quickly warm with anger. "He doesn't love you, and he never has!"

"What did you say?" Lola asked incredulously.

"You aren't married to Quinn Baxter. He's not going to be your husband!" Adrianna shot back, her voice rising with every word. "You're crazy if you think you're good enough for him! All you are is the woman who cleans his house! Nothing more! What you think is a lie!"

Lola's mouth opened and closed but no words came out. Instead, her fist tightened around the knife's handle, and she began slowly to walk down the steps toward Adrianna. Rage had taken control of her mind, moving her along with a will that was not entirely her own.

Adrianna could do little more than watch Lola descend the stairs. She heard the sound of Reuben's heavy footsteps behind her. In a matter of seconds, he would have hold of her, rendering her helpless for the moment that Lola would slide the long knife into her.

"What the hell's goin' on out here?"

Adrianna's heart sank in her chest at the sight of Jesse wheeling his chair through the door of his room. He had apparently been in a deep sleep. His usually well-combed hair was going every which way. His nightshirt hung crookedly from his shoulders and barely fell far enough to cover his knees. He held Cowboy tightly at his side by his collar. The dog began to growl deeply, his eyes locked tightly on Reuben.

"Jesse . . ." Adrianna muttered.

"How's a guy supposed to get any sleep with all this racket?" Jesse's eyes passed from one face to another as if he were searching for an answer. When he glanced at Reuben, the boy's eyes seemed to look past him, staring at something in the distance. When Adrianna turned to see what had grabbed his attention, she gasped; lying at the edge of the light was Gabe's unconscious body. Jesse's eyes suddenly found hers, confusion running wild across his face.

"Just go back to your room," she said quickly. Her mind was in turmoil. The thought of harm coming to the boy made her body quiver with dread. If she could just get him out of the room and back to bed, maybe he would be safe until Quinn came home.

"He ain't goin' nowhere," Reuben snarled.

"He doesn't have anything to do with this," Adrianna pleaded. She looked up at Lola, hoping for any sign that she understood. "Just let him go, and you can do whatever you want to me."

"We're gonna do that anyway," Reuben explained with an evil smile.

"I told you to shut up," Lola barked at the large man. His smile vanished but it didn't seem to Adrianna that he was angry; Lola certainly kept her dog on a short leash.

"That's all right, Adrianna," Jesse suddenly spoke up, all the while trying to keep Cowboy under control. "I'll protect you from this rabble!" From the gleam in his eye, she could see that he saw himself as one of the sheriffs in his pulp magazines. But this wasn't some dime novel; this was real life, and it was dangerous.

"It's too late for him anyway," Lola explained with a shrug. "He's seen and heard too much. Besides, I'm sick of always havin' to wait on the brat hand and foot. I sure as shit ain't gonna miss him."

"Let me do it," Reuben suggested. "I've always wanted a crack at that smart-ass kid." With that, the thuggish man took a step toward Jesse's chair, his hands clenching in spastic glee. Adrianna was amazed to see a smile cross Jesse's lips, anticipation dancing in his eyes.

"Get 'em, boy!" he shouted as he released his grip on Cowboy's collar.

With a sharp bark, the dog sprang at Reuben, covering the distance quickly. Every muscle in the animal's body was taut, the coarse hair on his back stood on end, and his mouth curled in a vicious snarl.

Before Cowboy could reach his target, the big man squared his shoulders and threw a back fist that struck the dog against the side of his head. There wasn't even time for Cowboy to yelp before he crashed hard to the floor, slid across the hardwood, and slammed into the wall with a thud. The loyal pet whimpered, tried to raise his head, but could only shudder before falling completely limp.

"Cowboy!" Jesse wailed.

Something deep inside Adrianna began to give way. As she watched Jesse, anguish coloring his face, the anger she had felt at Lola's interference in her life became a raging inferno. In that moment, she knew what she had to do. It was just as Jesse had told her when she was ill; she had to take control of her own life. She was not a coward!

Without another thought, Adrianna turned and headed up the stairs straight for Lola. In only a couple of strides she was a few feet from her foe. She paid the knife no mind; it wouldn't have mattered if Lola had held a gun. A look of surprise crossed over the housekeeper's face, and her mouth gaped in shock.

"What do you think —" was all Lola managed to get out before Adrianna raised her fist and brought it crashing into the woman's nose. There was a loud crunching sound, the cartilage breaking, and then crimson blood began to flow freely. Lola let out a howl of pain, and the knife fell from her hand to land on the stairs with a clatter.

"I hate you!" Adrianna shouted.

With all of the strength and anger she could muster, she fell on Lola as if she were a wild animal. In turn, Lola grabbed a handful of Adrianna's hair and yanked hard on it, but she felt nothing. Instead, Adrianna responded in kind, tugging hard enough at Lola's locks that she was sure she would pull hair out by the handful!

"Get her, Annie!" Jesse shouted his encouragement.

"Haw! Haw! Haw!" Reuben laughed and slapped his hand against his thigh.

Although she had never been in a fight in her entire life, Adrianna gave as good as she got. Lola slammed her fist into Adrianna's jaw; and, instead of going down in a heap or shouting in pain, she balled up her hand and struck the other woman.

"I'll kill you for this, you bitch!" Lola screamed.

"Not if I kill you first!"

Suddenly, Adrianna's foot caught on the steps. Grasping Lola's blouse, she held on tenaciously as she tumbled down the stairs. Her back slammed into the wall and pain shot through her body but, before she could try to think straight, she was lifted off the floor and slammed yet again.

Finally, she fell hard onto her back at the base of the stairs. She gasped for air, and darkness colored the edges of her vision, but she quickly shook her head and tried to get her bearings. Lola lay beside her, blood smeared across her face, her eyes blinking slowly.

"You'll not hurt anyone! Not anymore!" Adrianna shouted.

Rolling over, Adrianna threw herself at Lola. She straddled her, towering over her prone body. Grabbing her by the ears, she began to slam Lola's head into the floor, rage taking control. With each blow, she thought of Jesse and Quinn and all that this woman had done to them, all that she had tried to take from their lives.

It felt good!

Without warning, Adrianna was grabbed roughly by the shoulders and lifted off Lola like a sack of flour. She tried to hold on to Lola, but the hands that held her were insistent and finally wrestled her free. She was spun around to stare into enraged eyes.

"That done be enough!" Reuben bellowed.

Before that moment, Adrianna had thought little of her own death. To her, it had always been something far away. But now, it was bearing down on her as if it were a speeding locomotive.

"I'm gonna kill you for what you done to Lola!"

It was all Adrianna could do to close her eyes. No scream waited to escape her lips. No tears waited to slide hot down her cheeks. The fatigue and pain of her scrap with Lola began to seep into her joints. She only hoped that what was to come would be quick.

Suddenly, a loud crash filled the room, and Adrianna was dropped to the floor, collapsing in a heap. When she finally managed to open her eyes, what stood before her seemed to be some kind of a miracle!

There was Jesse . . . *standing!* In his hands were the remnants of a glass vase that had sat on a table near the foot of the stairs. On the floor before him lay Reuben, his unconscious body littered with shards of glass, water, and a few crumpled flowers.

"Jesse!" she managed, her voice little more than a whisper.

He stood unsteadily for a moment longer, his legs quivering and shaking, before he lost his balance and fell back into the wheelchair from which he had risen to protect her. The chair rolled slightly before coming to rest against the wall.

In a flash, she was up and to him, throwing her arms around him in a tight hug. The tears that had refused to come when she had been in Reuben's grasp now flowed freely; the difference was that these were tears of happiness.

"Oh, Jesse!" she cried. "Thank you!"

"I told you I'd save you." He smiled

broadly. "The sheriff always rescues the girl!"

CHAPTER 29

" 'Twas one of the best sing-alongs ever, I done do swear!"

Quinn smiled gently as he shooed Roy Long off the stool and toward the door. Even so long after the last paying customer had left, it wasn't unusual for Roy still to be at the bar. Quinn often let the older man hang around after the tavern was closed; it was always nice to have another voice as he tidied up the place, and besides, Roy spent nearly as much time there as he did at home.

"I think you might be on to something there," he nodded.

"That gal's one mighty fine pian'r player!" Roy remarked, trying to steady himself on shaky legs. For a moment, it looked as if he might tip over, but he held his balance. "If Gabe don't watch hisself, he ain't gonna have no job to come back to when that busted mitt is healed!"

"He still pours beer better than I do, so

maybe I'll be the one out of a job."

Roy laughed at Quinn's joke before tottering out the door and into the darkness, waving over his shoulder as he went. Quinn watched him until he was out of sight. *No doubt about it, I have a soft spot for the old drunk.*

Back inside the Whipsaw, Quinn spent the next forty-five minutes shutting the tavern down for the night. There was still much to be done; he cleared the empty beer bottles off the tables, tidied up the liquor bottles on the shelf, wiped down the bar counter, and counted the night's take before putting it in the office safe. All the while he worked, his mind was elsewhere. There was only one thing, one name that held a grip on his thoughts.

Adrianna.

Since they had lain together as man and woman, she had left a mark on him that would be there forever. Everywhere he went, in everything that he did, he thought about her. Tonight at the Whipsaw had been especially difficult; whenever he caught her eye as he moved around the bar, he had a hard time breaking his loving gaze. If he didn't hear her voice soon or feel her touch, he felt he might burst!

As he swept up a small pile of broken

glass, Quinn's mind was so focused on Adrianna that he didn't hear the Whipsaw's door open, nor did he hear the intruder's footsteps tap lightly across the wooden floor toward him. He became aware that he was not alone only when a man's voice spoke from behind him.

"I told you that you won't have her, and I meant it."

Without needing to turn, Quinn knew that Richard Pope stood behind him; that nasal voice was unmistakable. Anger flared in Quinn's breast at the man's gall in returning. He'd thought that he'd made it clear that Richard was never to show his face again. This time, he'd make certain that the man from Shreveport would *never* return!

As Quinn spun around, his fists were clenched tightly. He was determined to cause pain. He didn't realize that Richard held a pistol until a split second before the man fired. The noise was deafening. Even had Quinn been as quick as a jackrabbit, it wouldn't have made a difference.

The bullet slammed into the soft flesh of Quinn's thigh before crashing into bone. The force of the blow knocked him off his feet, and he fell to the floor with a thud. The pain was excruciating! The edges of his vision blackened, but agony seemed to prevent him from losing consciousness. Burning heat coursed through him as if he had been stuck with a branding iron. As his hand instinctively covered the wound, it became wet and sticky with his own deep crimson blood.

"You son of a bitch!" he hissed through clenched teeth.

"Do you think I'd really simply leave town with my tail between my legs?" Richard asked, ignoring Quinn's curse. He waved the gun about as he talked, the barrel swinging this way and that. "You've laid your hands upon me twice, and that is two times too many!"

Quinn's breath came in ragged fits; the pain, like sharp daggers, pierced his leg. For a moment, he had to rest his head on the floor and close his eyes to try desperately to regain his bearings. He would have to have his wits about him if he were going to survive this madman's attack.

"You have confused my dear Adrianna," the older man continued. "You and this piss-ant little town have managed to cast a spell on her, clouding her judgment and poisoning her thoughts against me, her intended husband."

"She . . . she doesn't want you," Quinn managed to say through the pain. "She —"

"Shut your mouth!" Richard shouted, cutting off Quinn's halting words. For a moment, he looked angry enough to raise the pistol and finish the job he had started, but instead he did something that curdled Quinn's stomach; he smiled and laughed heartily.

"What's so damn funny?"

"I find it amusing that you think you'll be alive long enough for Adrianna to be able to make choice between us," the man explained. As he spoke, Richard went behind the long bar and began to line up bottles of liquor on the wooden countertop. "The only choice that will be made this evening will be when I decide which way I wish to kill you."

Panic began to work its way through Quinn as quickly as the pain from his gunshot wound. He had to act, and he had to do it quickly! Suddenly, a flame of hope lit in his heart at the thought that Roy Long might have heard the gunshot. But that hope quickly turned to dread; if Roy *had* heard the shot, he was just as likely to come back to the Whipsaw, in which case Richard would shoot him as well. Quinn knew that if he wanted to get out of here alive, he would have to depend on himself.

The only weapon in the Whipsaw was a

small pistol he kept in the office, but in order to use it to protect himself, he would have to get to it first. Simply getting to his feet was going to prove a challenge, let alone getting out of the room alive. Richard had shown no remorse shooting him once; if he were to try to run for it, he had no doubt that the lawyer would shoot him in the back like a dog.

Quinn was pulled from his frantic thoughts by the sound of shattering glass. He looked up to see Richard flinging full liquor bottles to the far corners of the tavern, their contents spilling out onto the floor, tables, chairs, and even the walls. Bottle after bottle hurtled through the air before meeting the same fate as all the rest. One landed near him, soaking his shirt with whiskey. The room was soon filled with the sharp, strong smell of alcohol.

"What . . . what the hell are you doing?" Quinn managed to ask.

Richard's arm stopped abruptly, sparing a bottle of rum. "Isn't it obvious, my dear man?" he answered incredulously. He grinned before explaining. "I'm going to burn you alive."

"Ohhh . . . my head aches, *c'est la vérité!*" Gabe moaned as Adrianna helped him into a chair. His legs were rubbery and spots continued to dance before his eyes, but at least the ringing in his ears was subsiding.

"Take it easy," Adrianna explained.

"That is about all I *can* do." Gabe placed one hand gingerly on the knot growing ever larger on the back of his head. He winced as he touched it.

Adrianna's brow was still furrowed with worry. With Gabe's meager help, she'd tied up Lola and Reuben with rope she'd found in the pantry. Even though neither of them had yet to gain consciousness, the tightest knots held them. When Adrianna and Gabe were able, they'd fetch the sheriff; their attackers would pay for what they had done. Still, even with the immediate threat passed, a feeling of dread gnawed at Adrianna's gut. It was as if she somehow knew that the night's calamities were not yet over.

"I'm worried about Quinn. He should be home by now," she said aloud, rubbing her hands that were bruised from striking Lola.

"Quinn will be surprised about what's happened here," Jesse said as he rolled into the room in his wheelchair. Trotting along beside him, still a touch the worse for wear, was Cowboy. "We've got the bad guys all tied up. Even if they got loose, I'd just bust 'em on the head again!" he said proudly.

"Thank you for dispatching Reuben, *mon ami,*" Gabe nodded.

"T'weren't nothin'," Jesse drawled with a wink.

Even with all of this, Adrianna couldn't get the thought out of her head that something bad was detaining Quinn. The skin on the back of her neck was crawling with fear. The more that she thought of it, she knew that it wasn't her own well-being that was giving her worry.

It was Quinn's.

"I have to go to the Whipsaw," she said decidedly.

"What for?" Jesse asked.

"*Mademoiselle,* let's not be too hasty," Gabe cautioned. "We have no way of knowing if that ape was the only person Lola was using to try to do you harm. After all that has happened, I don't know if there is anything she would *not* be capable of. I wouldn't put it past that witch to have a couple more waiting outside the house right now, *n'est-ce pas?*"

"I don't care," Adrianna insisted. "Don't ask me how, but I just know that Quinn is in trouble. If I don't go to him right now, I'm afraid something terrible is going to happen to him. Reuben may have set thugs on him."

"On Quinn?" Jesse asked. "It would take a good-sized bunch to take him down!"

"I wouldn't put it quite the same way as he did," Gabe said, nodding at Jesse, "but Quinn is someone who knows how to take care of himself. I think it is far safer for us all to remain here and wait for him to come home."

As she weighed Gabe's words, Adrianna's mind was filled with memories of Quinn. It was as if she were at a motion picture. Moment followed moment with rapid precision, one more powerful than the next. As clearly as in a photograph, she could see his face as he slept beside her the morning after they had made love. A lone tear slid down her cheek. Angrily, she wiped it away with her thumb; she didn't have time to cry!

"I'm going," she declared and headed toward the door.

"Annie!" Gabe hollered. "Please, wait . . . !" was all she heard before she left the Baxter house, and Gabe and Jesse.

In seconds, she was out on the porch, rushing down the steps, and hurrying out to the street. She had pulled a sweater over her torn blouse, but her body was still battered and bruised from her encounter with Lola. She forced herself to run as fast as her legs would carry her. Even though she worried that someone lurked in the bushes, waiting to pounce on her at Lola's bidding, she had no time to be afraid.

She had to get to Quinn!

Quinn could only grit his teeth as Richard threw the rest of the bottles of liquor onto the Whipsaw's floor. The man truly seemed to be enjoying himself as he finished his destructive task. It would only be a matter of minutes before he set the whole thing ablaze.

Time was running out!

"Doing this isn't going to change how Adrianna feels about you," Quinn said, desperate to keep the man talking. If he could only bide his time, and prevent Richard from lighting the fire, he might devise some means to survive. "Killing me won't make any difference. After all, the reason she's here is because she was running away from you."

"That was my fault," Richard answered somberly. "I've not made many mistakes in my life, but that was one of them. Believe me, young man, I am the type of fellow who learns from his errors."

While his enemy talked, Quinn tried to lift himself up onto his elbows. Blood still oozed from his gunshot wound, and the pain still throbbed in time with his speeding heart, but he knew that he would have to overcome the discomfort if he wanted to live.

"I should have known better," Richard continued. He tossed one last bottle, smiled when it shattered, then wiped his hands against his suit coat. "Grief is such a powerful emotion. When someone has suffered a loss, say of a loved one, she is likely to look for a shoulder to lean on."

Quinn let the man ramble. Pushing with all his strength, he managed to move to a sitting position. Sweat covered his brow. Now, if he could just get to his feet . . .

"Unfortunately, grief can also be overwhelming. It can make even the most beautiful minds make ugly decisions. Take poor Adrianna, for example. With the death of her father, she became unbalanced and fearful. She ran away from me and ended up in this pathetic town with you."

Gritting his teeth, Quinn managed to roll gently onto his side and slide his good leg beneath him. A wave of pain washed over him, threatening to keep him from making his way, but he fought on. The next step was to drive himself upward, to gain balance on his one good leg, and then to get to the office as quickly as he could. He was about to make his move when Richard next spoke.

"When Charles Moore died, I thought she would be smart enough to know she needed a protector to take his place. It didn't occur to me that she'd become irrational. All my planning and the risk I took to do away with Charles was for naught!"

With the speed of the bullet that had wounded him, realization came to Quinn. *The bastard killed Adrianna's father!*

"What . . . what did you say?" he finally managed to ask.

"I suppose she told you about her father's passing," Richard said flippantly as he came out from behind the bar to stand before Quinn, the gun held menacingly before him. "What a tragedy. Even with all of his maladies, it was certainly quite a shock to her to find he'd expired in his sleep."

"Why?" Quinn asked. "Why would you do it?"

"Because he had what I wanted," Richard spat. "I was as much the reason for his success as he was, yet he received all of the accolades! Soon, I realized that with my hands on his money and his daughter, all of my dreams would come true. In his weakened state, it was a simple matter of getting him to sign his name here and there, making me the executor of his estate. Before the ink was even dry, he had made himself expendable."

Quinn's belly burned with ire and contempt. Through clenched teeth, he cursed at the man who was a threat to the woman he loved.

"You no-good, dirty son of a bitch!"

"All I had to do was place a pillow over his face one morning to get the job done," Richard said with pride. "Perhaps I erred in underestimating Adrianna's feelings for poor Charles, the old goat. You'd think she'd have been thrilled to have been released from the burden of caring for him."

Like a wild animal suddenly released from the cage in which it had been imprisoned, Quinn leapt off the floor and threw himself at Richard Pope. The pain that coursed through his body was no more than a gentle breeze, his only thoughts centered on getting his hands around the bastard's neck and squeezing the life from him! But, with surprising quickness, Richard lashed out, striking him on the side of his face with his pistol. He slumped to the floor, held awake only by the most tenuous of threads.

"I should kill you for the very audacity!" Richard fumed. "But a quick death is too good for a cur like you! Better for you to burn with this flea-infested hellhole you're so proud of!"

As he lay facedown on the floor, blood spilling from the cut on his cheekbone, Quinn could hear what was going on around him. The sounds came in a hurry; Richard's gun settling on the bar's counter, the rustling of cloth, and then the striking of a match.

What came next was the roaring of flames.

CHAPTER 30

Adrianna ran to the Whipsaw as fast as her legs would carry her. When she'd peered through the glass and seen Richard behind the bar, she'd known her premonition of danger had been well-founded. Stealthily, she opened the door in time to hear him say, *"All I had to do was place a pillow over his face . . ."*

Oh my God . . . Richard killed my father!

Adrianna stood in the doorway, frozen in horror. What she saw now paralyzed her: Richard with a gun in his hand, Quinn on the floor in a pool of blood, flames inching toward him. Bright crimson and dark orange flames licked up the walls as if they were starving men in search of food. New fires broke out everywhere a drop of alcohol had spread, until it seemed to cover every inch of the Whipsaw. Thick smoke began to billow upward. Through it all, the intense heat grew, threatening to consume everything it could reach.

She'd listened to it all, every sick and twisted nuance of Richard's vile plan to take her father's life and gain his fortune. With every word of his confession, her heart had ached with a pain she'd never have been able to imagine. Yet she'd been unable to find her voice, her only visible emotion the hot tears that blurred her vision and streaked down her face.

". . . thrilled to have been released from the burden of caring for him."

Even when Quinn had risen to his feet and charged at Richard, receiving a pistol-whipping for his efforts, she still couldn't move. For an instant, she wondered if it wasn't a dream, that she'd bumped her head when she'd fallen down the stairs with Lola, and that she'd wake up to find that none of it was real. But she knew this wasn't a nightmare.

"You bastard!" she screamed. "You heartless bastard!"

Richard turned to face her, a look of utter shock crossing his heavy face. "Adrianna, my dear . . ." he sputtered. "What . . . what in heaven's name are you doing here?"

"I heard everything you said, you no good son of a bitch!" she screamed with fury she'd never known before. She rushed at

Richard, paying no heed to the gun he still clutched in his hand, and began to pound her fists against his chest. "I hate you!"

Her last words seemed to do far more harm to the older man than her futile punches. With his free hand, he began to grab at her wrists, his brow furrowed with concern. "Stop this at once, dear Adrianna! It is not becoming a woman of your station!"

Adrianna couldn't hear a word he was saying. Between the thick smoke and the tears that flooded her eyes, she could scarcely even see him. Still, she kept on hitting him. Her mind was consumed with what Richard had done to her; he had murdered her father, stolen the fortune her family had amassed, wounded Quinn, and hounded her from the moment she'd left Shreveport. Enough was enough!

"I'll kill you!" she screamed. "I'll kill you for what you've done!"

Richard's hand flashed out with the speed of a serpent, striking her squarely in the mouth. The blow was sharp and painful enough to drive her from her feet, and she crashed to the floor a few feet away from Quinn. When she looked up at Richard, he glared back at her with eyes full of contempt.

"You have no one but yourself to blame for that, my dear," he chastised her coldly. "We will have to work on your manners. A woman such as you must know her proper limits."

As she listened to Richard, all around her the fire grew like a thing possessed. Flames licked at most of the tables and chairs and covered the long bar like a blanket. Ten feet away from her, the piano had begun to burn, smoke billowing from the closed lid. Even the seat where she had sat no more than a few hours earlier was in flames.

Turning on her side, she stared over to where Quinn lay. Dark blood seeped from a wound on his leg and oozed from a cut in his cheek that was surrounded by purple bruises. Even through the heat and smoke, she could see that he was gazing at her, a worried look in his eyes.

"Get . . . get out . . . of here," he pleaded.

"I won't leave you!"

Bang! Suddenly, the thundering clap of a gunshot split the wooden floor between them as it exploded in a shower of splinters. Adrianna was startled; even with the roar of the fire, the noise had been deafening. When she turned to Richard, she saw the gun in his hand.

"Don't speak to him!" the older man

ordered, his face a twisted mask of anger. "I won't stand for you defying me! A good wife would never defy her husband!"

Richard's words were more than Adrianna could bear. He'd spoken to her in such a way after her father's funeral, assuming that love and marriage were things that were not earned but simply ordained. What she had found in Lee's Point was the opposite: love was something that grew between two people, no matter their differences or upbringing.

Defiantly, she sat up, straightened her back and stared at Richard. "I am not your wife, and I never will be! I wouldn't marry you if you were the only man left in the whole country!"

"Don't say such things, dear Adrianna," Richard fumed. Her words had shaken his confidence, and his grip tightened on the pistol. "You're not in your right mind. This man has corrupted you."

"This man has done nothing but care for me from the moment he met me!" she argued, tears streaming down her face. "He's given me something that you could never give, no matter how much money you spent! He's given me love, and I have given it to him in return! If there's anyone that I am going to marry, it'll be Quinn Baxter, not you!"

As the mirror above the bar exploded from the heat, glass shards raining to the floor, Richard's sanity shattered with it. Like a rabid dog, he crossed the space between himself and Adrianna in an instant. Bending down to her, he began to slap her face and shoulders, one blow harder than the one before.

"You ungrateful wench!" he bellowed between blows. "After all that I have done for you! After all that I wished to give you, you have the audacity to speak to me in such a way! I'll make you regret that you ever said a one of those words to me!"

There was nothing that Adrianna could do to stop Richard from hitting her. She tried to raise her hands, but he brushed them aside like they were nothing but blades of grass. With every slap stinging her face, she grew weaker. If he didn't stop soon, she knew she would fall unconscious and be at his mercy. *But what can I possibly do to stop him?*

As if in answer to her unspoken question, movement to her left caught her eye. She'd hardly had time even to notice before Quinn suddenly lurched up off the floor and slammed into Richard's side, driving him away from her. The force of the blow drove the gun out of the older man's hand, and it skittered across the burning floor.

"Leave her the hell alone!" Quinn shouted.

"Quinn!" Adrianna yelled with a mixture of fear and joy.

Even in his weakened condition, Quinn was still in far better physical shape than Richard. Although his bullet-riddled leg made it hard for him to move, he stayed close to his foe. He threw a hard left to the Richard's midriff and then followed it up with a straight right that slammed flush against his nose, buckling his knees. Richard tried to answer with a feeble punch of his own, but Quinn merely swatted the blow away before throwing a left hook that cracked Richard's jaw. Still, he didn't go down.

"I'll . . . I'll kill . . . you . . ." Richard spat out of a blood-drenched mouth.

"You can try," Quinn answered. With all the strength he had left, Quinn threw a right uppercut that barreled into the man's chin with the force of a runaway locomotive. The blow seemed to lift Richard off his feet and he crashed to the floor flat on his back.

Adrianna gasped at the sight. All around them, the fire had begun to rage out of control. Fire crawled its way up the walls, tearing at the roof. The windows at the front of the tavern burst like ripe fruit, adding their noise to the cacophony of destruction. Beams and boards cracked and groaned, threatening to give way. Blistering heat seemed to radiate down to her very bones. With Richard now vanquished, the danger suddenly seemed even greater.

Quinn turned and hurried back to her, bending down to embrace her. His dirty, bloodied face loomed above her as he smothered her with kisses. "Are you all right?" he asked.

"I'm all right," she tried to reassure him, even though her face throbbed in pain, and her leg ached from her encounter with Rueben and Lola. "But we need to get out of here before it's —"

Before she could say one more word, another gunshot rang out, as strong as if a bolt of lightning had landed mere feet away. Quinn flew past her to land on the floor, his hand grasping agonizingly at his shoulder. In less time than it would have taken her to blink, crimson blood spurted between his fingers and raced down his elbow to the floor below. He'd been shot yet again!

"Quinn!" she screamed.

The only answer he gave her was to hiss

painfully between his teeth, "Get out of here."

She spun around to see Richard standing near the bar, his suit rumpled and his face a bloody wreck. In his hand was the pistol. Quinn's blow had knocked him down right next to his fallen weapon!

"That will be enough!" he raged through crimson teeth.

"Richard!" Adrianna pleaded, suddenly fearful that the older man would shoot Quinn again. "Don't do it, Richard! Please don't hurt him!"

"What makes you think I'm not going to just shoot the both of you?" Richard snarled. "After all I've done for you, I can't believe that you'd rush to him, you ungrateful little bitch! If this is the life that you have chosen," Richard barked, swinging his arms open to the burning Whipsaw, "then you do not deserve the generous gifts that I have offered you. I will give you just what you deserve . . . a painful death!"

With that, time seemed to stand still. Adrianna clutched at her chest as Richard raised the gun and leveled it at her. She expected the crack of the pistol, expected its murderous bullet finding its target in her heart, but another crack exploded across the dying tavern. Directly above Richard, a support beam that crossed the high room gave way, one of its ends entirely eaten through by the raging inferno that the man from Shreveport had ignited. Nearly as thick as a man's chest, the flaming beam crashed to the earth. Richard did not even have time to look up before the weight struck him and drove him to the floor. He screamed for only an instant before the noise, and he himself, were consumed by the out-of-control fire.

It took Adrianna only a moment to regain her composure. She hurried to Quinn. He looked up at her through tightly squinted eyes, his hand never leaving the wound on his shoulder.

"Oh, Quinn!" she cried. "We have to get out of here!"

Billowing black smoke curled around them as other beams began to give way, crashing onto the bar floor. They had only a matter of minutes, maybe no more than seconds, to get out before they too would share the fate that had befallen Richard.

"Go on without me," he hissed.

"I'm not going to leave you here!"

"I told you —" he started to say, but Adrianna was already hauling him to his feet. It was a struggle, but he helped her all that he could and was soon standing on one

439

good, but shaky leg. With one of Quinn's arms around her small shoulders, Adrianna led them toward the door.

They'd only gone a matter of feet before a beam crashed down behind them, shattering a table and a pair of chairs into kindling. It had missed them only by inches.

"Watch out!" Quinn warned.

As cautiously but as quickly as they could manage, they made their way toward the front of the tavern. The heat and thick smoke surrounded them, clinging to their clothing and threatening to pull them under. Adrianna's head swam with dizziness, coughs racked her body. Still, she steadily moved forward, inching ever closer to the door and the safety beyond.

Out of the smoke, a man appeared and drew Quinn's injured arm gently over his shoulder.

"Roy, you son of a gun! You came back," Quinn gasped.

"Course I did. I ain't never turned tail." Roy wrapped his arm around Quinn. "Come on, missy, this ain't the place to be right now, I done do swear!"

Roy helped her with Quinn and led them both out of the building and into the coolness of the night. Behind them, the fire seemed to grow even wilder in intensity; it was as if it had been saving its greatest fury until it knew that the two of them were safe.

All around them, shouts of "Fire!" rang out through the darkness, and the people of Lee's Point gradually scurried into the street carrying buckets. As the town came alive to fight the blaze, Roy gently laid Quinn down on the grassy verge of the street, and Adrianna knelt to try to staunch his wounds.

"I'm gonna run and fetch the lady doc," Roy explained. "That there wound looks like it done be more than the two of us can handle." With that, the older man was off into the dark.

Even as she worked to stop Quinn's bleeding, Adrianna's tears began to flow freely. With all that had happened, both here and with Lola, her nerves had been frayed raw. When she was finally able to see Quinn's face through the tears, she was surprised to see him smiling.

"What are you smiling about?"

"Because you're safe," he said simply.

"But look at all the hardship I've caused you," she answered. "Just because you knew me, you've been shot and beaten, and you've lost the Whipsaw."

"That's nothing but an old bar, anyway."

"But your father built it with his own two hands," she argued. "And what about Jesse?

You've been keeping it running so that he'd have something to support himself with when he was older!"

"He doesn't want it. He told you himself."

"But —"

"Hush!" he ordered her and she fell silent. He reached out and held her by the chin, keeping her eyes locked on to his own. They were so radiant, so piercing, that she knew she'd be lost in them for the rest of her life. "The only thing that matters to me is you. Not what my father might have wanted, not what anyone might think, and certainly not this bar."

"Oh, Quinn," was all she could say.

"I love you, Adrianna Moore," he said, setting her heart on fire with as much intensity as the blaze that raged behind them. "I love you, and I'll never let you go."

"I love you, Quinn," she answered through tears that flowed with joy.

As the roof of the Whipsaw collapsed in on itself, neither Adrianna nor Quinn looked up; instead they were absorbed in each other, their love the only thing on their minds.

EPILOGUE

"Hurry it up, will ya! We're gonna be late for the opening!"

Taking one last quick glance in the dresser mirror to make sure her hair looked just right, Adrianna lifted a shawl from the back of the rocking chair and hurried down the steps. Jesse stood at the bottom of the staircase, impatiently tapping his cane.

"It took you long enough," he complained.

"I have to make sure I look presentable today," she defended herself playfully. "After all, it is an important occasion. Besides, we've got plenty of time before it starts."

"That's easy for you to say. You're not the one that's got to hobble there with a cane. I know I'm doin' a lot better, but it's gonna be a while before I'm dancing a jig."

Adrianna beamed with pride. In the short space of a couple of months, Jesse had achieved an amazing amount of improvement with his legs. Through hard work, dedication, and even a fair amount of sweat and tears, he'd managed to work his way out of the wheelchair. He had then moved on to a walker and was now using a cane. With such progress, she knew it wouldn't be long before he was walking unassisted.

"If it's too far for you to walk, we could take the truck," she suggested.

"No way!" He smiled boyishly. "Today's the day for me to show off, too."

Laughing together, they made their way to the front door where Cowboy bounded up and barked, his heart set on accompanying them on their journey.

"Sorry, boy," Jesse said, sighing. "You're gonna have to sit this one out."

With obvious disappointment, the dog lay down on the floor and placed his head on his front paws.

Out on the street, Adrianna was struck by how beautiful the autumn day was. The sun shone brightly in a clear sky; its pleasant warmth setting her skin tingling. A soft breeze rustled the leaves, their colors turning ever-so-slowly from green to orange, yellow, and red. It was a perfect day.

As they walked, Adrianna realized how much she enjoyed Jesse's company. He had graduated from high school and would be leaving Lee's Point. He'd enrolled in the

State College at Baton Rouge for the coming term, a decision he'd made with both trepidation and excitement. She'd encouraged him to follow his dream, which he'd finally confessed was to become a writer. In her heart, she knew he'd make that dream come true.

"Sure is quiet around here today," Jesse commented.

"That's because everyone's already there."

"I hope so" — he nodded — "for Quinn's sake."

"For all our sakes." Adrianna smiled and took Jesse by the arm.

Looking around Lee's Point, Adrianna saw the same homes, storefronts, and other landmarks that had become familiar to her. Still, in the time that had passed since Lola Oxnard and Richard Pope had tried to destroy their lives, much had changed. After the sheriff had been called, Lola had been charged with attempted murder, as well as a few other offenses, and had been sentenced to spend a long time in prison. For his part in following his mistress's orders, Reuben had suffered a similar fate.

Richard's charred remains had been removed from the still-smoking embers of the Whipsaw. There was no way of knowing whether it had been the blow of the beam that had killed him, or if he had been burned alive in the inferno of his own making. The screams that had cut through the flame and smoke that night testified that either way, Richard Pope's fate had been painful. Regardless of how it had happened, Adrianna knew she would never have to be fearful of noises outside her window again.

"Thank goodness it's not much farther," Jesse groused.

"You're doing great."

Even with Jesse's still not fully strengthened legs, they covered the distance to town quickly. Rounding a corner, Adrianna could only smile at the sight that greeted her; there, sitting in front of Delmar's was her father's car, now fully repaired, with a "For Sale" sign in the window. *I certainly won't need that anymore,* she thought to herself.

Down another street, around another corner, and suddenly they were at their destination. Rising before them was the Whipsaw, better than before. New, it certainly was: crisp wood from the lumber mill made up the walls and ceiling, large panes of uncracked glass filled the windows, and a shiny coat of paint covered it all. The inside was even better; all the tables and chairs were new, the long bar was fully stocked with bottle after bottle of liquor, and a brand-new piano sat in the corner.

"Would you look at that," Jesse whistled, wiping his brow.

"It's really something, isn't it?"

"I'll say! Look at that sign!"

Adrianna followed Jesse's direction to the large banner that sat atop the tavern's roof. Bright and clear, it read "WHIPSAW" in tall letters. Nor was the wood warped or the paint chipped. It was perfect!

"Not half bad, if I do say so myself," a voice called from the front door. They looked up to see Quinn smiling back at them, his face full of pride. As it did every time she saw him, Adrianna's leaped with love.

"It's beautiful," she agreed.

"Hey, kiddo," Quinn called to his brother. "Why don't you head inside and see if Gabe can rustle you up a root beer? I think there might be a couple of cold ones around."

Quinn smiled as he watched Jesse walk, and then he made his way over to where Adrianna stood. He put his arm around her shoulder and pulled her to him. For a moment they were silent, admiring the new building.

"We can still call it 'Annie's Place' if you'd like," Quinn teased.

"Over my dead body," she exclaimed.

"It's your money."

"*Our* money," she corrected.

After the harm that Richard Pope had caused her, Adrianna had to admit that there was *one* thing he had done that had worked out for the best, even if she was certain he hadn't meant for it to. After he had swindled her father out of his fortune, Richard had drawn up legal documents naming her as the inheritor of *his* estate. He'd meant the document to have taken effect at their marriage, but he had been so certain of their impending nuptials that he'd signed the will and filed it. When he perished in the fire, all that had rightfully belonged to Adrianna was hers again.

When she had discovered that she was wealthy, Adrianna had had no doubt as to what she wished to do with the money. Quinn had tried to talk her out of it, insisting that he hadn't married her for her money, but she'd patiently explained to him that she wasn't giving it to him, but sharing; her life was no longer to be found in Shreveport, but in Lee's Point. With him.

"What does Gabe think of the finished product?" she asked.

"He's up on a cloud somewhere." Quinn winked. "Although I can't be sure if it's because of the new and improved Whipsaw or if it's because of what's going on with him and the doc."

Shortly after the fire, Gabe had finally summoned the courage to give voice to the feelings that had been roiling inside him from the very first moment he'd laid eyes on Sarah Bordeaux. He had been fearful to hear rejection and was shocked to find that the town's doctor shared his feelings but had been equally unable to speak them aloud. They'd been inseparable ever since.

"I know exactly how he feels," Adrianna said, slipping her arms around Quinn's waist and pulling him close. "Love can make the whole world turn upside down."

"Is that so?"

"It is." She smiled. "I love you, Mr. Baxter."

"And I love you, Mrs. Baxter."

Two months after that fateful night, Quinn and Adrianna had been married in a simple ceremony in the church on the outskirts of town. The whole town had turned out to wish them well and celebrate their love. Adrianna had only one family member who had been able to attend, her aunt Madeline from Mississippi. In the end, her aunt had come to visit her, instead of the other way around!

Tenderly, Quinn bent down and placed

his lips against hers. Reveling in the sweetness of their kiss, Adrianna knew that this was the man she was meant to spend the rest of her life with, enjoying all of the ups and downs with the passing of the years. What had happened in the past was just that — the past. All that mattered was their future . . . together!

"Well ain't that a sight!"

They broke their kiss to look back at the Whipsaw. There, standing before the door, his arms crossed over his chest, was Roy Long. He smiled his mostly toothless grin.

"What with all this kissin' and stuff goin' on, it's gettin' so that a fella can't even get hisself a good drink around here, I done do swear!"

ABOUT THE AUTHOR

Dorothy Garlock is one of America's — and the world's — favorite novelists. Her work has appeared on national bestseller lists, including the *New York Times* extended list, and there are over fifteen million copies of her books in print translated into eighteen languages. She has won more than twenty writing awards, including five Silver Pen Awards from *Affaire de Coeur* and three Silver Certificate Awards, and in 1998 she was selected a finalist for the National Writer's Club Best Long Historical Book Award.

After retiring as a news reporter and bookkeeper in 1978, she began her career as a novelist with the publication of *Love and Cherish.* She lives in Clear Lake, Iowa. You can visit her Web site at www.dorothy garlock.com.